HUNG

Scott Hildreth

DEDICATION

TO ALL CANCER SURVIVORS, THE LESS FORTUNATE WHO GAVE EVERYTHING ONLY TO FIND OUT SOMETIMES EVERYTHING ISN'T ENOUGH, AND TO THE FAMILIES THEREOF.
MY GRANDMOTHER BILLIE JEAN HILDRETH, MY AUNT GINA SILOR, AND TO BIKER BECKY.

THIS ONE IS FOR YOU.

BISCUIT

Standing in the courtroom with a Sheriff's officer on each side of me - my hands handcuffed, my feet shackled, and the two tied together by an interconnecting chain - caused me to feel more like a serial killer than a common criminal. As I waited for the judge to enter the room, I alternated glances over each shoulder and studied the officers.

I raised my hands slightly, pulling the chain taut which connected my hands to my feet. Somewhat frustrated at the entire series of events leading up to my arrest, additional jailhouse punishment, and being shackled and chained, I began yanking against it repeatedly, causing it to rattle through the steel ring in the center of the chain wrapped around my waist.

"Any chance of gettin' one of you fellas to take these fuckers off?" I asked as I gazed down at my shackles.

"Not a chance," bad cop responded under his breath, "And if you know what's good for you, you better quit fucking around with your restraints."

I stopped yanking on the chain and tilted my head to the left as I waited for good cop to respond.

The officer on my left shook his head and lightly chuckled, "After the shit you pulled this weekend, I don't think so."

I lowered my forearms and sighed, "*I* didn't pull a god damned thing. The cock sucker tried to steal my fuckin' cookie. Put yourself in

1

my shoes, fellas. I look like Hannibal fuckin' Lector here…"

As I began to explain myself, the door in the rear of the courtroom opened and the judge walked onto the elevated platform. An average looking gentleman roughly fifty years old with salt and pepper hair, he looked like a reasonable enough man. Hopefully he would see through the mile of shit the cops were certain to have placed out in front of him and have a little compassion for me. After quietly finding his seat and glancing down at the desk, he lifted his head and gazed my direction.

"This is a combination of an arraignment and the bond hearing for…" he paused and peered over the top of his glasses at the paper he held in his hands.

"Dalton Biskette. Mr. Biskette, you have been charged with speeding, reckless endangerment, resisting arrest, and since your incarceration of Friday evening, two counts of jailhouse battery. Do you understand the charges?" he asked under his breath.

"Yes, sir," I breathed.

"Be it known the penalty for these charges is a maximum of five years imprisonment, a $250,000 fine, or both. How do you wish to plead?" he asked flatly.

Five years for fuckin' speeding?

I swallowed heavily, knowing he was doing nothing more than trying to scare me. I decided trying to explain myself, using my wit and charm to the best of my ability - while trying to be respectful during the process - would be my best bet.

"How do I *wish* to plead, your honor? I *wish* to plead not guilty, but I'm well aware that ain't…I mean that *isn't* going to do me much good. I guess I'd like to plead guilty to the speeding, and speak my peace on the rest of the charges. Can I do that?" I asked as I did my best to shrug my shoulders.

He placed the paper on the desk, removed his glasses, and tilted his head to the side, "Absolutely."

As he clasped his hands together and provided what I was certain to be a sarcastic grin, I began to recite my best recollection of the events on Friday night.

"Well, I was headed to a meeting, and I was runnin' a little late. Kind of lost track of my speed, I guess. Next thing I knew, a cop was pulling me over. He uhhm. He had a little bit of an attitude; you know he seemed kind of mad about the whole speeding thing. Next thing I knew, there was about fifty cops screaming at me, and I was shot with a Taser. Unnecessarily, I might add, your honor..."

As I spoke, the judge appeared to be sorting through the paperwork on his desk. Before I had a chance to explain myself further, he raised his hand and interrupted.

"Officer Obie was unable to attend this hearing, and if his testimony proves *necessary*, we will reschedule. Are you aware, Mr. Biskette, the officer makes notes on his copy of the citation, providing his best explanation of the arrest and the events that led up to it?" the judge asked as he raised a beige piece of paper from the desk.

"I guess not," I shrugged.

"I have the officer's report, *and I quote*," he sighed.

"At approximately 1933 hours, while stationary at the 7000 block of Kellogg, observed motorcycle approaching at a high rate of speed. Removed LIDAR 001-00200 and directed toward oncoming motorcycle. Speed clocked initially at 133 MPH. After resetting device, clocked motorcycle at 128 MPH. Chase ensued, and motorcycle stopped without attempting to evade. DL, proof of insurance and registration were provided without incident. Identified suspect as Dalton Biskette. Upon stating arrest was *mandatory*, Biskette became belligerent and non-compliant. After backup officers arrived, repeated attempts to handcuff the suspect proved unsuccessful. Tasers were drawn, and suspect became more belligerent, screaming expletives while threatening officers with harm and anal intercourse. Eventually Biskette was brought down with Tasers from myself, officers Bryant and Moses; handcuffed, and transported to Sedgwick County Jail," he paused and lowered the paper to his desk.

"First and foremost, explain to me the necessity to be traveling on an occupied highway, in the city, at speeds in excess of one hundred and thirty miles per hour," the judge bellowed.

I cleared my throat and responded truthfully.

"I was late for a meeting," I sighed.

"A meeting?" the judge chuckled.

I nodded my head, "Yes, sir."

"You were traveling to a meeting at 7:30 in the evening?" he asked.

"Yes, sir," I responded.

He rested his hand on his chin and widened his eyes, "A meeting with whom?"

"The President. Had it just been with one of the fellas, I wouldn't have been goin' so fast," I explained.

"As I doubt you were late to a meeting with Barrack Obama, I'll ask that you explain further. The president of..." he paused as he turned his palms upward.

"The club, your honor. The president of the club."

"Evasive, Mr. Biskette. You're being evasive. It is part of the reason you're here. Specifically, who were you going to meet at 7:30 in the evening?" he asked.

"Slice. He's the president of the motorcycle club," I responded.

"Slice? Does *Slice* have a name," the judge sighed.

"I'm sure he does, your honor. It's just that I'm not aware of what it might be. Slice is all I know," I lied.

The judge shook his head, exhaled, and eventually locked his eyes on mine.

He sighed heavily as he began to dig through the paperwork on his desk, "You're going to plead guilty to the speeding?"

"Yes, sir."

Without looking up, he continued, "And the reckless endangerment."

"For the weaving in and out of traffic, I'm guessing?" I asked.

"That is correct," he responded.

"Guilty," I sighed.

"Resisting arrest?" he breathed.

I didn't see much value in trying to explain how I had told officer Obie and Moses I was going to beat their asses and butt fuck them if they tried to cuff me. If the judge wasn't going to bring it up, I figured it was in my best interest to just plead guilty and save a little embarrassment for us all.

"Cause I didn't want 'em to cuff me?" I asked.

"That is also correct," he said as he glanced up from his desk.

"Guilty," I responded.

Motherfucker…

This shit's adding up quick.

"Which brings us to the two incidents over the course of the weekend. Saturday, at the mid-day meal, you were observed beating another inmate to the point of unconsciousness. Would you care to explain?" the judge asked as he raised a white piece of paper from the desk.

I gazed down past the legs of my orange jumpsuit and focused on the little black slipper shoes they made me wear. After thinking for a long minute and exhaling all the air from my lungs, I glanced toward the judge and began to explain.

"I was wore out from the whole Taser thing from the night before, and I was hungrier than hell. I missed breakfast 'cause nobody bothered to wake me up, and I spent all mornin' miserable. Later on they called us for lunch, and I followed everyone into the chow hall. I was minding my own business, just eatin' my lunch, and some tatted up skinhead fella came and snatched the cookie off my tray and took a bite of it," I explained.

"Continue," the judge sighed.

"I smacked him, you honor."

"Smacked him? With your fist?" he asked.

I shook my head, "No sir."

"The inmate, Mr. Biskette, is *still* in the hospital," he said as he shifted his eyes to the paper he held.

"A broken jaw, broken wrist, his skull is fractured, let's see here," he paused as he picked up another piece of paper and studied it.

"It seems he has a concussion, and he's missing four teeth. With what did you strike him?" he asked as he lowered the sheet of paper.

"My head, my elbows, and maybe a knee or two," I responded under my breath.

"Over a *cookie*?" he snapped as he dropped the paperwork onto the desk.

"That ain't what this is about, no sir. It wasn't about *the cookie*. It was about *principle*. The cookie wasn't his, it was *mine*. And, while

6

we're here, I'd like to press charges on *him* for theft and the second fella I whipped for trespassing. He came in my cell without permission," I responded.

The judge sighed heavily and shook his head, "Historically, we don't charge inmates for battery, Mr. Biskette. Jailhouse fighting is a daily occurrence as is jailhouse theft. In this particular case, Mr. Biskette, I have no alternative but to charge you with battery, considering the degree of assault as well as the severity of the beatings you administered…" he paused and shook his head.

He turned his palms up, narrowed his eyes, and gazed at me as if frustrated, "I will not even address your ludicrous claims of self-defense or trespass. I had hopes you would be compliant, forthright, and willing to accept responsibility for your actions."

"I'll plead guilty to everything except whippin' them two fellas, your honor. I'll fight those charges till the day I die. They needed a lesson in respect, and all I was doin' was…"

The judge raised his hand in the air, "Stop speaking, Mr. Biskette. *Please*. It isn't your responsibility to teach anyone a lesson in anything, nor is there an allowance in the law for such acts. The laws are in place to *protect* people - even inmates in jail - from being assaulted. There are no such laws, however, allowing the administration of punishment to *teach someone a lesson in respect*. Consider yourself bound over for trial, and I'll set the bond at $50,000. If you're fortunate enough to have the means and methods to assemble $5,000, a bail bondsman may bail you out of jail under certain conditions and restrictions. And I will warn you, if there's another incident of violence during your incarceration, or during your period of probation, I will see to it that charges *are* pressed. And you *will* be on probation until the hearing."

"Have you any further questions?" he asked.

"If I pay the five grand, I forfeit it to the bondsman, is that correct?" I asked.

"That is my understanding, yes," he responded.

"And if I pay the entire fifty grand, all I got to do is show up to court, and they give all of it back?" I asked.

"That is correct," he responded.

"Well, if you'd let me make a couple calls, I'll just pay the fifty grand, save us a lot of trouble, and be on my merry little way," I grinned.

"Nothing, Mr. Biskette, would make me happier. I'll see to it the officers allow you a phone call. This hearing is adjourned," he said as he stood.

After the judge disappeared through the door behind him, officer bad cop tugged against my right arm and turned me toward the door.

"You've got fifty grand?" he chuckled.

"Got a lot more than that, but what I got ain't any of your fuckin' business, Boss," I snapped back.

"Being a 1%er must pay well. What are you guys into, running dope?" he asked in a gruff tone.

I glanced over my right shoulder and studied his name tag.

Kopic.

After turning away and taking a few shuffled steps toward the door, I grinned.

"Nope, we're into pimping bitches. One little gal makes us a ton of money. Got a weird last name, lemme think…" I hesitated and glanced up at the ceiling as if trying to recall her name.

"Hell, I can't remember it right now, but she can suck the skin right off a fuckin' apple. Crowd favorite, she is. She sucks off all the fellas

8

at the clubhouse, and all she wants in return is a gut full of cum. Got a puss on her a mile deep, too. She can take a cock for hours on end. Hell, sometimes she takes 'em two at a time – one in the twat and one in her tight little ass. What's her fuckin' name?" I paused and stared down at my feet for a minute.

"*Kopic*. That's it," I said as I glanced upward and toward the officer.

"Oh shit, that's *your* last name. Any relation?" I asked as I widened my eyes in false surprise.

As officer bad cop began to yank on my arm and threaten me with bodily harm, officer good cop attempted to settle him down.

I just grinned; feeling satisfied I'd got under his skin.

Most people are chameleons. They change their color and adapt to whatever their surroundings might be; afraid to be true to who they are, always cautious of what others might think.

Me?

I'm Dalton Biskette, known as *Biscuit* to my friends and brothers, and I never change.

Never have.

Never will.

BISCUIT

After Otis brought the bail money, we got my bagger out of impound and headed to the bar. Luckily, there were no scratches or scuffs on the bike, and I was able to ride away without having to beat someone's ass for scratching my Harley. In much need of a drink, but in more need of a little pussy, I fixed my focus on the waitress at the shitty little bar Otis picked for our afternoon drink.

"So if it ain't purple, what the fuck do you call it?" I asked as I stared at her purple fingernails.

"It's gray," she said as she spread her fingers apart and pressed them onto the table.

"Looks purple to me," I shrugged, "I fuckin' like it. It makes your eyes look deep blue. Well, almost deep blue. God damn, I like lookin' at you."

"Thank you," she grinned.

"Hell, thank *you*. I just got out of jail, and seein' you is the best thing to happen to me today, so far that is. That fine fingernail polish just adds to it," I nodded as I raised my glass of vodka.

"Oh my god. Jail? What for?" she asked.

"Ridin' my bike about a hundred and fifty miles an hour down Kellogg, beatin' the fuck out of a couple dozen cops, and kickin' the shit out of a skinhead gang while they had me locked up. Huge misunderstanding if you ask me. I'm a lover, not a fighter," I grinned as I reached up and pulled against my beard.

"So you're a bad boy. We get a lot of bikers in here, and most of them are just phonies. You're the real deal, huh?" she asked as she twisted her hips back and forth.

I took a swallow of vodka, chased it with a drink of Red Bull, and grinned as I lowered the can onto the table.

"As real as it gets," I sighed.

She glanced toward Otis, and then shifted her eyes to meet mine. After a short pause, she smiled, "I like your beard."

"Appreciate it," I said as I glanced toward Otis and winked.

The beard was a love or hate thing for women. There didn't seem to be much in between. Since I let it grow out ten years prior, it had become my trademark. Now full, well-trimmed, and long, it was a magnet for some, and a means of repulsion for others. The ones who liked it *loved* it, and the ones who didn't seemed to simply *hate* it. As the waitress stood and stared, I ran my fingers through the bottom of it, doing my best to fluff it up.

"Lemme guess," I sighed as I twisted myself in the booth, turning my body to face her directly.

Now facing her, I gazed up and down her frame as if I was trying to memorize every inch of what I was seeing. Probably in her early twenties, she was every bit of ten years younger than me. Roughly five foot six with brown hair and an average build, her face made up for what her body lacked. She was cute as hell, and had an extremely long torso in comparison to her rather short legs, another huge plus in my book. After watching her nervously paying attention to my expressed interest, I fixed my eyes on hers and reached for my glass of vodka.

"Guys take advantage of you. They never really care what you *want*, or try to listen to what you even *think*. All they want you for is arm candy, or eye candy, and maybe to - excuse my French - but to fuck. And you like fuckin', but you want more. You want someone who *understands* you and *appreciates* you," I said flatly as I raised my glass.

"Oh my god, this is insane. It's like your psychic," she squealed.

"My boyfriend, well, he's not *really* my boyfriend, we just hang out sometimes," she paused and stared down at the floor for a moment.

She glanced upward with an almost expressionless face.

"All he cares about is, you know," she said as she wagged her eyebrows.

I nodded my head and turned toward Otis. If I was able to measure his level of disgust on a scale of one to ten, he'd have tipped the scale at an eleven. Otis and I were about as close as any two men could be, but he didn't totally agree with my constant efforts to hit on every woman I encountered. As far as I was concerned, it was me just having fun and being myself.

"Oh I know," I said as I shook my head, "Probably what, in his early twenties?"

"Yeah, twenty-two," she sighed.

"Hell, that's part of the problem. You're fuckin' with a boy, and you need to do yourself a favor and see how a *man* treats you. Men are more appreciative," I said as I turned toward the booth and reached for my Red Bull.

"Oh really? So what's the big difference?" she asked.

I glanced over my left shoulder and studied her until she seemed to become nervous. As she started to fidget, I grinned and released the can.

"The difference? The *big* difference? I tell you what; I'll explain it to you. With a boy, you never know what you're gonna get. It's anybody's fuckin' guess – hell, half the time, he doesn't even realize what he's gonna do. With a man, a *good* man, you'll know," I said, hoping she'd ask for an explanation.

And, before I had a chance to wipe the moisture from my hand to the thigh of my jeans, she did just that.

"And how would I *know*?" she asked.

I lifted my legs and shifted sideways in the booth. Now facing her, I glanced down at her feet and slowly shifted my gaze along her body and stopped when our eyes met.

"Because a man would tell you what to expect, that's how. You know, with me, there are four things I'll never do. I'll tell you two of 'em now and the other two after you get on the back of my bike and go for a ride," I responded.

Silence.

"One, I'll never lie to you. And two, I won't come in your mouth without askin' permission," I said as I kicked my legs over the edge of the booth and turned to face Otis.

"Oh wow, I wasn't expecting that," she said as she nervously glanced toward Otis.

As she shifted her eyes toward me, she continued, "Okay. I have two questions. Well, one question and I guess a statement."

She paused and moved toward Otis' side of the booth. Now standing on the opposite side of the booth, she rested her hands on the edge of the table, leaned forward, and peered up at me.

"What kind of bike is it?" she asked.

"Only kind there is as far as I'm concerned. It's a Harley," I responded as I reached for my vodka.

As I held the glass in my hand and waited for the *statement*, I gazed beyond her, toward Otis. Sitting in the booth with his arms crossed, he shook his head and grinned. This wasn't the first time he'd seen me do the exact same thing I was doing now. For whatever reason, giving half the information now and the other half later seemed to work well for me; it catered to the curious side of women.

"You said you were going a hundred and fifty down Kellogg. A Harley won't go a hundred and fifty," she grinned.

"The fuck you say. Mine will, and it'll do it in a damned hurry. And in the lap of luxury, I might add. It ain't one of them uncomfortable crotch rockets," I said as I took a sip of vodka.

"It's nice, huh?" she asked.

I nodded my head, "Let me tell you what. It's like ridin' a marshmallow down the road. And not one of those little bastards you put in a cup of hot chocolate either. It's like one of them big fuckers you toast over a campfire. Now my man Otis here and I got to discuss some business. Here's two questions for ya. When do you get off work, and what was the statement you were gonna make?"

"I get off at three," she grinned.

She leaned down and rested her elbow on the table. After looking over her shoulder, she cupped her hand to the side of her mouth. As I turned my head to the side and tilted it her direction, she responded under her breath.

"You won't have to ask my permission. You know, for the thing you said earlier. I'd just let you," she whispered.

I raised my hand to my mouth and responded as if telling her a secret, "You know what? That's the funny part. I'd ask for permission anyway. It's just how I roll."

"See you at three," I said as I leaned into the seat and glanced at my watch.

After what seemed like all of an eternity, but was no more than a second or so, she stood, smiled, and walked away.

"You make me sick sometimes," Otis chuckled as she disappeared into the kitchen.

"Organizing a piece of puss is natural for most men. You ought to try it sometime," I responded.

"You and I both know all you're going to do is fuck her. That's it. You ask me, it's fucking mean," he said as he reached for his beer.

"Ain't nothin' mean about it. If I lied to her, it'd be different. I gotta live with myself, so lyin' is out of the question. She's a big girl, she'll be fine. So anyway, where was I?" I asked as I grabbed my second glass of vodka.

"The cookie," Otis responded.

"Oh yeah, the cookie. So this dumb fuck with a swastika on his forehead walks up and stops right in front of me. I got a chicken leg in my hand, and I glance up at this Jew hatin' skinhead and cough out a laugh. *Can I help you?* I ask. He reaches over, grabs the cookie off my tray and promptly takes a fuckin' bite. I'm sittin' there in fuckin' shock; my eyes as big as a couple of pie tins. Who the fuck does such shit?" I shrugged.

Otis raised his eyebrows, apparently wanting to hear the rest of the story, "Obviously some dumb fucking skinhead. So what happened?"

"Well, first of all, the cookie was a chocolate chip. I mean, had it been oatmeal or some nasty ass shit, maybe things would have been different, but it wasn't, so it ain't. So he's holding my cookie and gettin' ready to take bite number two, and I know I gotta make a move

16

and make it quick. And, I know from bein' around fuckers like the Corn Dog and some of the other fellas who've done time in the joint not to smack this fucker with my hands. So, I stand up and head butt this prick. Busted his nose open like a ripe fuckin' plum. After that, I commenced to whip the shit out of this stupid fucker. Hell, he didn't know what hit him. Afterwards, I picked my cookie up off the floor and sat down like nothin' happened. Whole thing didn't take two minutes. I finished my half eaten chicken leg and ate what was left of my cookie with this bloody fucker lying next to me. Hell, I thought I was in the clear. Was I? *Fuck no*," I paused and shook my head, frustrated that I got caught.

"Cameras?" Otis asked as he lifted his beer bottle.

"You been in this jail down here, have ya?" I asked.

"No, just stands to reason they'd have 'em," he shrugged.

"Sure as fuck do. God damned chow hall is littered with 'em. But at this point in time, I don't know that. Not yet, anyway. So, they came around checkin' everyone's knuckles for cuts, and when they didn't find any, they let us all go back to our cells. Then, they took that fucker to the hospital. Five minutes after I got to my cell, they came and arrested me. I said what the fuck you fellas gonna do, put me in jail *inside* the jail? They didn't bother anwerin'. Took me and locked me in the drunk tank till the next morning," I paused and took a drink of my vodka.

I slid the glass to the side and leaned on the edge of the table, "Next morning comes, and they let me out. Maybe an hour after I got back to my cell, one of his little minions comes up and asks *you the one who beat the shit out of Zippy?* Fuck, I didn't even answer. This brain surgeon had some shit about Hitler tattooed on his neck, it was pretty obvious who he was and why he was at my cell door. So I grabbed this walkin' abortion by his ears and head butted his ass. About ten kicks to

17

the gut and a head stomp later, and his ass was done. You know, finding out his partner's name made it all worth it. Hell, had I known his name was Zippy; I'd have whipped his ass just for that alone. Anyway, this pile of shit is layin' at my cell door, and to make sure no one else would to try and fuck with the Biscuit during my little stay, I glanced around the cell block and pulled down my little orange suit. All these fuckers are staring at me wonderin' what I'm gonna do. You wanna guess what I did?"

I leaned back in my seat, turned my palms upward, and waited wide-eyed for Otis' response.

"You pissed on him," Otis responded as he lifted his bottle of beer.

"See? I can't get one by ya, Brother. You god damned right. I pissed on that motherfucker while the whole cell block watched. I hadn't so much as stuffed my hankster back into my little suit and the goon squad came running in, tackled me, and cuffed me. Left me in the shackles and chains till I went to court," I shrugged and shook my head as I recalled trying to walk in the shackles.

I picked up my glass of vodka and stared at the half melted cubes of ice, "You know, if you try and take a normal step in them fuckers, you'll fall flat on your nose."

"What's that?" Otis asked.

"Them shackles they hook to your feet. Tricky little fuckers to walk in, I'm tellin' ya," I responded as I lifted my glass and drained the remaining vodka.

"Fifty grand seems kind of high for speeding through town. You must have really pissed some people off," Otis chuckled as he slid his empty beer bottle toward the edge of the table.

"Ten more minutes," the waitress said as she reached for Otis empty

18

beer bottle.

"You need another?" she asked Otis as she lifted the bottle from the table.

Otis glanced at me and shrugged.

"I think we're good. If you're talking ten minutes, that is," I responded.

"Ten or less," she responded.

Well, I guess now's a good time to test you.

"Make it less, understand?" I barked.

"Uhhm, okay," she responded immediately.

Yeah, she'll do just fine.

BISCUIT

Many years in my younger days were spent wondering if something was wrong with me. I had never been in a relationship, and never really wanted to be for that matter. As far as I was concerned, trying to tie myself down to fucking one woman was like deciding which one food I wanted to spend the rest of my life eating on a daily basis. If the world offered me various foods, eating only one seemed senseless. Consequently, if there were women who were *willing* to fuck me, forcing myself to be satisfied with only one made absolutely no sense what so fucking ever.

"Oh my god…I'm going…to do it…again," she wailed as I continued to flick my tongue against her clit.

With my index finger sliding in and out of her well lubricated ass and my thumb doing the same with her pussy, I continued to wedge her clit between my upper lip and tongue. As I rolled her little nub between them with precision, she moaned as if she were dying.

"Holy fuck…holy fuck…" she bellowed as she bucked her hips up and down.

As she lowered her hips and relaxed, collapsing onto the lounge chair, I pulled my head from between her legs and gazed down at her motionless body.

"I can't believe…you can do that…for so long," she breathed as she attempted to sit upright.

I cleared my throat and coughed a light laugh, "If licking pussy was a crime, I'd be doing life in prison."

She sat up in the chair and sighed. Her hair was a mess. The sun beat down on us through the cloudless sky, and her body was covered in sweat. Her swimsuit bottom at the edge of the pool, and her top askew across her b-cup titties from all the writhing around in the lounge, she looked young and confused.

"You alright?" I asked as I stood.

"Just kind of dizzy. Holy crap, you're really good at that," she sighed as she ran her fingers through her hair.

"Oh wow," she giggled as she pointed toward my crotch.

I glanced downward.

My cock was rigid, and the fabric of my swim trunks was stretched as tight as a violin string. After a few minutes in the pool, she had wanted to sunbathe, which led to me betting her I could make her orgasm six times from licking her pussy. Whether I could or not was irrelevant, her accepting the bet got my foot in the door – sexually speaking.

Standing in front of her with a cock so hard it could be used to cut diamonds; it appeared I had every ounce of her attention.

"Tends to get excited when I do that," I grinned.

"You like it? Doing it?" she asked without looking up.

"Love it," I responded.

"Can I see it?" she asked as she leaned forward and tilted her head toward the bulge in my shorts.

"Thought you'd never ask," I responded as I reached for the drawstring.

I untied the knot, and pulled down on the waist of my shorts as she fixed her eyes on the prize. After gripping my cock with one hand and pushing down on my shorts with the other, I finally managed to pull it from confinement.

"Holy crap," she gasped as it sprung free.

"What?" I asked, attempting to seem surprised by her shock.

Her eyes widened as she leaned forward and gazed at my cock. After a long minute of studying it, she glanced upward.

She swallowed heavily as she covered her mouth with her hand, "That's huge."

"Yeah, it kind of is. And we're on a time crunch. Right now, your little twat is about as wet and ready as it'll ever be. Come here," I said as I kicked my shorts to the side.

"Right here? In the backyard?" she said as she glanced over each shoulder.

"I just sucked on your pussy for thirty minutes; don't start that high and mighty shit now. And take that top off so I can play with your titties," I said as I motioned toward the bathhouse.

She stood from her seat, glanced around the pool nervously, and sighed. As she reached up to remove her top, I began to stroke my cock.

"Do you have a condom?" she asked as she tossed her top on the concrete beside her bikini bottom.

"If God wanted me to wear a condom, I'd have been born with one wrapped around my cock. I don't wear 'em. Ever," I said flatly.

"I'll take my chances with diseases. I *know* I'm clean, and I'm gonna *guess* your clean," I shrugged.

"I am, but..." she said through her teeth.

"You ain't got to worry about gettin' pregnant. I got fixed a long time ago," I sighed.

"Really?" she asked as she tip-toed across the hot concrete deck.

Quickly becoming irritated at the fact I wasn't already powerfucking her wet pussy, I sighed my response heavily, "Yeah, *really*."

"Uhhm, I dunno," she said as she gazed down at crotch.

Still gripping my cock in my hand, I shrugged my shoulders and grinned, "You gotta risk it to get the Biscuit."

That didn't sound as good out loud as it did in my head.

Standing just a few feet in front of me, she bit into her lower lip, shifted her eyes toward my cock, and grinned as she glanced upward. She nodded her head once. It was all I needed. I slapped my palm against the wall of the bathhouse. As she shifted her eyes toward my hand, I reached for her hair, pulled her into my shoulder, and breathed my sexual demands into her ear.

I'd found out from nothing more than experience, trial and error, and being slapped a few dozen times what worked best for convincing women to comply with my sexual demands. *Asking* them to do things exposed me to the possibility of a *no* response. *Demanding* they do something could potentially backfire, and often did just that. *Suggesting* they do something seemed to work well; and proposing my desires in the form of a stern whisper rarely did nothing but satisfy us both.

With her hair in my hand and my lips against her ear, I turned her head to the side with a slight tug.

"Put your hands against the wall and brace yourself, Cassie," I breathed against her ear, "I'm going to fuck you until you collapse into a pile, and no matter what, don't move your fuckin' hands."

I inhaled a shallow breath, exhaled into her ear, and continued, "Do you understand me?"

"Oh fuck. Uhhm, yes," she whimpered.

As she turned to face the bathhouse, she raised her hands in the air and breathed her concerns in the form of a dry whisper, "But what if... what if it doesn't fit."

"Press your hands against the fuckin' wall, Cassie," I growled into her ear.

"Oh shit. Okay," she said as she slapped her hands against the wall.

I let go of my cock and tugged against her hair hard enough to get her attention. After tilting my head to the side and inhaling a shallow breath, I pressed my lips lightly against her ear and exhaled heavily.

"Spread your legs as wide as you can, slide your hands down the wall a little, but don't you dare take them off that fuckin' wall, no matter what," I whispered.

As she began to resituate herself, I continued.

"Now, arch your back and stick that sweet little pussy of yours up in the air so I can shove my tongue in it. Understand?" I breathed into her ear.

"Uhhm, okay," she muttered.

I released her hair, bent at my knees, and gripped her ass in my hands. As I spread the bottom of her butt cheeks apart with my thumbs, she slowly lowered her shoulders and bent over. Without warning, I pressed my face into her swollen pussy and began tongue fucking her as deep as I was able to.

There was no doubt in my mind God put me on the earth for one thing and one thing only.

Fucking women.

For him to grace me not only with a cock the size of a cucumber - but a five inch long tongue - could only mean one thing.

He wanted me to please women sexually.

Not one to argue with God's will or question his intention for having me on this earth, I decided to embrace his wishes and do just that.

As my tongue slid in and out of her pussy, she moaned and groaned while she repeatedly bent her knees, pressing her ass into my face. After a solid five minutes of tongue lashing, she had no less than two orgasms, and was whimpering like a lost puppy. I pulled my tongue from her pussy, licked along the crack of her ass and up her back, and eventually rested my chin against her shoulder.

"Turn your head to the side," I breathed.

Breathing heavily, and still confused from her repeated orgasms, she tilted her head to the right and blinked her eyes a few times.

"Open your mouth," I whispered against her earlobe.

Without speaking, she opened her mouth.

I slid my index and middle finger into her mouth as I reached down and gripped my throbbing shaft in my hand. As I slowly worked my fingers along the surface of her tongue, I pressed the tip of my cock against her dripping pussy.

"If it hurts, bite down on my fingers," I said.

Her eyes widened and she attempted to speak.

"Shhhh," I whispered into her ear.

"As hard as you want. Now remember, no matter what, don't move those fuckin' hands," I said through my teeth.

She nodded her head as she began to suck my fingers.

There's no doubt some women have small pussies, while others have larger ones. My experience had taught me that regardless of size, preparation was paramount to my success. A good amount of foreplay and a little tongue fuckin' allowed me to do what many guys with large cocks couldn't.

As I slowly pushed the tip of my cock into her wet pussy, she moaned in delight.

A few slow shallow strokes with about half the length of my shaft, and she began to suck on my fingers like she was sucking a cock. Two or three strokes with three fourths of it, and she was wailing like she'd just won the lottery. As it was apparent she wasn't going to be biting my fingers any time soon, I slowly pulled them from her mouth and allowed her to scream in delight as I continued to work myself deeper and deeper into her pussy.

Now slowly and steadily fucking her with every inch of my swollen manhood, I reached up and began lightly pinching her nipples with my fingertips. With each light pinch, she groaned and twisted her body in pleasure. I pressed my face against hers as I continued to fuck her slowly and steadily.

"Take that big biker cock like a good little girl," I breathed against her neck.

"Oh fuck…I uhhm…will…I will," she moaned.

The inner wall of her tight wet pussy working against every inch of my cock was almost more than I could handle. As I pulled my head rearward, positioning my mouth against her right ear, I slid my hands along her sides and down to her hips. Rubbing the tips of my index and middle fingers into the depressions of her hips while I continued to fuck her, she began to writhe against me.

"When you get ready to come, I want you to scream, do you understand me?" I whispered into her ear.

"Yes…I…I understand," she moaned.

I slowly fucked her as deep as I was able, my hips pressing against her round twenty-two year old ass with each stroke.

"You like that big cock?" I grunted as I continued to thrust myself into her.

"Oh fuck yes," she responded.

"I like that tight little pussy of yours. I'm going to fill you with cum, you know that, right?" I groaned.

"Uhhm yes...please..." she sighed.

I gazed downward, studying her ass as I thrust myself into her half a dozen more times with long, slow strokes, watching my glistening cock slide in and out of her pussy with each rearward thrust of my hips.

"I might pull out and come all over those cute little titties," I said under my breath.

"Oh Jesus...." she said through her teeth.

"You move those hands and I'm going to stop fucking you. Don't fucking move 'em," I growled into her ear.

"Oh fuck...I won't...I...promise," she stammered.

"Maybe I'll cum all over that pretty face or in your mouth. You're a little cock hungry slut, aren't you?" I breathed into her ear.

"Uh huh. I am. Whatever you say. Yes..." she responded as I continued to pound myself deep into her.

"You tight pussied little bitch," I whispered against her neck.

I pressed my lips to her ear and exhaled, "I'm going to pump you full of cum you sexy little whore. You're going to fuck me whenever I tell you to – you're my on command pussy – do you fucking hear me?"

"Okay..." she sighed, "Whenever...you...want. Your cock feels... so...good"

I slowly pulled my hips rearward as I glanced down at my cock. As each inch of the shaft slid free of her pussy, I smiled in satisfaction. Holding still with only the tip of my cock penetrating her, I exhaled into her ear heavily.

"Scream like you're trying to wake the fuckin' dead, do you fuckin' understand me?" I growled.

She exhaled her response, "Okay…"

In one thrust, I buried myself balls-deep into her pussy. As I continued to press my fingers against her hips, I pounded myself steadily in and out of her wet mound. With my tightening nut sack striking her clit with each stroke, she began to slap her hands against the wall. Steadily working my hips with the precision of a male stripper, I felt her pussy begin to contract around my throbbing shaft. As she tilted her head rearward and began to moan, I released her right hip and slapped her ass with my hand.

"Louder," I demanded.

"Oh fuck…Oh my…fuck…" she screamed.

I relaxed and closed my eyes. One other thing God seemed to grace me with was the ability to reach orgasm on command. All I needed to do was relax and focus. If I had a clear mind and a good piece of pussy, and I was able to cum whenever I wanted to. To please her, satisfy myself, and make the experience as enjoyable as possible, as she began to reach climax I exhaled and unloaded every drop of cum I had in reserve into her warm wet pussy.

"Ohhh…." she groaned as her legs went weak.

I gripped her hips in my hands and held her upright as I continued to have miniature climaxes inside of her. As she all but collapsed into my arms, I lifted her up and prevented her from falling.

"Good shit, huh?" I sighed as I slid my cock from her dripping pussy.

"Huh?" she gasped.

"The cock. Feels good, huh?" I breathed into her ear.

"You have no idea," she sighed.

I lifted her from her feet and walked around the front of the bathhouse. Almost as if she were in shock, she gazed at me silently as I carried her to the doorway. After I kicked the door open, I walked through it and into the shower. As I lowered her to her feet and turned on the water, she looked up and spoke.

"So, you said earlier you didn't date or anything," she said under her breath.

"That's right," I nodded as I ducked into the shower.

"Get in here, it'll feel good," I said as I rinsed off in the cool water.

She stepped beside me and began to rinse off, smiling the entire time.

"But you said while you were fucking me I was your uhhm, your *on command* pussy," she said.

"You are," I responded as I stepped free of the shower stream.

"So, how's that work?" she asked as she rinsed her hair.

I turned to face her, shrugged my shoulders, and widened my eyes, "It means whenever I want to fuck, within reason, you'll do it. You're going to fuck me whenever I want. Understand?"

"Uhhm. Okay," she responded.

"You like that big cock, don't you?" I asked.

"Oh fuck, I love it. It's just. I don't know, it just feels different. You know, *good* different. I've never come so hard in my life," she grinned as she stepped away from the shower.

"Ever had two cocks at once?" I asked as I turned toward the door.

"Huh? Two at the same time? Uhhm, *no*," she snapped back.

"If I ask you to, you'll do it for me, understand?" I said over my shoulder.

"You mean two guys fucking me at the same time?" she asked as she attempted to catch up with me.

"Yep," I responded as I reached for my shorts.

"I dunno. I mean…" she began.

I shook my head, "If I ask you to fuck me and one of the fellas, you'll do it. Understand?"

"I'll uhhm. I mean I *might*," she shrugged as she picked up her bathing suit bottom.

"If I ask you to, you'll do it for me, *understand*?" I repeated as I pulled up my shorts.

"Okay, yeah. I'll do it. Just don't, I mean, just don't like…tell anybody," she shrugged.

"It'll be our little secret," I grinned.

"Cool. So, what now?" she asked.

"Now? We'll swim for maybe fifteen minutes or so, and then we'll fuck again. How's that sound?" I responded.

"Again? Oh wow. You can do that?" she asked as she pulled her top around her cute little titties.

"Sure can," I said as I dove into the pool.

As the icing on the proverbial cake of life, God graced me with one more gift, the one that convinced me my time on this earth was to be spent doing nothing other than fucking women.

Within fifteen minutes of having sex, I would recover fully; and be ready for another round. There was really no other reason for me to possess this quality but to fuck like a rabbit. I swam the length of the pool, smiling to myself, knowing I had added yet another woman to my long list of willing sexual participants.

As my lungs began to burn, I came up for a breath of air. After catching my breath, I stared up at the clear summer sky and smiled.

HUNG

Thank you, God.
I won't let you down.

BISCUIT

I stood in the corner of the shop with a bottle of beer dangling loosely from my fingers as four men stood in a semi-circle listening to me tell a story. If there was a way I could get paid for telling stories, I'd damned sure quit building Harley engines and give it a try. For now, I did it to satisfy me and entertain those I enjoyed spending time with. As I waited for someone to prompt me to continue, I raised my beer bottle to my lips and took a slow drink.

"So what happened?" Pete grunted, "God damn, you always do that. You fucking *start* and then make us beg ya to continue. Just tell the fuckin' story, asshole."

"Watch that mouth, Brother Pete. My lips was parched, and I needed a drink. I've been tellin' this fuckin' story to everyone I bump into since last week when it happened. My fuckin' throat's raw from all the talkin' I been doin'," I said as I lowered the bottle of beer.

"So I tell this bitch *follow me to the truck*, and I turn for the door. Now I don't know if she's followin' me or not, but I keep on fuckin' walkin' like I know she's back there. When I step through the door and out into the rain, and I don't hear the door slam behind me, I know she's comin'," I paused and glanced around the group.

"So I walk to the truck, open my door and climb inside. Like a trained pro-fuckin-fessional, she just glides right into the truck and leans back

33

in the seat. Bitch don't say a god damned word. She just fixes her eyes on my crotch and stares. *So just how big is it?* She asks. *Well, now's a fine time to ask* I respond. She glances up and rolls her fuckin' eyes at me. Right there in my own god damned truck, this gal's fuckin' rollin' her eyes. So I'm thinkin' *fuck it*. I reach for my belt, unbutton my pants, and pull out the hankster. She lays eyes on it, and all of a sudden they're bulgin' out of her head like one of them fish at the store you can buy in a little plastic bag. *That's right, lady. Every inch of it* I sighed. *Every fuckin' inch,*" I paused for effect and took another drink.

"Damn it, Biscuit. Get to the fucking punch line," Corn Dog sighed.

"Ain't no punch line, brother. This is the damned sacred truth. *I skin it,*" I said as I slapped my hand against my forearm.

As soon as I slapped my arm, Pete's eyes widened, "Holy shit, what happened?"

"I'm fuckin' tryin' to tell ya, and I'd be done with the story and halfway home if you rude pricks wouldn't be interruptin' me every time I took a breath," I sighed.

"So, anyway. She stares at my cock for a while, exhales a breath for so long she fogs up my windows, and then she looks up. *You ain't gonna punch me in the face are ya?* She asks. *Why the fuck would I punch you in the face?* I ask her. She shrugs her shoulders and stares at me. *You've bet me twenty bucks you can deep throat my cock* I say to her. Before I can even try and decide why she'd ask such a thing, she tells me why. Pete, run and get me a beer, I'm fuckin' dyin' here," I said as I raised my empty beer bottle.

"Don't tell any more of it till I get back," Pete said as he turned toward the fridge.

"So what bar was it?" Otis asked.

"That one on Douglas. The Shamrock," I responded.

"Truck parked in the street?" he asked.

"Yep," I nodded.

Otis shook his head as he raised his beer to his lips.

"You're fucking crazy," Toad said as he shook his head from side-to-side.

"I said don't tell anymore till I got back," Pete grunted as he stepped to my side.

"I ain't said a word. Now hand me that beer before I got to admit myself in the hospital for strained vocal cords," I said as I reached for the beer.

"So anyway. This gal says *well, most guys end up smacking me at some point in time. I was just checkin'*. I stared down at her and said *what the fuck you mean most guys smack ya*? She shrugs her shoulders and says *well, I'm just a magnet for that stuff. So do you promise you won't hit me?* I stared at her for a long minute and shrugged my fuckin' shoulders. *I can't make any promises, but I sure ain't plannin' on it* I tell her. Then I studied her for another second and said *If it's any reassurance, you'd be the first.* She sticks her hand in her mouth and…listen up Pete, god damn it, this part is crucial," I barked as Pete turned to face the door.

"Sorry, thought I heard somethin'," Pete responded.

"I'm sure you did, you weird prick. There's twenty Sinners in this shop, I'm sure you heard a lot of somethin's. If you wanna go play out in the street, go ahead. If you wanna listen to me, pay fuckin' attention," I growled.

"I'm listenin'," Pete nodded.

"Okay, so this gal is hot. Maybe forty, got long brown hair, big fuckin' titties, long legs, and a pretty face. So she turns kinda to the side where I can't quite see her, sticks her hand in her mouth, and pulls somethin' out. Now at this point in time, I can't see it. But when she looks up," I paused and took a drink of beer.

"She ain't got any teeth on top. Nary a one. Nothin' but fuckin' gums. Now I start thinkin' about how much extra room there's gonna be in her mouth for my fat cock, and what it's gonna feel like getting a gum job, and…"

Otis scrunched his nose and bit his lower lip as he interrupted, "She pulled out her fucking dentures?"

"God damn it, Otis, if you want to tell the story, I'll let ya. But don't fuckin' interrupt me when I'm tryin' to," I sighed.

"Continue," Otis said under his breath.

"Dentures?" Pete asked.

"Listen up, fellas. At this point in time, she's agreed to suck me off for a twenty, got in the truck, asked me if I'm going to punch her face, and pulled out her dentures and has 'em in her hand. Is everyone caught the fuck up?" I asked.

Four heads nodded.

"Alright. So she looks up and says *got anywhere I can put these?* And she opens her hand. I act like it's a daily occurrence and I shrug my shoulders. *Put 'em in the glove box* I say as I reach over and open it. Now remember fellas, I got my cock out, and I'm in the middle of the fuckin' street in my truck. She glances at the glove box, reaches in her mouth and pops out the bottom row. So now she's sittin' there without a tooth in her god damned head. Hell, most fellas would be grossed out, but I just wanna *feel* it. You know, smooth gums on my cock. So, she shuts the glove box door and says *I like it rough. I want you to force me to suck you off.* My eyes widen and I grin at her. After a second I ask *just how rough?*" I lifted my beer and took a long drink.

As I lowered the bottle and hooked my thumb on my belt, all eyes were on me.

"She turns to me and grins. Then she says *rough as fuck*. Hell, I felt like I won the jackpot. *You got the right man* I said as I grabbed her head and shoved it into my lap. So, I got her head in one hand and my cock in the other. I'm tryin' to force feed this bitch my cock, knowin' she ain't gonna get half of it down her throat, and then…I'll be dipped in shit… here comes the huge fucking shocker, fellas…"

"Husband shows up?" Pete said.

I shook my head as I took a drink of beer.

"Barfed?" Corn Dog said.

"Nope," I said as I lowered my beer bottle.

"She swallowed it?" Otis sighed.

I nodded my head, "All the way to my nuts. Now remember, she said she likes it rough. But I swear to God himself. Fuckin' this gal's throat was like fuckin' a jar of jelly. No resistance at all. She says she likes it rough, and I can't force her to do a damned thing. Hell, her face just falls down to my lap and back up she goes. Now I know why guys smack her in the mouth, there ain't nothin' else to do if she likes it rough. Fuckin' gal's a human jackhammer. So she's goin' to town on my cock, and moanin' and groanin' and my nuts are covered in slobber, and I'm thinkin' this is the best twenty bucks I ever spent – and because it's a bet – I can still say I ain't never paid for pussy. Anyway, I'm about to bust a nut, and I get all grabby…"

"So I reach under her shirt for a fist full of them titties, and she starts gruntin' and tryin' to pull off my meat. I'm two seconds or three strokes from a happy endin' and I ain't havin' it. She's gruntin' *no no no*, and

I'm forcing her head down on my junk thinkin' *yes yes yes*. So I got an elbow on the back of her head, and I reach up under her top and pull on that wire at the bottom of her bra to let them big titties out. You know, just pull it up and over the nips and let 'em pop out," I paused and took a sip of beer as I glanced at each man.

Standing with their eyes wide and waiting for the next bit of the tale, they stared in awe.

"And I lift that bastard back, and *pop*. Out comes two fake rubber titties. Fell right out onto my dusty ass truck floor. I'm starin' at these rubber fuckers tryin' to decide what happened, and she's tryin' to pull off my cock, so I just bury my elbow into her head and blow a load into her throat – you know, because she says she likes it rough. I'm thinkin' this is all part of the *I like it rough* act. After I let her up for a breath, she's cryin' and all embarrassed," I paused and shook my head.

"I'm feelin' bad for her. She's got cum dribblin' from her lips, and she ain't got a tooth in her head, her god damned teeth are in the fucking glove box, and the only tits she has are layin' on the dusty assed floor of my truck beside my boots."

"Flat chested gal, huh?" Pete shrugged.

I shook my head, "Fuckin' cancer."

"Oh God damn. No shit?" Toad asked.

I nodded my head, "Yep. Said she had a double whatever they call it. Hell, I felt terrible. We sat for a long bit afterward and talked about it. God damned shame anyone has to go through that, if you ask me. I told her it didn't matter as far as I was concerned; I told her she was pretty with or without tits. You know, it's god damned sad about the cancer, but she's a great gal. Her name's Billie Jean. Hell, I ended up gettin' her number and added her to the list," I shrugged.

"But here's the *really* good news," I said as I lifted the bottle of beer.

"What's that?" Otis asked.

"She said she'll do club parties. Ends up she gets some weird satisfaction from sucking dude's cocks. Anyway, if any of you fellas want a gum job, she's ready," I grinned as I raised my bottle of beer.

"I'm out," Toad said as he turned away.

"Me too," Otis sighed.

"Count me in," Corn Dog nodded.

"I'm good as long as it's Wednesday or Thursday," Pete grinned.

"See, you two fellas are going to miss out," I said as Otis and Toad walked away.

"They don't know what's good for 'em," Pete hissed, "A blowjob's a blowjob."

"Amen," I nodded, "And one without teeth is a rare occurrence indeed."

"Agreed," Pete grinned.

"Now huddle up, fellas. I'll tell ya about my run in with a skinhead gang while they had me locked up," I said as I raised my beer bottle.

As I gazed blankly at the bottle, I realized it was empty.

"Pete, get me one more," I sighed as I raised my empty bottle in the air.

As Pete walked toward the fridge, I glanced around the shop. For me, telling the stories was like reliving them. Another chance to have the same amount of fun as I had actually had doing what it was I told the story about.

And I was good at it.

Pete handed me the cold bottle of beer and I placed the empty in the trash can behind me. Telling stories about being in jail, drinkin' a beer, and being surrounded by my brothers – hell, life couldn't get any better.

Without a doubt, being a Sinner was my calling in life.

Well, that and fuckin' bitches.

BISCUIT

I carefully pulled the brush along the edge of the wooden door trim, being cautious not to touch the wood with the bristles of the brush, but taking time to ensure the *Revere Pewter* paint underneath the new coat of *Chelsea Red* was covered completely. After I reached the bottom of the trim I took a few steps back and admired the room.

The red paint was a refreshing change. The pewter color had only been on the walls for roughly four weeks, but the red really set the room off and made everything pop. Masking off the trim was always an option - but I took pride in doing everything by hand - a steady hand and a little caution provided me with tremendous satisfaction. My nostrils flared as I took a long deep breath and gazed around the room blankly.

The smell of success.

After carrying the paint, drop cloths, and brushes to the garage I went into the kitchen and washed my hands. Alt-J's *Left Hand Free* played from my iPod, providing further proof that the art of creating good music had not been lost in the modern age.

Music was my only outlet, my only escape. I hadn't had a television in my house for almost fifteen years. Although I'd watched television at some of the Sinners homes, and when we were on the road I often watched it in the hotel, I viewed my life as much more simple if I didn't have access to a television or watch the news.

As a teen I decided to stop, and I never regretted my decision since making it - when so many of my brothers were depressed about world events I was none the wiser. Often, subjects being discussed were several months or even a year old before I learned they had even happened. I lived with much less grief and seemed to have a fairly steady emotional state as a result.

As I dried my hands I heard my phone beep. Modern technology was without a doubt the downfall of society, but having a telephone was mandatory for a Sinner, and I accepted it as a useful tool.

I scrolled through the text message from Otis and typed my response.

Be there in fifteen, Brother.

I slipped the phone into the front pocket of my jeans, unplugged my iPod, grabbed my keys, and walked out to the garage. After plugging my iPod into the pigtail on the stereo of my bike, I fired it up and opened the garage door.

As the Black Key's *Sinister Kid* blared from my saddlebag mounted speakers, I pulled out of the garage and onto the street. My neighbors had come to accept the fact I was a biker and rode a loud as fuck Harley, but they'd never quite understood my need to play the music I did as loud as I chose to. As the thumping bass shook the handlebars slightly, I rolled back the throttle and leaned into the first curve leading out of my neighborhood.

Riding a Harley wasn't something I chose to do because I thought it was cool, or because I felt a need to be surrounded by others who supported me. It became a way of life from the first time I rode a bike at eighteen years of age. From that very first day, I had ridden every day possible. To me, riding cleansed my soul. A thirty minute ride alone could take me from the foulest of moods and insert me in my own star-filled heaven. Whatever it might have been that had me upset quickly vanished – and never returned – after a full-throttle ride down the highway.

Riding and music, my two much needed outlets.

As I pulled into the parking lot I noticed Otis hadn't arrived yet. I parked the bike on the sidewalk, kicked the kickstand down, and let Jimi Hendrix's *Red House* finish playing before I turned off the key. Jimi's music provided a constant reminder of the talent that was lost – never to be replaced – as a result of drug use. The talented musicians who had died as a result of drug overdoses over the years sickened me.

Janis Joplin, Jimi Hendrix, Jim Morrison, Nick Drake, Sid Vicious, John Bonham, Shannon Hoon, and Amy Winehouse, all dead for no good reason other than the fact they didn't know when to stop using drugs and start living life.

Me?

Never used the stuff and never planned on starting.

As the music stopped and the next song began, I turned the key and stepped over the seat. After reaching over and locking the bike, I walked into the empty bar. After a quick study, it seemed four people would be joining Otis and me, none of which provided me a feeling of threat or a sexual interest. I walked to the bar, sat down, and ordered a drink.

"Double vodka and a can of Red Bull when ya get a minute," I said as I sat down on the bar stool.

"Be just a second," the bartender said over her shoulder.

Turn around so I can get a good look at ya.

No more than a thirty second wait later, and she slid a can of Red Bull and a glass of vodka in front of me. Half zoned-out and listening to Peter Gabriel's *Solsbury Hill*, I glanced up and blinked as my eyes attempted to come into focus.

God damn....

Cute as absolute fuck, probably tipping the scales at a hundred and ten pounds, and all of five foot three, the bartender had perfect complexion, smooth skin, beautiful green eyes, and fire engine red hair with two purple stripes – in the front. A definitive line across the center of her head from left to right separated the back half of her hair, which was brown. The entire multi-color scheme of unnatural hair colors repulsed me.

I puckered my face like I'd just bit into a lemon and turned away.

God damned waste of a fine lookin' girl if you ask me.

I reached over my shoulder, fumbled for my glass of vodka, and sighed as I finally felt the cool glass in my hand. As I took a drink and tried to wash the sight of her from my mind, Otis stepped into the bar.

Otis was a strange man. Satisfied by simply living life, he wasn't a typical biker, nor was he a typical man. He didn't have an Ol' Lady, only had a girlfriend during his high school years, and never took the time – or had the desire – to try and pick up women. He was definitely one of the club's strong points, and was often the man a brother would go to in a time of need. His advice was well thought out, never pre-prepared, and always considerate of who it was that was receiving it. The fact he wanted to meet me *to talk* had me a little concerned, but only a little.

I stood from the bar stool and opened my arms, "Big O, what's shakin'?"

"Just needing to unwind. Let's go over and sit in one of those booths, I don't need the bartender listening to what we're talking about," he said as he tilted his head toward the booth on the other side of the bar.

I patted him on the back and turned toward the bar, "No argument from me, that stool is as hard as a wedding day cock."

I grabbed my vodka and Red Bull, anxious to get away from the walking box of crayons behind the bar.

"Place don't seem the same without Avery and that other chick workin', does it?" I asked as we walked toward the booth.

"Sure doesn't," Otis said as he sat down.

The night we all met Avery, Otis staged a fight between Toad and Pete. Hell, Toad was kickin' the absolute shit out of Pete, and I had no idea why. Toad will fight a man just for the sake of doin' it, but fightin' one of your brothers generally requires a good reason. Come to find out later Otis set it up just so Slice could see how the poor gal handled the outburst.

That damned Avery is good for Slice, no doubt about it. She keeps him grounded, and his mood swings are almost non-existent now. Personally, I don't need a woman to keep me grounded, but for some of the fellas, it's a necessity. Although I never would have guessed Slice would be one of those fellas, I was pleased to see him commit to Avery, and more pleased to see how he changed after they moved in together.

The big tittied friend of Avery's was a totally different story, and nothing short of a sexual train wreck. As I laughed to myself at the thought of her, I leaned forward and grinned, "Sure you heard about Corn Dog and that poor girl who worked here, huh?"

"I've heard some, yeah," Otis nodded.

"They're inseparable now. He's been fuckin' that poor girl six ways from Sunday. Talked to him after the meeting the other day. Said he's been schooling her on sucking cock, and it sounds like she's got quite the sexual appetite. Anyway, he's making up for the five years of lost time he spent in the joint," I said.

45

Otis seemed a little off his game. He slowly nodded his head as he looked beyond me and into the bar, "I'm sure he is."

As he waved his hand in the air, I continued, "You know, every one of the fellas is fascinated by that girl's big fucking titties. But me? I'm fascinated with the fact Toad wrapped her head in god damned Saran Wrap, fucked her until she was damned near dead, and then took her to the Dog's house, dropped her off, and she ain't fuckin' left yet. Hell, until the Toad dropped her off, she'd never met Corn Dog."

"I'll take a couple of Michelob Ultras and bring him another can of Red Bull and a few iced double vodkas," Otis said as the waitress walked up.

I turned and glanced over my shoulder toward the waitress. Tall and far beyond gorgeous, she appeared to be in her mid-twenties and all of damned near six foot tall. If I was a guessing man, I would guess she was one of Avery's volleyball sisters from the college.

The waitress grinned as she shifted her eyes from Otis to me, "Sounds good. You guys aren't going to shoot the place up, are you?"

"We might after we get a few drinks in us," I chuckled.

She glanced over at Otis and studied him for a long minute. Knowing Otis wasn't going to make a move on this girl, and feeling like I damned sure needed to, I cleared my throat.

"God damn…" I sighed as I shifted my eyes up and down her frame.

"What?" she snapped back as she turned to face me.

"Your eyes. They're the craziest blue I ever seen," I responded.

She shrugged her shoulders, "Contacts."

Colored contact lenses, I had a little experience with them and it wasn't good. In fact, it kind of freaked me out at first. I never understood why a person felt a need to try and be someone or something they weren't. My eyes were hazel, and I never had a desire to have them be anything but what God gave me.

"Figures," I grunted as I shifted in my seat.

"Be back in a minute," she said.

I leaned forward and shook my head, "Nothin' against the Dog, but I wonder about that fuckin' girl, Sloan. Damned thing can't have a lick of proper upbringing in her. Personally, I wouldn't fuck her with Pete's cock, and he's a nasty fucker. Corn Dog's pounding that shit like each day's his last, so I guess I'll say good for him; and from what he was sayin' she's become mighty fine at sucking cock. Oh, shit, I almost forgot, I got a story to tell ya."

Otis grinned and nodded his head. He generally listened to my stories and seemed to enjoy them, even if he'd heard them before. As I started to tell my tale, I couldn't immediately remember if I'd told him in the past.

"So, speaking of suckin' cock, there was this girl; she gave the best fuckin' head ever. Damned thing was like a trained professional, and probably should have had a college course on how to properly suck a cock. She could take my meat all the way to the balls, stick out her god damned tongue, and curl it around my nut sack without missin' a beat," I paused and waited to see if he looked uninterested.

He grinned and waited for more.

"So, this bitch had the most beautiful blue eyes. And, because she had no gag reflex, I could fuck this girl's mouth just like I was fuckin' a pussy. Anyway, when I'd pound her throat with my cock, I'd look down into her eyes, and after she bat those long lashes and revealed those damned eyes a few times, I'd just explode. She knew her eyes were my biggest weakness, and she was right," I ran my fingers through my beard and waited for a second to continue.

He leaned into the table and waited for more.

"So one night, she's down on her knees, and she's going to town on my cock. Just a slurpin' and a suckin' like this one's her last. Hell, I'm lookin' up at the ceiling like I got no interest in watchin' her, which couldn't be any further from the truth. My problem was this," I paused as the waitress walked up.

She slid the drinks onto the table. Although I couldn't immediately identify the name of her perfume, I had smelled it in the past, and really enjoyed it. As my mind drifted away at the thought of her scent, she spoke.

"Here you go, two iced vodka doubles, a can of Red Bull, and two Ultras. Anything else?"

I stared at the drinks and inhaled a shallow breath through my nose.

"Other than being like super big, you don't look like a biker, I mean not *really*," the waitress asked.

I grabbed the bottom of my cut and tugged on it proudly, "Never thought I was super big, but thanks, *I guess*."

"I uhhm, I was meaning him," she responded with a laugh.

"Oh," I sighed.

Otis seemed offended. As he lifted his beer and tilted it her direction, he replied, "I don't know that bikers look *any* certain way to be quite honest. I look the way I look and I'm a biker. One has nothing to do with the other."

"Oh, I didn't really mean anything by it, I was just. I don't know. You know, trying to make conversation. Do you know Avery?" she asked.

Good recovery.

"Sure do, she's a good friend," Otis nodded.

"Well, we're not *close*, but I played volleyball with her. I'm a senior this year and she's a year older than me. I just heard she was like dating one of the guys in your gang," she responded.

Volleyball?

Senior?

I glanced over my shoulder and gazed at her as she spoke. She was a damned fine specimen of God's ability to grace us from time to time with the equivalent of a human Grand Canyon or Niagara Falls. She was a natural beauty, and I was quickly becoming tired of her main focus being Otis.

Otis shook his head, "Club. We're a *club*, not a gang. A motorcycle club."

"Oh, I thought you were a motorcycle *gang*. What's the difference?" she asked.

"There isn't one. Gang sounds bad, and club sounds less like we're criminals, so we like to call it a club," Otis responded.

"So you *are* a gang?" she sighed.

I shifted in my seat and raised my finger to my lips, "Shhh. Don't tell anybody."

"Oh, I won't. You can trust *me*. I'm Kat," she grinned.

I grinned and looked down at her shorts. Her legs were a fucking mile long.

"Like a pussy cat?" I asked.

"Kind of, but with a K. Katrina, Kat for short," she giggled.

"I'm Biscuit, that's Otis," I said as I shifted my eyes up to her fairly large breasts.

"Biscuit? Why Biscuit?" she shrugged.

"Why not?" I shrugged.

49

"Well, it's nice to meet you guys. I'll leave you two alone for a while. If you need me, just holler, we're not real busy. I'll probably stop by in a few and see if you're doing alright."

She turned and walked away. As she walked, I continued to stare, hoping she'd turn around and see me, but she never did. After a long minute of studying her walk, I turned around and grabbed my vodka.

"Meeefuckingyow. Kat, huh? She's a hot little number," I said as I lifted my glass.

"Where were we?" Otis asked.

"Hold up a minute, I've got to clear my mind of evil thoughts. I'm gonna poke that little bitch, mark my words, brother," I said as I took a drink of the vodka.

I chased it with Red Bull and shook my head, "I was face fucking my blue eyed girl."

"The professor of oral pleasure," Otis grinned.

"She damned sure was," I nodded, "Could have given a college course on it for sure."

"Okay. So I've got my cock down her throat, and she's staring up at me, knowing if I look into those beautiful blue eyes for more than a few seconds I'm gonna shoot my load. Me? I'm lookin' up at the ceiling, countin' them little popcorn dealios they spray on up there. Now she's suckin' away, and I'm on about two thousand five hundred and fifty-three, knowing I can't last much longer. I glance down just for a quick second, and luckily her eyes are closed," I reached for my vodka and let Otis absorb what I'd said.

"So, I reach down and grab blue eyes by the ears. Now, I got her ears in my hands, and I start pounding my cock in and out of her throat like I'm gettin' paid. Hell, I'm watchin' that fucker disappear in her mouth, amazed by the sheer talent of this girl, and I pull it out and shove it back in. Then, I pull out, and shove it back in balls deep. She don't gag or whimper or nothin'. Hell, this is turning me on like a motherfucker, so I turn it up a notch."

I raised my eyebrows, inviting Otis to imaging what might be next. While he was dreaming of my next move, I stood from my seat, held my hands in front of my hips, and started fucking the air, imagining her head in front of my cock.

"So I'm shoving my cock balls deep into her throat, pulling it out, and shoving it right back in, and it builds up that throat snot like a motherfucker," I said as I bucked my hips back and forth.

Otis wrinkled his nose, "Throat snot?"

"Yep. What, you never heard of it? It's that goop down deep in their throats. Hell, you probably ain't got a cock big enough to find it, but ole Biscuit does," I chuckled as I continued to thrust my hips back and forth.

"So anyway, I'm pounding away and things get kind of slippery. So I pull back…"

"And I don't realize it at that exact minute, but my cock slides all the way out of her mouth. So I go to shove it back in, thinkin' the tip is still in her mouth, and the head hits her top lip, and the fucker's all covered in slobber and throat snot, so it shoots up the side of her face and sticks her in the eye," I hesitated and shoved my hips forward as if I was poking her in the eye with my cock.

"Now, initially, I don't think nothing of it, other than the fact I just poked her in the eye with my cock. So I pull my hips back and prepare to shove her throat full one more time."

"And she looks up and opened her eyes…"

51

I widened my eyes and grinned. Otis sat, shaking his head and grinning.

"And she's starin' back at me smilin', ready for the cock, and she's got one brown eye and one fuckin' blue one. I got my cock in my hand, starin' back at her, and I blink my eyes, not sure if what I'm seein' is what I'm seein'. Nope, she's still crouched down there, with her mouth open, starin' back at me with one brown and one fuckin' blue one – ain't got a fuckin' clue of what's happened. Now this freaks me the fuck out, because the entire reason I like this girl, other'n the fact she can suck a golf ball through a garden hose, is that she's got them crazy blue eyes. And I glance down, blink one more time, and my eyes focus on my big fat cock. And the tip of my rod's got a little transparent blue dot on the end of it."

"Contacts?" he asked.

"Yep. That's when I learned about 'em. Fucked it right out of her god damned eye," I said with a laugh as I slipped back into my seat.

"That's a hell of a story," he chuckled.

I reached for my vodka, took a drink, and nodded my head, "Damndest thing I ever seen."

"So what was all *that* about?" a voice from behind me asked.

I glanced over my shoulder, "What?"

She grinned and held her hands in front of her little shorts and began bucking her hips like she was riding a cock. She looked like Beyonce, Britney Spears, and Madonna all rolled up into one very well-tuned dancer.

"God dayumm," I howled as I watched her put on her show.

After a few more well-timed thrusts of her hips, she slapped her hand against her ass and locked eyes with me.

I'm gonna fuck you ragged, you sexy little bitch.

"I just thought it was funny when you were doing it. I'm sorry, I'm just bored," she giggled.

"You can come over here and fuck the air any fucking time you want," I responded.

"Is that what you were doing, *fucking the air*?" she asked.

Her eyes locked on mine and her mouth curled into a cute little smile. I wanted her, and I wanted her bad. Something about her made her seem like a tease to me, but I knew she was far from it. I decided to take a chance, reveal a little about the story, and see what she had to say about a little sexual innuendo.

"*Here*? Yeah, I was fucking the air," I said as I pointed down to the floor.

"But in the story I was tellin', I was fuckin' a girl's mouth," I said as I pointed up toward her face.

"Sounds fun," she giggled.

It always *sounds* fun, but it ain't every woman who can actually take a foot long shoved in and out of their throat. Time, I suppose, would tell. Hopefully, it'd just be a matter of time, and I'd have her just where I wanted her.

Her eyes still fixed on mine, she tried to turn away. Her gaze stayed stuck as her body twisted around.

"I probably ought to go clean some tables before I get myself in trouble," she sighed.

I kept my eyes locked on hers as she walked away. After walking halfway across the bar, she grinned and turned away.

"Damn, Biscuit. Looks like she likes ya," Otis laughed.

"Sooner or later, they all do," I responded as I reached for my vodka.

"Probably those damned gauges you have in your ears," he said as he tossed his head my direction.

"Naw. It's the beard, my charm, and that big cock I'm rockin'," I laughed.

"So what'd you want to talk about?" I shrugged, realizing we hadn't even spoken about anything significant.

"Nothing, I just needed to unwind. I'm good now," he sighed.

I shrugged my shoulders, "You sure you're alright, Brother?"

"Positive," he nodded as he lifted his beer bottle.

"How long you want to stick around?" I asked.

"Drink this and go?" he shrugged as he raised his bottle of beer.

I nodded my head and glanced over my shoulder. Kat stood at the corner of the bar staring at me like she was starving and I was the only available next meal.

"I might stick around until she gets off," I said as I tilted my head her direction.

Otis raised one eyebrow, "Trial's tomorrow."

I nodded my head. Sydney's brother was given a life sentence for admitting he'd kill a rival gang member if they rode into town with a rocker claiming territory. Seemed like a far-fetched case to me, and from what Avery said, he was pretty much forced into saying it on one drunken night in a bar with an undercover ATF agent. We had all agreed to go to the trial together to support him. Trial or no trial, my focus, at least for the time being, was Kat.

"You see her fuckin' legs?" I asked as I tossed my head her direction.

Otis nodded his head as he finished his beer. He seemed off his game.

"You sure you're alright?" I shrugged.

He sighed and tilted his head rearward, "My old girlfriend, Sam. Her mother died. Just wanted to try and let it all settle. Just trying to make sense of it."

Otis' only love was Sam. They split up when he was in his early twenties, and she moved away to New York, and married some rich fella. Now hip deep in kids, and living the high life, the last thing Otis needed was to see or think of her again. He never quite recovered from losing her, and whether or not he'd ever admit it, he missed her dearly.

"Oh shit, your sweetheart? Damn, Brother, I'm sorry. What happened, if I might ask?"

"Aluminum foil. It was an accident," he sighed.

I shook my head.

Aluminum foil?

Hell, maybe she got crushed in a machine at work, I thought.

"Damn, did she work at the Reynold's Wrap factory or something?" I asked.

He shook his head, "No, she was cooking and went to pull some aluminum foil off the roll, and it cut her wrist. She bled to death before the ambulance arrived."

Shocked at the thought of a woman dying from such a freak accident, and further shocked thinking the woman was Sam's mother, I stood from my seat and opened my arms.

"Well, when a deal like that happens, you just got to stand back and realize that this world we're living in ain't ours, it's His; and things like that are just proof of it. His plan's much bigger'n this," I said.

He hugged me and slapped his hand against my back, "Appreciate it, Brother."

"See you in the morning," he said as he stepped back.

"Long as I'm done with her," I laughed as I turned around and glanced toward Kat.

"Just don't fuck her in the eye, and everything'll be fine," he chuckled over his shoulder as he walked away.

Thinking of Brother Otis being in pain didn't set well with me. He wasn't one to reveal his feelings, nor was he a person who complained about *anything*. He had texted me and wanted to meet, which meant he was bothered by the death of Sam's mother, as he should be. Trying to decide if he was more uncomfortable about the death or Sam's undoubted arrival into town was anyone's guess, but my opinion was he was worried about possibly running into Sam.

Either way, Otis never did anything he didn't want to do - if he happened to stumble onto Sam, he'd react in a manner supporting what he believed was in his best interest. As I lowered myself into the seat and reached for my vodka, feeling guilty for not having provided him a little more ear and a lot less mouth, Kat slipped into the seat across from me.

"So, what's your story?" she asked as she sat down.

I widened my eyes and stared like a sex starved idiot.

"Who me?" I asked as I pointed to my chest.

She tossed her hair over her shoulder with the back of her hand, "Yeah. You. What's your deal?"

"Deal? I dunno. Don't guess I got a *deal*. I'm just a biker who likes havin' fun, suckin' down a little beer, and tryin' to see how much Red Bull I can drink before I have a heart attack," I responded as I lifted my glass of vodka.

Her blue eyes were driving me insane, even if they weren't blue underneath her little contact lenses. As she sat and studied me, waiting for her mind to come up with another question to ask me, I daydreamed about doing the windmill with her. Her long legs and participation in sports would probably make it effortless.

"My dad's a cop," she said flatly.

"Excuse me?" I snapped back as I spit about half my vodka onto my hand and forearm.

She nodded her head, "Yep. Wichita P.D."

"Well, that's a nice how do ya fuckin' do. Damn, where'd that come from?" I asked as I wiped my hand on the leg of my jeans.

She shrugged her shoulders and sighed heavily, "I don't know, just thought I'd get it out of the way."

"Just had a run in with the cops a week or so ago," I chuckled as I glanced at the back of my hand.

"What did you do?" she asked as she leaned forward, and rested her tits on the edge of the table.

"Late for a meeting with the fellas, was going about a hundred and a half down Kellogg, resisted arrest, got Tased, cuffed, hauled to jail, and then kicked the shit out of a skinhead gang while I was locked up. Typical weekend for me," I shrugged.

Still leaning forward on the table, she glanced up and blinked her eyes a few times before answering.

"I'm not even going to lie, I *love* bad boys," she cooed.

"Well, I'm about as bad as it gets. Now, you spilled your guts about your pop being a cop, I guess I'll just cut right to it, you know, eliminate all the guesswork so to speak," I said as I lifted my glass of vodka and peered over the top.

Still pressing her tits into the top of the table, she batted her eyelashes a few times and smiled, "Okay. You're not going to scare me."

"We'll see," I sighed.

I took a sip of the vodka and chased it with a swig of Red Bull. As I sat the can down to the side, I leaned onto the edge of the table and curled my index finger into my palm, hoping she'd scoot a little closer to the center.

I wanted to smell her while I spoke to her.

She did just that, and as I inhaled a whiff of her perfume, I decided she must have sprayed a little more on herself while she was away. Maybe this was just meant to be.

"I don't commit to anyone, and I'll never be anyone's exclusive *anything*, or whatever you call it nowadays," I whispered.

She gazed at me as if hypnotized.

"Okay," she breathed.

Well, that went fairly well. Let's see how long she lasts…

I inhaled a short breath, exhaled, and glanced over each shoulder. The bar was still empty, and in fact, had two less people than the four who were in it when I entered an hour before. I turned to face her and inhaled through my nose.

Couture La La. That's the scent.

I grinned at my recollection of her perfume, and continued, "I've got a five, or maybe a six inch tongue, and a twelve inch cock about as big around as your wrist. I don't believe in love, I think marriage is a fuckin' joke, and I don't like cops. I've always wanted to fuck a cop, but never found one willin'. Lookin' at you *now*, I think I'd settle for the daughter of a cop, but that's all you're gonna get. *Fucked.* I can promise you it'll be fun, no strings attached, and we can keep doin' it for as long as you want, but it'll never be nothin' more than fuckin'. You in or are you out?"

She didn't blink an eye. As the edges of her mouth curled upward, she fought against it and began to speak.

"I like bad boys, and I hate my cop father with a passion. He despises people like you; which makes me like the thought of your twelve inch dick that much more. I'll challenge you on the tongue, because I don't think any human has a tongue that long, but the thought of it excites me. I've never been on the back of a bike, but I'd like to, and until now, I never really thought I'd even *talk* to a real biker. The bottom line, *Biscuit*, I'm in. *Your move*," she said in one uninterrupted sentence without so much as becoming short of breath.

Still positioned in the center of the table no less than eight inches from her face, I sat and stared.

Fuck, I like this girl.

For once in my life, I was at a loss for words. To mask my sudden stupidity and buy some time to come up with something to say, I reached for my glass of vodka.

"First things first," I sighed as I sat up straight.

"It ain't a dick. It's a cock. Little boys and short dudes got dicks. Mine's a *cock*," I grinned as I raised my glass to my mouth.

I took a short drink, more for theatrics than for the need to take a drink. I slid the glass to the side and widened my eyes slightly.

She reached for my vodka, slid it across the table, and lifted it to her mouth. As she peered over the rim, she tipped it up and drank the remaining liquid from the glass. After she wiped her mouth with the back of her hand, she grinned and set the glass to the side.

"I've been off work for ten minutes. From here on out, the d-word will be off limits. Now, you think you and that third leg of yours are up for a ride?"

She batted her eyelashes and waited for a response.

I swallowed heavily and raised my right hand in the air.

"What's a man gotta do to get a bar tab in this joint?" I hollered.

She grinned and leaned back into her seat. As I studied her face, and continued to stare at her overly blue eyes, the bartender slapped the tab onto the table.

"Here you go," Crayon box huffed.

I didn't even bother to turn around.

"Thanks," I said under my breath.

"You leaving?" she asked Kat.

Kat nodded her head, "With him."

"Like your beard," Crayon box said.

"Like your hair," I lied as I reached for my wallet.

"Thanks. Just got it done," she replied.

I pulled a fifty dollar bill from my wallet and pressed it on top of the thirty dollar tab.

"Keep the change," I said.

You can use the tip to fix your hair.

"Ready?" I asked as I stood.

She stood and nodded her head, "Yep."

As I watched her turn toward the door, I began to wonder if *I* was ready. Something about Kat made me feel like if I was ever going to meet my sexual match, I'd just done it.

If her willingness to perform was equal to her ability to talk a quick line of shit, I guessed it wouldn't be long and I'd know for sure.

And I was more than ready to try and find out.

KAT

I had been raised under the thumb of my overly protective police officer father, and never allowed to live life with the feeling of being free. Everyone I dated, hung out with, or even had a cup of Starbuck's coffee with was placed under a microscope and examined. None stood up to his expectations, and if I didn't remove them from my life, he made their lives so difficult they decided to leave on their own.

Going to college was the best thing to ever happen to me, and although the campus was only forty miles away from my parent's home, I opted to stay in the housing immediately off campus, claiming the drive back and forth from their house was more than I could handle when combined with my homework.

I could never decide for sure which it was, but either my hatred toward my father's strict rules, the fact he was a cop, or my mother's subservient nature caused me to have a desire to only date bad boys, and the older the better as far as I was concerned. Until I had spent some time talking to Avery, I never really considered a biker, and typically migrated toward military men.

My first three years of college were spent with a former Marine ten years older than me who was the most controlling, overly abusive, and mentally exhausting prick to ever walk this earth. Even though we broke up six months prior, he insisted on kicking my door in every time he got drunk and all but raping me upon entering the house. Finally, after beating the girl he had as a side piece for our entire relationship, he was arrested and thrown in jail for battery and domestic abuse.

Now free of his grasp, I felt a need to spread my sexual wings, and see what else the world had to offer. A relationship was the furthest thing from my mind, considering my difficulties with Kyle. I wanted a bad boy, sans the abusive behavior. I'd seen the Sinners in the town I lived in on a daily basis for the last three years, and although I viewed them as the baddest of bad boys, I hadn't really looked at any of them as a viable option until recently. Avery's explanation of the club, the men, and their loyalties sparked my interest; and Biscuit's arrival in the bar with Otis couldn't have come at a better time. Now half-drunk, horny as hell, and standing in Biscuit's living room, I wondered if I had possibly let my alligator mouth overstep the abilities of my hummingbird ass.

Standing on one side of the island in his kitchen while he stood on the other, I watched his mouth move as he spoke. The words he spoke made very little sense; it seemed my mind's focus was on his lips and beard. He'd claimed in the bar that he had a six inch tongue, and when I questioned him later, he said he knew how to use it quite well. I'd never considered myself to be one of the women who was intrigued or turned on by *beard porn*, but with him standing a few feet from me, each minute that I spent studying him caused me to be more and more attracted to the thought of him licking my pussy – something Kyle had never done. As he finished saying whatever it was he said; he began to laugh.

Naturally, I laughed in return.

"So, what do you think?" he asked.

I think I have no idea what you just said, that's what.

I grabbed the bottle of beer and squeezed it in my hand. It was luke-warm and not of any interest to me. I released the bottle, inched a little closer to the island and grinned as I lowered my hand to my waist.

"I think my leg itches," I said as I bent down slightly.

He stood on one side of the kitchen, and I stood on the other. Hidden from his view by the island in front of me, I slid my finger beneath the fabric of my shorts and along my pussy – just to check.

Holy shit, I'm soaked.

Attempting to hide the joy of finding my wet pussy, I reached for the beer with my left hand and lifted it to my not so willing lips. As I drank the warm filth, I scratched the inner part of my thigh and raised my right hand to the bar.

"Probably a fuckin' mosquito. They're bad this summer," Biscuit said.

All I saw was tongue.

"So is your tongue really six inches long?" I asked.

He wiped his hand along his beard and stretched his jaw a few times, opening his mouth wide as he did so. A few seconds later, he stuck out his tongue. If he so desired, it appeared he could lick his eyebrows with it. After twirling it in a circle and curling the tip of it while holding the remaining five inches still, my mind wandered away to all of the possibilities. I imagined him bringing me to climax with it.

My knees buckled slightly.

"Oh my," I sighed.

"Wanna try it out?" he asked as he shrugged his shoulders slightly.

Do I ever...

Incapable of speaking, I simply nodded my head.

"Go into the living room and lie down on the couch," he said as he pointed toward the room behind me.

All I heard was *lie down.*

I turned toward the living room, walked briskly to the couch, and flopped onto my back. As my head rested into the rather comfy decorative pillow, I bent my knees and rested my feet against the cheeks of my butt. In hindsight, I probably looked like an overeager prostitute.

"You might want to take them shorts off," he said as he walked into the room.

I rolled off the couch and removed my shorts and panties with one good tug. Still wearing a shirt and bra, but not really worried about anything but feeling his tongue inside of me, I jumped back onto the couch and made myself comfortable.

"Where do you want me?" I asked.

"Right there's fine," he responded as he knelt down beside me.

"Now you ain't gonna freak out and start comin' by here odd hours of the night or anything are ya?" he asked.

"Not a chance," I responded as I shook my head from side-to-side.

"You sure?" he asked.

"Promise," I responded.

"Deal," he said as he placed his hand against my inner calf.

As he pulled my leg to the side, I closed my eyes and waited. His soft beard slowly slid along my inner thighs and toward my embarrassingly wet pussy. As the tip of his tongue lightly touched my pussy lips, my entire body tingled and I almost sprung from the couch.

"You're fucking soaked. Were you standing in the kitchen thinking about this?" he asked.

I nodded my head.

Please, please, do that again.

The tip of his tongue slowly began to work its way from the bottom of my pussy to the top, stopping at my clit each time. After flicking against my clit a few times, he'd start over. With my eyes closed, my ass pressed into the couch, and my pussy against his face, I slowly slipped into some weird sexual bliss.

As I focused on his very predictable pattern of licking, he stopped.

"Ready?" he asked.

Having no idea what he was asking, but ready for whatever it was he was willing to offer, I responded, "Uh huh."

I wasn't.

I wasn't even close.

No one could have prepared for what he did.

He shoved his tongue deep inside of me. With it fully inserted into my vaginal cavity, he curled the end of it, flicking it against my g-spot. With each flick of his tongue, my body went into shock. After three or four flicks, my eyes opened wide and I prepared to explode.

"Oh my…" I wailed.

He raised his hand in the air to silence me, but never stopped doing what he was doing.

As he steadily fucked me with his thick tongue and tortured my g-spot with the tip, I wondered if there was any way I could convince him to be my boyfriend. If there was a heaven, and I had never been quite sure there was, I was now in it and a few seconds from meeting God.

I stared at the ceiling, arched my back and bit my lower lip.

My body began to convulse into the craziest feeling I had ever felt. To describe it as an orgasm wouldn't do it justice; I had orgasms a thousand times, and this wasn't one of them. It was more like an experience than a feeling. As I bucked my hips and released my lower lip, I began to wail.

As my cries increased in volume, he moaned into my pussy as if to encourage me to continue.

The tip of his tongue continued to stroke my g-spot as he tongue fucked me into a state of semi-consciousness. I bellowed out into the room as my body shook and my mind attempted to catch up to the feeling inside of me.

In and out his tongue worked.

Up and down my hips bucked.

Chills ran throughout my body and caused every muscle I had worked so many years to develop to contract and release repeatedly. Roughly four orgasms into the ordeal, I opened my eyes and let out a blood curdling scream.

The orgasm that every other orgasm in the future would be compared to.

I collapsed onto the couch and closed my eyes, slightly embarrassed at my screaming.

"I'm…sorry," I said under my breath.

"For what?' he said as he raised his head slightly.

"Screaming," I responded in a whisper.

"I like it. Let's me know I'm doing my job," he grinned.

"Wanna see my cock?" he asked.

My head bobbed up and down like a wind-up toy.

He rolled off the edge of the couch and unbuckled his belt. After removing his jeans, he turned to face me.

The size of the bulge in his boxer shorts was supportive of his claim. With wide eyes and an eager attitude, I swallowed heavily and stared.

"Oh my god. It's uhhm. Wow," I said as I gazed at his shorts.

"Shit, I've got cock for days. I got cock I don't even need," he said as he pushed the waist of his boxers down his thighs.

As the material cleared the twitching shaft, what appeared to be a third leg hung heavily between his legs. I gazed down and blinked my eyes, uncertain if what I was seeing was some kind of a joke or if it was real.

After kicking his shorts to the side, he glanced up and grinned. With his eyes locked on me, and my eyes glued to the eighth wonder of the world, the sound of his raspy voice confirmed this was no joke.

As he spoke, I shifted my eyes to meet his.

"Big fucker, ain't it?" he asked with a laugh.

I glanced downward, stared for a long second, and forced myself to look away as I nodded my head repeatedly in affirmation. As much as I felt a desire to speak, I couldn't. I had my reservations on fucking him now, hell there was probably no way that thing was going to fit inside me...

But I had to know.

"Does it, uhhm..." my voice was dry and nervous, "...get bigger?"

"Afraid so. If you want to bail out, now'd be the time," he began.

My eyes still fixed on his lower region, I shook my head. I didn't want to bail out, I wanted to get started.

My brother rode bulls professionally when we were younger, and I'd been to a few rodeos in my day. I had no earthly idea why I did it, but as I attempted to shift my eyes from his now rigid cock, my right hand slowly raised into the air. In hindsight, it was probably some subconscious connection between the signal to release the bull from the chute and my willingness to at least attempt to ride his stiff dick.

Cock.

Correction. His stiff cock.

"You got a question?" he asked as his eyes followed the path of my slowly rising hand.

"Nope," I shrugged as I slowly lowered my hand, "I'm ready to ride."

KAT

Every girl in college wants a boyfriend with a big dick – well, at least the girls I talk to. No one really says they can't wait to see if so-and-so has a tiny penis. They all look at guys and say things like *I bet he has a big dick, look at how he walks*. I never really considered that a man might exist who had *too much* dick – until now.

I exhaled onto the countertop as his cock slowly penetrated me. It didn't feel like I was being torn to shreds, but it damned sure felt different than Kyle's dick. I closed my eyes and took a short choppy breath as I bit my lower lip, hoping in time it would become a little less painful.

"Just go…"

"…slow," I sighed.

"I won't hurt ya if that's what you're worried about, but listen up," he said as he leaned forward, pressing his massive chest onto my back.

His beard pressed lightly against my cheek. I felt his breath against my jaw as he continued to slowly push further and further into me. The feeling was an extremely strange sensual pain unlike anything I had ever experienced. As his warm breath encompassed my ear goosebumps rose along my arm. I tilted my head to the side as my entire right side began to tingle.

"I'm in charge. *Me*. You're gettin' fucked and I'm doin' the fuckin'.

You need to understand that. We clear?" he breathed into my ear.

"Jesus…yes, I understand," I murmured.

"Good, and don't forget it," he breathed against my neck.

"Won't. I won't," I sighed.

Slowly, carefully, cautiously, almost magically, he withdrew his cock from inside of me. As I opened my eyes and exhaled, I felt it slowly begin to fill me again. As I bit my lip and prepared for the pain, he pulled back. A few slow short strokes later, I relaxed, exhaling heavily onto the countertop. Although I hadn't realized I was tense, the almost immediate relaxation of my muscles made clear my degree of apprehension regarding his huge cock. The process continued with short slow strokes for a few minutes, and the pain was entirely gone.

Being bent over the kitchen island with a big tattooed burly biker fucking me from behind on the night I met him sounded wild and crazy, but it wasn't so bad. The kindness of his sexual approach was a nice change from what I was used to, and definitely not what I had expected.

Maybe bad boys aren't so bad after all.

"Lift your left leg up a little," he said as I felt his hand against my right inner thigh.

Half hypnotized by his slow strokes and the feeling of his fat cock inside of me, I opened my eyes and gazed blankly into the kitchen.

"Huh?"

He leaned forward and pressed his beard heavily against my neck.

"Don't make me keep repeating myself, Kat. Lift up your fuckin' leg," he growled against my ear.

Not knowing what he meant, but afraid of pissing him off, I lifted my leg slightly. As I did, his hand grasped my lower calf and raised my leg a few feet from the floor.

"Kick it up on the countertop," he said flatly as he continued to slowly fill me with his throbbing shaft.

"Whaaa?" I muttered, feeling totally lost at what he wanted me to do.

He gripped my head in his massive hand and turned it to the side, pressing his face against my cheek as he did so. The roughness was a little more of what I was used to with Kyle, and definitely a turn on. Now with his mouth totally enveloping my right ear, he growled into my ear.

"You never been bent over the kitchen counter before?" he breathed.

His warm breath against my ear caused me to moan in anticipation, "Uhhm. No."

"Well, I'll make sure you don't forget this anytime soon," he growled as his hand slid down to my ankle.

"Throw your leg up on the counter," he demanded.

Without question, I raised my right leg and kicked my foot onto the countertop. As I resituated my left foot, and shuffled a little further away from the island, I bent my leg and pressed my knee onto the cool surface of the counter. Gripping the edge of the granite in my hands tightly with my chest slightly raised from the counter, I wondered what was next.

Not near as slowly, but in a very predictable manner, he began to *fuck* me. As I inhaled a deep breath and widened my eyes, I decided the niceties had been cast aside.

"You like that big cock?" he asked as he pressed his chest against my back.

"Uh huh?" I grunted in return.

"You got a nice little pussy," he growled, "I'm going to stretch it out and make that little fucker mine."

Oh god.

"God damned right. *My* little pussy," he moaned as he released my hip and slapped my ass lightly.

Oh hell yes.

"I'm going to ruin you. You know that, right?" he asked as he began to increase his pace and force.

"Uh huh?" I grunted, knowing full well I wasn't far from being ruined already.

"Sexy little bitch," he said as he slapped my ass a little harder.

"Oh hell yes," I moaned.

"You like that?" he asked as he slapped my ass again, much harder than before.

I coughed a breath as my eyes widened from the slap, "Yes," I shouted.

"Tell me what you want, you little bitch," he said as he forced his cock deep inside of me and held it on place.

"Slap my ass," I bellowed.

With each forceful stroke of his cock his hand came down against my ass in the same spot. After about six strokes and an equal amount of slaps, my right butt cheek was on fire and my pussy was beginning to tingle from the inside out. As I felt his hand against my ankle, I closed my eyes and tried to focus on the orgasm which began to rush through me.

His hand lifted my ankle from the counter, and began stretching my leg high into the air.

No, no, don't move me, I was getting ready to...

With my ankle gripped tightly in his right hand, he held my leg almost straight in the air. Now fucking me at an odd angle, and fucking me deeper than before, the tip of his cock pounded into and past my g-spot with each stroke. An entirely new feeling, and a very satisfying on indeed, I bit my lower lip and let him continue to do what he seemed to be extremely good at.

Fucking me.

"You know what I call this?" he asked.

Afraid to break my sexual concentration, I shook my head, but didn't respond.

"The windmill," he chuckled.

"Hits that magic spot each time, huh?" he asked.

"Uh huh," I moaned.

"You get ten more strokes, little girl. You better get your business done by the tenth. Ready?" he bellowed.

What? Ten? Why?

He pulled his hips rearward until the tip of his cock was resting against my outer pussy lips.

"One," he said as he slammed his cock into me.

My g-spot tingled all the way up my spine. I hadn't even realized he pulled out until his voice echoed into the room.

"Two," he shouted as he thrust himself deep inside of me.

Oh god.

"Three," I heard him shout.

My entire body began to tingle and my mind went strangely blank for some time. With my ears ringing and my head tingling, it was as if I had been transported into some other galaxy altogether. Outer fucking space or somewhere. Although I could still hear him, it seemed he was distant. His shouting continued.

"Four," he bellowed as the underside of his cock pressed against my throbbing clit.

His war-like cries into the empty room added to the entire sexual experience. As he shouted numbers and filled me with cock, my body began to rush into an orgasm that was certain to kill me.

"Five," he screamed as his lower torso slammed between my widely spread ass cheeks.

The anticipation of the tenth stroke was killing me. Something about his counting did exactly the opposite of what I expected. Instead of making me nervous, it caused me to focus, making the climax much more satisfying than anything I had ever experienced. The build up to the climax exceeded any orgasm I had previously experienced.

And I began to explode.

As my pussy started to contract heavily, I felt *it*.

From deep within my soul, it wanted out. To be released. I began to climax heavily, my entire body convulsing and tingling. With my eyes closed and my mind as focused as I could make it, I bit my lower lip and hoped for the best.

"This big fat cock is gonna ruin' you, girl…" he growled into my ear.

He was right. Incapable of responding, I attempted unsuccessfully to open my eyes. As I began to nod my head, his thickness filed me repeatedly.

"Six, seven, eight, nine, ten," he screamed as he bucked his hips back and forth, the tip of his cock dancing along my g-spot with each inner thrust.

My body shattered into a million sexual pieces all over the kitchen with the last stroke. Although I initially didn't realize I was doing so, after a few seconds I heard myself screaming. I finally regained control over myself, attempted to bite my lower lip, and the screaming stopped.

At that instant I realized he wasn't even close to being done.

"My fucking pussy," he grunted as he thrust himself into me again.

Yes yours.

"Thirteen, fourteen, fifteen, sixteen…" he shouted as his cock continued to take ownership of what was already rightfully his.

And his already thick cock began to swell to twice its girth.

My body convulsed into an orgasm completely capable of causing world peace, ending a holy war, or turning water into wine.

And he exploded inside of me.

As I shook and blubbered like a mental patient, I felt as if my mind had turned to jello. I *knew* very little for certain.

But I knew *one* thing.

Once a girl gets fucked *right*, there isn't any turning back.

She's ruined.

BISCUIT

Axton Bishop was without a doubt one of the best motherfuckers ever allowed to walk this earth. Dealt a shit card in life as a kid, and growing up with an abusive old man, he earned the nickname Slice from the kids on the street. They taunted him for the scars that littered his back where his old man had cut him as punishment for doing nothing more than being a kid.

Most kids exposed to the punishment would have turned to a life of crime, drugs, or both. Axton? He quit drinking, never used drugs, and picked up the books. His home filled with bookshelves of books he'd read at least once from cover to cover, he was one of the smartest men I had ever met, and the president of the MC for one reason and one reason only.

No one on this earth was more capable of keeping the Sinners in line.

I respected Axton as if he was my father, and in many respects, he was.

"When are you going to grow up," Axton chuckled as he closed the ledger and slid it to the side.

"*Grow up*? Shit, Slice," I said as I stood from my seat.

"I grew up when I left home at the ripe old age of fifteen. Ain't nothing wrong with a man havin' a little fun," I said over my shoulder as I walked toward the door.

"I'm gonna toss this empty in the shop before you tell me to. You know why? Because I'm all grown up and I don't need you to remind me, that's why," I said as I opened the door to the office.

One of Axton's pet peeves was people throwing empty beer bottles in the trash of his office. I didn't know one thing that made him angrier than having someone do it, and we all knew it. From time to time someone would forget, and when they did, the wrath of Axton came down on them like a lightning bolt.

After tossing the empty bottle in the shop trash, I got another beer from the fridge and walked toward the office. I'd brought Axton up to speed with stories of jail, Billie Jean, Cassie, and Kat, and as always, he found minimal humor in my actions. It had been a week since Kat and I met, and in that week we had fucked no less than ten times. If God ever produced a woman built solely for fucking, Kat was definitely her.

In many respects, she was a female version of me.

Put on this earth to satisfy the needs, wants, and sexual desires of men.

And I intended to use her for what God placed her in front of me for. Fucking.

"So anyway, I'm thinkin' this gal's a shoe in for the 2015 twat of the year award," I said as I walked into the office.

"I'm sure she is," Axton sighed.

"Get her name up on the garage wall if she ain't fuckin' careful," I grinned.

"From what Avery can tell me, you'll have your name carved on the stalk of her father's rifle if you're not careful," Axton said as he tilted his chair back on its hind legs.

"Pffft," I hissed as I waved my hand his direction.

"A thirty-three year old man – and a 1%er at that – fucking the twenty-two year old daughter of a cop isn't a great fucking idea in my book, Biscuit," Axton sighed.

"I ain't thirty-three yet, and she's twenty god damned two," I said as I lifted the beer bottle.

"Well, shit. That fixes *everything*," Axton chuckled.

I shrugged my shoulders and took a drink of the cold beer.

"Look, I'm not trying to raise you, but you're one of the few men here I'm close to. Toad's still about half his former self from the shooting, Otis is worried about Sam's mom and who fucking knows what else, and I sure as shit don't need you spending any more time in jail or getting shot by a biker-hating father of a god damned college girl," Axton growled as he lowered his chair to the floor.

"I'm with ya, Boss," I said as I tilted my bottle his direction.

"I'm god damned serious, Biscuit," he responded.

I'd never been one to allow *any* man to tell me what to do, but I certainly gave Axton's wishes good long consideration. He was as wild and as rough as any man, but he was an extremely sensible human being, and seemed to have a sixth sense about trouble. Although I was pretty damned sure Kat would never say anything to her father, a man could never be positive of anything when it came to a woman.

"I'll have another talk with her about the cop," I sighed.

"Be a damned good idea," Axton nodded.

"What you thinkin' about Sydney's brother? He's a stand up fella, ain't he?" I asked as I leaned into the edge of the table.

"Well, I sure as fuck wouldn't be asking for him to be brought in as a patch if he wasn't," Axton hissed.

"Just checkin'. He seems like good people. Hell, you know me, Slice. Hard for me to trust anybody except you, the Toad, Corn Dog, and Otis. We'll see how he does, I suppose. Big fucker though, ain't he?" I asked.

"That he is. I think he'll surprise you. I've spent some time checking him out, and he got nothing but good reports from everyone I could talk to. I think he'll not only make a good Sinner, but he'll damned sure become one of the short list," Axton said as he stood and picked up the ledger.

"Good to know," I said as I stood.

"I'll have another talk with Kat," I said as I lifted my bottle in the air.

"You do that," Axton said over his shoulder.

"Alright, Boss. I'll leave you to it," I said as I opened the door to the shop.

"Few days here, and we'll have a vote on Jack," Axton said as he turned to face me.

"Sounds good. I'm gonna go build a 103 incher and try to rekindle my shoe box. Fuckin' cops got fifty grand and it ain't settling too well with me," I shrugged.

"Cops are going to have a lot more than that if you don't talk with that girl," Axton chuckled.

"I might be half stupid, but I got good ears. I heard you the first ten times," I laughed as I walked into the hallway.

"Ears with extra fucking holes in them," Axton said as he closed the cabinet door.

I finished my beer and tossed the bottle into the trash. Axton was right, I needed to talk to Kat and make sure she didn't tell her dad anything about me. Having a cop on my bad side wasn't something I wanted, needed, or could deal with properly.

Bikers and cops didn't mix well.

Bikers and the *daughters* of cops, on the other hand, seemed to mix real well.

Maybe too well.

KAT

Certainly no newcomer to having sex, I found it remarkable that Biscuit had left such an impact – sexually speaking. I was incapable of ridding myself of thoughts of him fucking me, and in all of my time away from him, I spent the majority of it thinking about the last time we had sex.

Convinced his big cock, long tongue, stamina, and willingness to try out every sexual position in the book was the reason for my mindless stumbling through the hallways of my college campus, I wandered aimlessly to my next class.

"You look like shit, Hooker," Jennifer said with a laugh as I sat down beside her.

"Haven't slept in a week," I said over my shoulder as I lowered my book bag to the floor.

"Still boning that biker every night?" she whispered.

I nodded my head and grinned, "Oh yeah."

"You're crazy. He's going to cut you in little chunks and put you in a steel drum in his basement," she said under her breath.

I scrunched my nose, narrowed my eyes, and tilted my head her direction, "He's a biker, not a serial killer."

"What's the difference?" she shrugged.

Her shit talking was beginning to annoy me. I realized Biscuit and I were only fucking, and we weren't technically in a relationship, but to hear her talk the way she was about him irritated me.

"Seriously, he's pretty demanding when we're fucking, but he's really a nice guy. And he's funny," I explained.

"Get a picture of him yet?" she asked.

"Yeah, I took some the other day. He had on a wife beater, jeans, and some cool red suspenders. We were in the parking lot of the bar. He was just standing there and glanced over his shoulder, and I snapped a few pics. He got half pissed and made me suck his cock for it…Hold on," I said as I reached into my book bag.

"He made you suck his cock because you took pictures of him?" she shrugged.

"Uh huh," I said as I scrolled through my phone for the pic.

"Here," I said as I handed her my phone.

Her eyes widened as she stared down at the screen of the phone.

"Holy Jesus. He looks mean. In like a really hot way. Dear god. Have one of his face?" she asked.

"Yeah, here," I said as I flicked my finger across the screen.

A pic of his face I had taken on the same night appeared. She stared at it for a few seconds, flicked back to the pick of him glancing over his shoulder, and back to the one of his face. After a few seconds, she lifted my phone slightly, licked the screen, and handed it back to me.

"What the eff, Jen?" I snapped.

"Nothing. Good lord. I'm a sucker for guys with beards. Holy shit, Kat. Sorry. But yeah, I might need to borrow that later," she chuckled as she reached into her book bag.

"Nope. Not gonna happen," I said as I stuffed the phone into my bag.

"Text it to me," she said over her shoulder.

I shook my head and laughed, "No."

"Hooker," she said between her teeth.

"Skank," I responded under my breath.

Jennifer and I had been friends since my freshman year. We not only played varsity volleyball as teammates, but shared the same major, and had virtually every class together. We were close, but we didn't share the same views on all subjects, men included.

She was relieved when Kyle and I broke up, and even more at ease when he was placed in jail for abusing the girl he was fucking on the side. In the grand scheme of things, she wanted me to be happy, safe, and loved. Personally, I was willing to settle for happy, safe, and being fucked really hard, but that was a different story altogether.

As Mr. Salisbury walked into the classroom, I blinked my tired eyes and tried to remember where we'd left off. A lazy glance over my shoulder toward Jen revealed her jokingly reaching for my book bag, and I responded by kicking at her hand playfully.

"Stay out of there," I whispered.

"I can't," she said through her teeth.

Her playful nature after seeing his picture made me feel better about everything between us. I realized not every woman would see Biscuit as being attractive, but the fact she did allowed me to feel my decision to spend time with him wasn't some crazy childish decision I had made.

Maybe it was a childish decision, but at least I was doing it with someone *hot*.

Someone hot who also had a big cock.

Not just *someone*.

A biker with a big cock.

A biker with a big cock and a magical tongue.

As Mr. Salisbury began to speak to the class, my mind did what it had been doing for the last two weeks. It drifted off to thoughts of lying on my back with Biscuit's face between my thighs and his tongue tickling my g-spot.

I didn't know when he intended to stop fucking me, but if I had any say in the matter, it wouldn't be any time soon.

He didn't lie when he told me what he was going to do to me on the first night we had sex.

There was no doubt in my mind.

I was ruined.

BISCUIT

Being a patched member of a 1% club isn't as easy as getting a tattoo, buying a Harley, and donning a pair of boots. It's a way of life, a commitment, and more responsibility than most men can rightfully fathom. Select few men make it into 1% clubs, and even fewer are worth the salt in their sweat when it comes to being a true brother.

Jack's being voted into the club went without a hitch, and now he was a fully patched member of the Selected Sinners MC. As Otis and Toad took him on a grand tour of the clubhouse, I stood in the corner of the shop doing what I did best.

"Alright. So I got her foot in my hand, and I'm stretching it up in the air like a rubber fuckin' band. I'm about balls deep in this poor gal's pussy, and I lean forward and bite the bottom of her ear and I ask her, I say," I paused and took a swallow of my beer.

"*You know why that twat of yours is throbbin'?* So she turns her head to the side and her god damned eyes are watterin', and she whimpers to me."

I shrugged my shoulders, narrowed my eyes, and did my best to resemble a twenty-two year old college girl, "*No,* she says."

"*It's throbbin' because you got a foot of Sinner cock in ya,* I tell her," I lowered my shoulders and slapped Pete on the shoulder as I began to laugh.

Out of my peripheral I saw Toad, Otis, and Jack walking up to the group. As I started to turn their direction, Otis taped me on the shoulder.

"Biscuit," he said as he patted my shoulder.

"What's shakin' O?" I said as I turned to face him.

"Man wanted to talk to ya," he said as he patted Jack on the shoulder.

I glared at Jack, wondering what his problem might be. Big or not, he damned sure wasn't big enough to fuck with me. There wasn't a man on this earth who I'd ever backed down from, and my first sure wasn't going to be some 200 pound swole up weight lifter. After giving him a good solid minute of the ole Biscuit stink eye, I sighed and shifted my eyes to meet his.

"What can I help ya with?"

He stood his ground, tilted his head toward me, and responded, "Heard you were the one who put the money on my books."

I shook my head and started to turn away, "Money came from the club."

"Heard you were the one who *sent* me the money. The money the club raised for me. *You* were the one who put it on my books," he responded.

Wondering what his major malfunction might be, I glanced at Otis, turned toward Toad, and then back to Jack, "You got the right fella. Is there a problem?"

He extended his hand and narrowed his gaze, "Just wanted to personally thank ya for sending it. I appreciate ya. If you ever need anything, just let me know. Name's Jack. *Big Jack.*"

That's what I was thinking. You didn't want none of this, did ya, big fella?

"Biscuit. Stick around and have a beer," I chuckled.

He crossed his arms in the standard prison posture pose, "I'll be back. Just got to see the boss about my cut."

"I'll be right here," I said over my shoulder.

A few minutes later, they returned. As Otis and Toad stood behind, Jack approached me and stood quietly until I turned around.

Well, at least he's respectful. He might not be all that bad after all.

"What's shakin' Big Jack?" I asked as I turned his direction.

"We were thinking about heading into town to the bar. Fellas and I were wondering if you'd want to roll with us?" he asked as he uncrossed his arms.

"Always up for a drink, sure. You ridin' that old Softail of Toad's?" I asked.

He nodded his head, "All I got for now."

"Well, get you a frame, and I'll build you a big inch motor for nothin'. How's that? You're goin' to roll with the big boys here, you can't be ridin' that bobbed out softie all over the place. Damned thing ain't got enough power to get out of its own way," I chuckled.

"Appreciate it," he nodded.

"Well, let's roll," I said as I turned away from the fellas I was talking to.

"Fellas, we'll catch up next time. I got shit to do," I said over my shoulder as I walked out to the bagger.

As I reached the parking lot, I gazed over at Toad. Sitting on his bagger with the motor idling, the bike was rumbling like a top fuel dragster. His new cams sounded good, and provided him with plenty of power. No match for my bike, and probably no match for Otis' either, it suited him well. I glanced at Otis as I fired my bike up, and then turned toward Jack.

Riding in even numbered groups was much more satisfying to me than riding in odd numbers. Odd numbered groups when riding two abreast always left one man in the rear alone. Riding in even numbered groups always left me feeling like it was truly a group of brothers riding together.

As the four of us rode out of the lot, I pulled to the front, glanced over my shoulder, and grinned.

"Loser buys the first round," I said as I twisted the throttle to full throttle.

As the bike lurched forward and I slid around the corner onto College Drive, I guessed *someone* had to be in the rear – at least this time.

And it damned sure wasn't going to be me.

BISCUIT

Hands down, winning will always beat losing, no matter what the stakes might be. I arrived about a full minute ahead of the group, and had time to get off my bike and strike a winner's pose at the front door before they even rolled into the lot. As they rolled up to the edge of the sidewalk, I exhaled and looked at my watch as if I'd been there for a week waiting.

"Throat's parched, fellas, you finally ready to get a drink?" I asked as Jack shut off his bike.

"Fuck you, Biscuit," Toad said as he got off his bagger.

"God damned thirsty, that's what I am," I said as I opened the door.

The fellas walked past me and over to a booth on the right side. I followed close behind, knowing the sweet taste of a free drink is always more savored than one a man has to purchase. As I sat down in the booth, Toad turned toward me and cleared his throat.

"Otis tells me you been fucking some college girl who works here. What the hell's wrong with you, Biscuit?" he asked.

I laughed as I reached up and stroked my beard, "Shit brother, ain't a damned thing wrong with me, wait 'till you see her. I think you'll agree Biscuit's doin' pretty damned good with this one, college girl or not. We've been fuckin' like a couple of Catholic rabbits. That girl's got the sexual drive of a three peckered billy goat."

Otis nodded his head, "She is cute as fuck."

91

"Right now, I think I'd fuck anyone who agreed to hold still long enough for me to poke 'em," Jack laughed.

"And that'd be about ten seconds worth, it's been quite a stretch for me," he said as he leaned into his seat.

I turned toward Jack as I tried to imagine spending ten years or whatever in prison without pussy. Hell, a weekend was enough to make me jittery.

"I bet you're hornier than a fourteen year old boy who just found daddy's Playboy collection," I said as I slapped my hand against his shoulder.

"Pretty damned close," he chuckled in response.

"Kitchen closes in twenty minutes if you want food. If not, the bar's open till two. Want to see a menu?" the waitress said as she walked up to the table.

"You fellas wanna just get some beers?" I asked.

Otis shook his head and laughed, "Get fucking *Budweiser*. I don't want Toad trying to order beers. We'll end up with some pale ale orange apple cider bullshit."

"Four Bud's?" the waitress asked.

"Hold up, now. *God damn.* Do we look like four beers is going to do us much good? We'll drink four of them fuckers before you can get back to the bar. Make it twelve. We'll go through the first four in about a *minute*," I growled.

She looked like she needed to be riding a pole at the amateur night for MILF's at the strip club. Five foot six, and a hundred pounds, thirty of which was tits, she was damned near as ugly as a mud fence.

She cocked her head to the side and grinned, "I'll bring eight and as soon as you set your empties at the side of the table, I'll bring four more.

92

You don't want to drink hot beers, do you?"

"Smart girl right there," I responded as I pointed at her, "Make it eight."

"Be right back," she said as she walked away.

"So you fellas take any long rides? Go to Sturgis?" Jack asked.

I leaned forward and began to speak, and before I got a word out, Otis responded.

"Don't go to Sturgis, but we make some pretty good runs. Austin for the ROT Rally, and down to Phoenix for the Arizona Bike Week. Some of the fellas go down to Daytona, but it's a long ride and still winter here when that fucker pops off," Otis replied.

"No Sturgis, huh?" Jack asked.

Toad shook his head and chuckled, "Sturgis became a trailer-fest. Every swinging dick in the country drags his bike there on a trailer and then rides the fucker around town for a few days. Some of the fellas head up there alone, but we don't make a club run."

Jack nodded his head and grinned as the waitress shoved the beers to the center of the table. I reached for a beer and raised it to my lips as I wondered how long it had been since Jack had a drink of cold beer.

"Never cared for that rally myself; bunch of amateurs," Jack said as he took a swallow of beer.

I agreed wholeheartedly. Sturgis had gone from the best biker gathering in the USA to the most fucked up dipshit fest in the nation.

"Here's to being free, riding hard, and sleeping on a soft bed," Jack said as he raised his beer bottle in the air.

We all tilted our bottles toward his and took a drink. After no more than lowering the bottle from my lips, Jack swung his beer to the center of the table again, and grinned.

"And here's to Slice's Ol' Lady Avery. Without her, I'd still be eating Star Crunch and drinking cold instant coffee in my cell," he said as he tilted his bottle forward.

"Damned fine woman right there," I agreed.

A few seconds of silence was my invitation, and as the fellas continued to drink their beers, I figured I'd break Jack in right and give him one of my best stories. I leaned into the center of the table, inhaled a deep breath, and as I exhaled, began telling my tale.

"So, we were supposed to leave to go to the ROT Rally in about a week. There was this cute little Asian bitch working at this Thai place, and at the time, I hadn't fucked me an Asian yet. So I'd been goin' in there and bein' sweet on this little bitch," I said.

I glanced around the table. All eyes were on me, just like I liked 'em to be. As I lifted my beer to my lips and held it in place, I continued, "So she's a little fucker 'bout four foot nothin' and has these little titties that look big because she's so damned tiny. Had an ass about the size of a Jonathan apple, but on them skinny little legs and against that eighteen inch waist it looked like Kim fucking Kardashian's ass. So anyway, we're a week out, and I head in there to get me some Asian pussy before the run."

"So I get in there, and she ain't my waitress, this other cute little chick is. But that ain't what this is about. So I order my food and get that spicy peanut chicken shit they sell. You guys eat Thai food?"

"Had some," Toad nodded.

Jack shook his head and laughed, "Don't fuck with the stuff."

I turned to Otis. His face filled with disgust.

"Well, lemme tell ya, it ain't spicy, it's fucking *hot*. So anyway, I order this shit, and after a bit, a big plate of it shows up. Now I'm about half pissed this little Vietnamese princess ain't working, so I gobble this shit down. Now I'm waitin' on my check, and my gut starts making them noises. You know them noises when you *know* something's gonna happen and it ain't gonna be good?"

Jack nodded his head and lifted his beer, "Like after eatin' a burrito out of the toilet."

"What the fuck are you talkin' about?" I snapped back, "A *toilet* burrito?"

Jack chuckled, "Contraband. If you get caught with them, you go to the hole, so you can't leave 'em out in the cell, and you need to keep 'em cold anyway. So the Mexican's would steal the food from the kitchen and smuggle it to the cells and make up burritos. They'd sell 'em for stamps and store. They'd come wrapped in a piece of plastic, like from a garbage bag. The end was tied and it'd be airtight, and we kept 'em in the toilet to keep 'em cold until we wanted to eat 'em. Toilet's kind of like a 'fridge in the joint. Got sick on a few of those fuckers, that's for sure. Sorry for interrupting, go ahead."

"You ate shit out of a toilet?" I asked.

Jack nodded his head and grinned.

"Didn't have a choice. Food, drinks, everything. You tie a string to it, shove it in the toilet, and pull it out when you want it. If the cops come, you flush it. After they leave, if they don't find the end of your string, you pull it back out of the sewer and either eat it or drink it."

I narrowed my eyes as I tried to imagine eating anything out of a toilet, "God damn."

"Go ahead," Jack said, "I apologize for interrupting."

You're alright in my book, big boy. I like it that you're already schooled in the respect department.

I took a quick drink of beer and continued, "Okay, so I'm waitin' on my check, and my gut's a rumblin' and makin' noise, and I know it's time to go. I reach into my wallet, pull out a twenty, and drop it on the table. I run out to my bike and ride that fucker home like I'd stole it. Whole way, it's a coin toss as to whether I'm gonna shit my pants or make it on time. I pull that fucker in the drive, hop off, and run into the house, dropping my pants as I'm runnin'."

"So I get into the shitter, and just explode. A miracle I even made it, I'm tellin' ya. So for about four hours, I got the shits. Now for situations like this, I keep them pills, the anti-diarrhea stuff, *Imodium AD*. I take about ten of those fuckers and finally it stops."

I took another quick drink and raised my hand to silence the group from another interruption. As I set my bottle back onto the table, I widened my eyes and continued.

"So that ain't even the story, the story's *this*. I took so many of those damned pills that I didn't shit for a week, and we got the rally comin' up in two days. Finally, it came. When it did, it was a week's worth, and about the size of a ten year old boy's arm. Fucker ripped my ass to shreds. Now, although I finally took a shit, I'm in pretty sad shape and I got a hemorrhoid the size of a Johnsonville Bratwurst hanging out of my ass."

"God damn," Jack chuckled, "That's a bitch. And the run's a few days out?"

I nodded my head and grinned, "Precisely. Two days until we're gonna spend ten hours on the road, and I've got a little friend hangin' outta my ass like I just gave birth. So I know I can't make it with this hot dog hanging out of my ass. Hell, I can't even sit down. Sleepin' on my belly and shit, and I fuckin' *hate* sleepin' on my belly, I'm a back

96

sleeper. So I get me a rubber glove and I poke this fucker back up in there. Hell, after a few minutes, I feel pretty good and forget it's even there. I stand up and take a few steps," I paused for effect and leaned into the table.

"And *bloop* - out the fucker comes. Another rubber glove, poke him back in there, and everything's fine. Take a few steps and *bloop* - out he comes again. Now I *know* I can't ride to Austin with my finger in my ass, so I start to thinkin'. And all of a sudden it comes to me, so I have Tater come get me in his truck and take to me that dildo shop out east. After a look around a bit, I find one of them butt plugs. Did you know they come in about ten different sizes?"

"Had no idea," Jack laughed.

"Well they do. Picked me out a little red number on the small side of things. And it had this little ring in the end made it look like a pacifier. So Tater takes me home, and I glove up, shove the hotdog inside, and poke the little pacifier in my ass. After I wiggle around a bit, it feels pretty good. Now as far as I'm concerned, problem's solved. I'm a day out and ready to ride. Just for shits and grins, later on that night, I reach back there to check on things, you know, make sure everything's where it should be. And I'll be damned if that little ring, you know the part you hold on to? It's fucking gone!"

Jack's eyes widened, "Huh?"

"Yep. Fucker sucked right up there in my ass. So, now I got to go fishin' for this little fucker. I glove up *again*, stick my finger up there, and fish around and find it. I pull her out, wash her up, and grease it with Vaseline and poke it back inside. Couple a minutes, and *bloop*. You guessed it, it disappears."

"So I just say fuck it. At this point in time, I feel pretty good, other'n knowing I got a butt plug in my ass. I hop on the bike and ride out to the snow ski and mountain climbin' store out on Central. Buy me one of those spring loaded carabiner D-rings. After I rode home, I gloved up one last time, found the little fucker, pulled it out, and hooked that D-Ring to it. Then I shoved her back in, and let the hook just hang out of my ass."

Jack shook his head and narrowed his gaze in apparent disbelief, "Rode to Austin with a rappelling D-ring hanging out of your ass?"

"Sure as fuck did, left it there for a fucking *week*. Don't know if it was a conscious thing, or just because I had that little rubber plug in there or what, but I didn't shit for a week. When we got home, I reached back, grabbed the D-ring and gave it a tug. Damned thing popped out, and my little friend the hotdog was gone. Problem solved."

Jack reached over and slapped his hand against my shoulder, "You're funnier than a motherfucker," Jack chuckled.

"Club joker, that's me," I grinned.

"Holy. Fucking. Shit. Now, *that's* a woman," Jack whistled.

I turned to face the door. A six foot tall blonde supermodel walked into the bar, clearly out of place in a bar with a bunch of bikers. As I studied her and began wondering if she could lift her thirty-six inch long legs over her shoulders, Otis stood and turned around.

"Sam," he hollered.

"Sam!" he screamed again as she walked to the bar.

Holy shit, *that's* Samantha.

She turned around. As she made eye contact with the Big O, she looked like she'd seen a ghost.

A few minutes later, Otis brought her to the table and introduced her to all of us. Meeting her did little but fuel my desire to fuck Kat again.

As she sat in the booth and laughed and talked to Otis about old times, I stared blankly at the walls and tried to figure out what it was about Kat that made her a better piece of ass in my mind than any of the other women I had fucked recently.

Coming up with nothing she possessed other than an extremely eager attitude and a long set of legs, I was pleased when Otis and Sam stood to leave.

Knowing Otis was going to knock off a piece of *for old time's sake* pussy, I turned toward Jack and Toad and yawned.

"Fellas, I'd be lyin' if I said I was tired. But, I'm tired of lookin' at you two fuckers. I'm gonna piss, hop on my sled, and head to Kat's house. I'm in dire need of some pussy," I said as I glanced toward the bathroom.

"It's damned near midnight," Toad said as he looked at his watch.

"Good. That'll leave me damned near eight solid hours to fuck her before she's got to get to school," I said as I turned toward the bathroom.

As I walked to the bathroom, I realized I had yet to talk to Kat about her father. Tonight probably wouldn't be a good time, I just needed to get laid, not piss anyone off. Maybe next week I'd say something when both of our minds were clear and she had the ability to listen to what it was I had to say.

For now, I simply needed her to be no more than what she was.

A piece of pussy.

KAT

Predicting my former boyfriend Kyle's sexual actions was easy. He'd climb on me, fuck me, and climb off. From time to time, he'd demand I suck his dick, and he'd hold my head with his hands while I did so, making sure to make me as uncomfortable as possible during the entire process. Predicting what Biscuit was going to do, however, seemed to be nothing short of impossible.

The long list of sexual offerings Biscuit chose from seemed to be very vast, and to be brutally honest, as far as I was concerned I never wanted to be fucked in a bed or in the missionary position again as long as I lived.

"Get up here and sit on my face," he said as he bent over backwards and rested his shoulders and the back of his head on the table.

The deck off of the apartment jutted out to the side, and hung from the exterior wall for all the world to see. Every apartment in the building had a similar deck, and they were situated directly above, below, and beside each other. Mine was approximately eight feet by eight feet, and was just large enough for the small glass table and four chairs I had positioned on it for sitting and enjoying the evening air or having a drink.

As much as I wanted to do what he asked of me, the flimsy table, at least in my opinion, wasn't suitable for both of us to be fucking on.

"I think it might collapse," I shrugged.

"Get the fuck out of here," he chuckled as he rolled onto his side and stood.

He turned toward the table and began inspecting the legs, upper portion, and the surface of the glass.

"Get this fucker at Home Depot?" he asked as he examined the table.

"Wow. As a matter of fact we did," I responded.

"Well, it'll do just fine," he sighed, "Toad's got one just like it at his place on the back deck, and I stood on the bastard one Sunday and told a story. Motherfucker never collapsed on me, so it ain't gonna collapse here."

"Now ride my fuckin' face," he said as he lowered himself onto the table again.

"But, we're *outside*," I explained as I peered over the edge of the deck to the deck beside us which was not more than ten feet away.

I glanced to my left, toward my other neighbor's deck which was the same distance away.

"I don't give a fuck. It's seventy-five out here, and about ninety god damned degrees in your apartment. I been ridin' all day, I'm hot, and it's fuckin' midnight. Grind that sweet little pussy on my beard, I ain't gonna *ask* ya again. Now get to work," he said in a demanding tone.

I glanced over my left shoulder, and then turned to my right. All of the decks I could see in both directions were empty, which wasn't surprising. It was almost one o'clock in the morning. Somewhat reluctantly, I unbuttoned my shorts, pulled them down past my thighs, and kicked them to the side. After pulling off my panties and tossing them on top of my shorts, I walked toward the table and peered down at Biscuit.

Lying there on his back with his face pointed straight up at the sky, he grinned and stuck out his tongue.

"Just sit down here like you're gettin' on a chair," he said as he closed his eyes and patted his hand against his beard.

"This seems weird," I sighed as I glanced out at the pond situated directly behind the deck.

"Don't seem weird to me. Eatin' pussy is damned sure more natural than eatin' a fuckin' hamburger," he said flatly.

"Fuck my beard, Kat," he sighed.

As if I had no choice, and feeling no differently, I backed up to the table, straddled his chest, and squatted down on his face. As my butt cheeks rested against his face, he reached up and shifted me slightly, then shoved his tongue against my pussy.

As soon as I felt the tip of it against my swollen mound, I spread my legs slightly and relaxed.

Oh dear God.

His tongue pressed deeper and deeper, finally reaching the sweetest of spots. The tip of his tongue tickled my g-spot while the girth of it satisfied my pussy like no vibrator or dildo ever could. Somewhat nervous at first, ten seconds of his torturous tongue caused me to forget everything but being satisfied by his ability to please me orally.

As I exhaled and arched my back, I peered up at the clear star filled sky. His tongue repeatedly searched inside of me for a place to tease as I held my breath, bit my lip, and prayed to last another thirty seconds before I reached climax. The build up to the orgasm was almost more enjoyable than the orgasm itself, but so far about ninety seconds was my record on orgasm denial.

Being quiet during climax had never been one of my strengths, nor

103

had prolonging the build-up. When it was time to have an orgasm, I had no control. The two sexual assurances in life, for me anyway, were that I was going to have the orgasm when the time came, and I was going to be vocal about it.

As Biscuit began to moan into my thighs, his tongue danced in and out of my now soaking wet pussy. Just to solidify my place on the night's orgasmic calendar, I reached down and began to play with my clit. Five or so seconds later, I felt my body began to reach the brink.

It was all but over.

"Oh holy fuck…" I moaned.

He began to moan more aggressively into my thighs. His beard against my inner thighs caused me to tingle all over as he forced his tongue in and out of my pussy.

"Jesus Biscuit…Jesus…I…" I wailed as I closed my eyes.

He pressed his tongue deep, held it there, and began some new procedure on my g-spot. Instead of flicking the tip of his tongue against it once and retracting it, he now held his tongue in place, and flicked the tip of his tongue against my sensitive g-spot over and over. I opened my eyes and stared up at the sky as my body convulsed and my toes began to curl.

"Holy…shit…" I squealed as I heard the table creak beneath our weight.

My pussy began to tingle from the inside out, and my mind went blank. When I came back to my senses, my entire body felt as if it was on fire, and I was standing beside the table wide-eyed with my hands raised to my mouth.

"What the fuck did you get up for?" he asked as he stood.

"What the fuck just happened?" I asked.

"Well, I was doing *the flicker* and you screamed, came all over my face, and jumped up," he said as he wiped his beard with his hand.

"The *what*?" I muttered.

As if I was some inexperienced sexual idiot, he raised one eyebrow, turned up his palms, and shrugged his shoulders slightly.

"*The flicker*. It's when I hold my in tongue deep and tease your g-spot. You like it?" he asked.

"Uhhm, yeah. That's an understatement," I murmured.

"Well, we better keep at it before your pussy goes all back to normal," he said as he reached for his belt.

I was still floating round somewhere in the star-filled sky as I watched him remove his boots, jeans, boxer shorts, and shirt. Now standing at the edge of the deck naked as the day he was born, I stared at him realizing it was the first time I had actually studied him while he was fully naked. Covered in tattoos and muscles, his cock hung between his legs like another limb altogether.

"Come here and give me a hug. And take that shirt off, I wanna see those big titties," he said flatly.

"Huh? A hug?" I asked.

"Yeah, a fuckin' hug," he responded.

I pulled off my shirt and removed my bra. Somewhat self-conscious about my large breasts, I crossed my arms over my chest as I approached him, unfolding them as I stepped in front of him. As my arms wrapped around his upper body, he reached down and lifted me from my feet.

With his hands against my ass, and his forearms along my thighs, he held me above the floor in his arms. Slowly, he began to lower me slightly as he released my left leg and obviously guided his cock into my throbbing and overly anxious pussy.

As I felt his cock penetrate me, I gasped in slight shock. In this position, it felt huge. With each additional inch of his girth inside of me, my eyes widened slightly in disbelief. When he was finally all the way in, I felt as if the tip of his dick was in my chest.

"Holy shit…this…feels….weird," I stammered.

"You'll get used to it," he said with a nod.

"Ready?" he asked.

Eager to have him fuck me senseless, I nodded my head and bit my lip.

Holding me in his arms and moving me up and down as if I were a rag doll, he began to raise and lower me onto his stiff cock. To ease the process and minimize the pain, I spread my legs wide and extended them beyond his hips.

With his massive hands cupping my ass, he began to thrust his hips up and down, pressing his upper thighs against my butt cheeks. The sound of skin on skin echoing into the night was almost as big of a turn on as him fuckin me on the deck.

"Who's little pussy am I fuckin', Kat?" he asked as he pounded himself in and out of my dripping wet pussy.

"Yours," I whimpered.

And, as much as he'd never admit it, my pussy was just that.

His.

"Stick those big titties in my face," he said as he lowered his chin.

I reached up with one hand and raised my right boob. Immediately, he bit into my nipple, and began nibbling on it was he continued to fuck me hard. His cock now sliding in and out with ease, and my nipple between his teeth, he pulled my ass cheeks wider as he thrust his hips up and down with perfect rhythm.

I could feel myself running down my leg as the cool night breeze blew across the deck. I closed my eyes and focused on the tingling feeling that was running violently between my nipple and my pussy. Within a few seconds, I felt my inner lady bits start to tingle, and I knew it was all but over.

"You better scream when you have that orgasm," he grunted as he released my nipple from his teeth.

I nodded my head and opened my eyes.

"You like that big cock?" he asked.

I nodded my head and grunted.

He pressed his face against mine and bit my earlobe as he stuffed me full of cock.

"You're a cock hungry little bitch, aren't you?" he breathed into my ear.

"Yes," I whimpered.

"Scream it," he demanded.

"I uhhm…I'm a…cock hungry…little…"

"Bitch…" I cried.

"Scream it!" he demanded as he pulled his hips rearward and held them there.

I arched my back, stared up at the sky, and screamed at the top of my lungs, "I'm a cock hungry little bitch!"

He released me from his grasp, lowered me to the floor, and spun me in a half circle in one fluid motion. Now facing the table and slightly confused, I felt his hand against my upper back.

As I bent over onto the table, I felt his cock slide easily into my wet willing mound.

And. He. Began. To. Fuck. Me. To. Death.

His hips slapping against my ass, and his balls beating a tune against my clit, I bit my lip and pressed my chest into the cold glass. The sound and smell in the air was nothing but sex. His hand slapped against my right butt cheek, and it was all I needed. Immediately, my body began to convulse, and my pussy began to contract around his swollen cock.

"You like it when I slap that ass?" he bellowed.

"God yes!" I blurted. "Slap it again."

His hand came down with tremendous force, forcing me slightly to the side.

"Oh…holy…"

My mouth opened wide, and my mind wanted to scream. My voice, however, went silent and my throat emitted nothing but a little squeak. As he continued to pound himself in and out of my aching pussy, I had orgasm after orgasm after orgasm. Almost to a point of passing out, I felt his cock begin to swell.

"Oh god, do it. Come in me," I begged.

And he did.

As he erupted into me, I had another orgasm - a long, steady, inner orgasm that lasted for thirty seconds. Not only did it cause my ears to ring, it made my eyesight go black for a few seconds. As he held his cock deep in me and didn't move, I felt it slowly going limp.

It was over.

The smell of the sweet summer air filled my nostrils as the cool breeze blew against my soaking wet inner thighs.

After a few minutes of silence, I exhaled and stood.

I glanced in his direction and smiled.

"We're just *fucking*, right?" I asked.

"Yep," he responded as he glanced down at his bare feet. .

"And as long as I don't get attached, you'll keep fucking me, right?" I shrugged.

He glanced upward and nodded his head once, "Yep."

"I fucking hate you," I chuckled.

Nothing could be further from the truth, but for the sake of my sexual sanity, I figured I could play the game.

"That's what I like to hear," he grinned.

Well then, I'll keep lying.

BISCUIT

I stood in the shop, bent over a bench, grinding the tabs off of an exhaust bracket. As I watched the wheel on the grinder grind the metal into a shower of sparks, I heard Axton's voice over the sound of the grinder.

"God fucking damn it Biscuit, I told you to take care of that fucking cop," he shouted.

I released the safety pedal of the grinder and stood silently as it came to a stop.

"Huh?" I said, knowing full well what he had said.

"The girl you're fucking's god damned father. I fucking told you," he screamed.

The veins in his neck were standing out as he screamed. He was madder than I had ever seen him.

"Fuck, Slice, I forgot. I'll get to it," I said as I placed the exhaust shield on the bench.

"Well, go do it. He's out at the fence in riot gear," he bellowed.

My eyes widened and my heart began to pound out of my chest, "Huh?"

"You heard me. He's parked in the street, leaning against the gate. He's in a fucking truck, looks like he's off duty, but he's got on a vest and his fuckin SWAT gear," he said as he gazed down at the floor and shook his head.

"Maybe it's not him," I shrugged.

He glanced up and shook his head, "You dumb fuck, bringing that shit to our shop. It's him, he asked for you *by name*. Dalton Biskette. Sound familiar?"

"God damn," I sighed as I attempted to peer past Axton and into the parking lot.

"You've got ten fucking minutes," he sighed, "Get him gone or I'm going to shoot you both."

"Got it, Boss," I nodded.

"I'm not fucking joking," he grunted.

"I'm headed out there now," I said as I began to walk to the lot.

The last thing I wanted was Axton upset with me. The next to the last thing I wanted was to be shot. And the thing next to that, and highest on my list of shit to hate to deal with in real life, was to be talking to the cop father of a twenty-two year old college girl I was fucking.

As I walked into the lot, I glanced up at him. Kat should have warned me. He looked like Otis in SWAT gear. If I was going to whip him at any point in time, I'd either need a big stick or a gun. I figured my best bet was to be as mean as I could and stand my ground. I wasn't about to let him try and intimidate me, cop or not.

Fucking fuck.

"Dalton Biskette?" he said in a typical cop voice.

"Depends on who's fuckin' askin'" I responded in my best *fuck you* voice.

"Officer Chadsworth, Wichita PD," he barked.

"Don't mean fuck to me, cop," I barked back as I reached the fence.

He placed his hands on his hips and stared.

I reached for the same cock I'd fucked his daughter with the night before, scratched it, and stared back.

I hated cops.

And, rightfully so, cops hated me.

BISCUIT

I had never backed down from a fight in my life, and I'd been in more than I could ever count. I'd been in biker brawls, stand-offs with rival clubs, and involved in nothing short of what cops would describe as *gang wars*. Through all of this, for my thirty-two years on earth, not one man had ever intimidated me.

And I didn't see that changing any time in the near future.

The oversized cop pressed his hands onto the sides of his hips and stared, "I'll make this simple, Biskette. You're going to stop seeing my daughter."

"Don't know what or who you're talking about. I don't *see* anybody, cop. I got a list of about thirty or so girls I *fuck*, and if you'll give me her name, I'll pull my little black book out of my cut see if she's on the list," I said as I crossed my arms in front of my chest.

He pursed his lips, widened his eyes slightly, and lowered his hands. As his right hand hovered over the grip of his pistol, he inhaled a long, deep breath.

"Smart-ass, huh? Well, that's fine. Katrina Chadsworth is her name, ring a bell?" he asked.

"Nope," I responded.

He shook his head and exhaled an audible sigh, "Listen, I'm not going to stand here and dick around with you. You don't like cops, and

I don't like pieces of dirty ass shit who fuck my daughter. You can't win this fight. I'm not going to go into details of how I run an investigation, but I will say this. You're alleged to having a six inch long tongue and being hung like a mule. It's *you*, and I know it's *you*. Now, what I'm telling you is this…"

He paused and raised one eyebrow before he continued, "It stops today."

I uncrossed my arms, lowered my hands to my sides, and rolled my shoulders rearward as I flexed my chest and biceps, "If having a big cock is a crime, you better arrest me now, cop."

"I'll put it terms you can understand, Biskette. Keep fucking with her, and I'll put a bullet between your eyes. It's that simple. This conversation is over," he said as he turned away.

"You threatening me, cop?" I hollered as he walked toward his truck.

He opened the door to the truck, paused, and peered over his shoulder, "That's not a threat, Biskette. It's a view into what your future holds. Try me, and your buddy Bishop in there'll be burying your ass."

How the fuck do you know all of our names?

Creepy ass cop.

He nodded his head once, climbed into the truck, and drove away. I stood for a long minute, gazing beyond the fence and into the street. I wasn't about to let any man tell me what I could or couldn't do, but something about getting shot between the running lights by one of Wichita's finest had me second guessing whether or not fucking Kat was what I needed to be doing with my spare time.

Axton's hand on my shoulder startled me slightly, and caused me to understand I was truly out of my comfort zone with Kat's father stopping by to see me.

"So, I'm assuming you got it resolved?" Axton asked.

I nodded my head and sighed, "Guess so."

I turned to face Axton and crossed my arms in front of my chest, "Listen to *this* shit. That motherfucker said if I contacted her again he was gonna shoot me."

"Jesus Christ, Biscuit. Well, what'd you say?"

I gazed down at the ground for a moment and thought. As I glanced upward, I responded, "I said a lot of shit, but after *that* I didn't really say anything."

"Motherfucker rendered you speechless, huh?" he chuckled.

"Somethin'," I shrugged, "And it ain't funny."

"So, what are you going to do about the girl?" Axton asked as he turned toward the shop.

As I started following him across the lot, I considered his question. I really didn't know what I was going to do. I had no desire to get into a pissing match with a cop, and I damned sure didn't want to get shot by some overeager protective father.

But I'd be damned to hell if I was going to let him tell me what to do. Whatever I decided was going to be *my* decision based on what I thought was in *my* best interest.

"Well?" Axton asked over his shoulder as he stepped through the garage door and into the shop.

I swept a few of the loose rocks away across the parking lot with my boot and glanced his direction, "I'm thinkin'."

As I continued to gaze down at boots and kick random rocks across the lot, I continued, "I think I'm gonna finish this bracket, see if it fits, and then ride over to her house and fuck her. You know, to see if I like it as much as I remember likin' it. If her pussy's as good as I remember it bein', I'll keep fucking her. If it ain't, I'll stop. But I ain't stoppin' because some fuckin' cop told me to."

Axton coughed a laugh and shook his head, "No pussy's worth dying over."

"You ain't fucked this gal, so you don't know. Her twat's worth quite a bit," I laughed, "Lemme ask you this, Slice. Same situation, what'd you do?"

I reached down, picked up the exhaust shield, and waited for his response.

He crossed his arms in front of his chest and inhaled a deep breath. As he exhaled, he grinned, "Well, I'd have probably already left, and about now I'd be fucking her. There isn't a man alive that's going to tell *me* what to fucking do."

"You're right," I said as I tossed the exhaust shield onto the bench, "I'm going to head that way now. This bracket can wait."

"Devil looks after his own…" Axton said under his breath.

"Sinner forever, forever a Sinner…" I breathed as I walked toward my bike.

And, as much as I knew I was a sinner to the bone, I didn't believe what I was doing with Kat was sinning, criminal, or warranted getting shot by her father. If her father decided to shoot me, maybe he'd do it while I was nuts deep in his daughter's pussy.

And I could die a happy man.

KAT

It seemed whenever life was going good, either my father or Kyle stopped the flow of things, never allowing me to enjoy much more than a day or two of happiness without interruption. Having both of them intervening in my life at the same time, however, wasn't something I thought would ever happen again.

But somehow, it had.

"I have no idea how you got out of jail, but I *really* don't want you here," I said as I raised my hands in front of my chest.

"I've been locked up for a fucking month, and I need some pussy. Put your fucking hands down, get your ass over here, and suck my fucking cock," he said as he pushed his way past me and sat down on the couch.

"Seriously, Kyle. I'm seeing someone. It's over. Just leave," I begged.

He unzipped his pants and pulled out his dick, "This thing isn't going to suck itself you dumb bitch, get the fuck over here."

I walked briskly toward the couch, stopped in front of him, and crossed my arms. I glanced toward the front door, which was still open. I glanced at Kyle. He disgusted me. After inhaling a breath of courage and exhaling harshly enough for him to hear me, I said what I had to say.

"Put that little joke of a dick of yours back in your fucking pants and get the fuck out of here!" I fumed as I pointed toward the door.

I hoped the month in jail, the pending charges for abuse and battery, and his desire to stay out of jail would cause him to listen to me, grant my wishes, and leave.

"You stupid bitch, I told you to suck my fucking dick," he said as he stood.

He stunk of a combination of sweat and laundry soap. Wearing jeans, lace up camouflage boots, and a wife beater, he looked every bit of the Marine he used to be.

The blur of his arm in front of my face startled me. He grabbed my hair in his hand, pulled my head rearward, and slapped my face harder than he ever had in the past. The impact of his hand caused my ears to ring, and within a few seconds I tasted blood in my mouth. As much as I tried not to cry, I felt tears begin to roll down my cheeks.

"Now see what you made me do, you dumb cunt? Hell, I came over to give you some lovin', and you made me smack your dumb ass. Get on your fucking knees," he said as he shoved against my head with both hands, pushing me to the floor.

On the floor crying, feeling there was no way out of the situation I was in, I wanted him to just die. I hated him, the thought of him, and even the smell of him. As he held my head with his hands, he pressed his dick into my face and bellowed his demands into the room.

"Put. My. Dick. In. Your. Cunt. Mouth. It don't get any simpler than that, Katrina," he sighed.

As he smashed his half-soft dick into my face, I considered biting it, and wondered if I could make it to the open door before he caught me. I glanced to the side and tried to remember where I left my phone, hoping I could make a mad dash across the floor and get to it before he grabbed me. As he began to bark out more commands, I attempted to stand.

He shoved against my head and slapped my face again.

"You stupid bitch. You can't suck my dick if you're not on your knees," he sighed sarcastically.

"Kyle, stop. You're hurting me. Just get the fuck out," I cried.

The sound of him screaming in response was muffled by the sound of my door slamming and another person's screaming. As I glanced up and toward the door, my heart began to pound rapidly.

"Get your hands off the girl," I heard Biscuit shout.

Thank God.

Within two steps, he was grabbing Kyle by the shoulders and spinning him around.

"Get in the kitchen, Kat," I heard him demand.

Somehow, I ended up in the kitchen. The small apartment was open, and I stood mere feet from where Kyle and Biscuit were, watching everything. As Biscuit held Kyle's shoulders in his hands, he spoke in a very demanding tone and everything began to happen extremely fast.

"What's the fuck's going on, Kat?" Biscuit shouted over his shoulder.

"Who the *fuck* do you think you are?" Kyle growled, "I'm a U.S. Marine, and I'll kick the absolute shit out of you."

Beat his fucking ass, Biscuit.

"Shut the fuck up," Biscuit growled in return.

"He's trying to rape me," I cried.

"You crazy bitch," Kyle sighed.

"Listen, I was just…" Kyle continued.

For being as mean as he was to *me*, Kyle seemed like a big pussy when it came to fighting a man. He wasn't attempting to do anything to free himself from Biscuit's grasp, and, from where I stood, it seemed he was going to try and negotiate his way out of things.

With his back facing me, Biscuit shouted, "Kat?"

"He was trying to rape me. He slapped me hard, twice," I sobbed.

He looked like he released Kyle as he quickly turned around and studied me. Standing in the kitchen crying with a swollen bloody lip and what I suspected were two very prominent hand prints on my face, my crying increased to an almost full sob. As Biscuit's eyes met mine, they widened and he immediately spun around to face Kyle again.

And all hell broke loose.

It looked like a scene out of one of the Jason Statham movies - if Jason Statham was six foot tall and had a beard. As Biscuit spun around, his right knee lifted in the air, and he swung it into Kyle's stomach or crotch, I couldn't tell for sure. As Kyle bent over from the impact, Biscuit clenched his hands together in a huge fist and swung it upward into Kyle's face.

Kyle stumbled rearward and landed on the couch.

And, within a half-second, Biscuit was on top of him, beating him savagely on his face with his hands.

"You motherfucker. I ought to fucking kill you," he screamed as he beat him.

Kyle was either unconscious or dead. He didn't even lift a hand to defend himself. For as tough as he portrayed himself as being, he sure didn't look the part now. I had no idea of what I *should* have felt, standing there watching Biscuit beat Kyle, but I felt relieved, honored, and protected. Not one single shred of my being felt sorrow or compassion for what he was doing to Kyle.

"Beat his ass, Biscuit," I shouted.

After a few seconds, Biscuit stopped punching him, bent down, and appeared to be kissing him.

And Kyle screamed a cry like he was being tortured.

Biscuit turned his head to the side, spit something on the floor, and picked Kyle up from the couch. As he drug him toward the door by the hair and his half-removed jeans, he spoke to me in a remarkably calm tone.

"Open the door, would ya?" he asked flatly.

I ran past them, grabbed the door, and pulled it open. As I turned around and made eye contact with Biscuit, he shook his head and grumbled out a growl that sounded like a rabid pit bull.

And he dropped Kyle to the floor.

"You son of a worthless cock sucking bitch," he said as he began kicking Kyle's face with his boots.

I stepped out onto the hallway between my apartment and the adjoining apartment, and glanced around nervously. After several swift kicks to the face, Biscuit picked up Kyle and slapped him a few times.

"Can you fuckin' hear me, you little bitch?" he shouted as he slapped him.

Kyle groaned.

"I need you to answer me, motherfucker. You hear me?" Biscuit growled.

His face, arms and shirt covered in blood, Kyle moaned.

"Either answer me, or I'm going to toss you on the floor and boot your ass again," Biscuit said as he slapped him again, "Can you fuckin' hear me?"

"Yeah," Kyle moaned.

Biscuit held Kyle rather limp body in his hands, and pressed his face within inches of Kyle's.

"Good. Now listen up. I'm tellin' you once. You ever come in contact with her again, for *any* reason - and believe me, I don't give a fuck what it is - I'm gonna find you. And don't worry you little punk assed bitch, I won't kill you, but I'll make you one solemn promise; you'll wish you were fucking dead when I get done with your ass. I'll have the fellas I run with butt fuck you until you can't hold your shit in, and then I'll come and cut your fuckin' hands off – both of 'em. You fuckin' understand me?" he growled.

Jesus.

I swallowed heavily at the thought of what Biscuit said. Something told me he was far from joking.

"Yeah," Kyle moaned.

"Tell me what's going to happen if you ever come in contact with her. Tell me what I said," Biscuit hissed.

"Cut my…cut off my…my hands," Kyle muttered.

"And?" Biscuit asked as he shook Kyle violently.

"Butt…Uhhm, butt fuck me," he whined in response.

"That's right," Biscuit growled.

Biscuit shoved Kyle through the door, past me, and onto his back. I turned toward where Kyle landed and gazed down at him, pleased the ordeal was over, but worried about Kyle's bloody body being on the landing of my third floor apartment. I glanced toward Biscuit as he walked past me, grabbed Kyle's boots, and promptly drug him toward the steps. Somewhat confused at what was next, Biscuit didn't keep me wondering for long. After a swift tug on Kyle's legs, he drug him feet first down the steps, Kyle's head thumping against each step as he did so.

The sound of it was almost grotesque.

Almost.

But I despised Kyle and his ability to call rape by another name. Men seemed to think if they ever fucked a woman or had a relationship with her, that it provided an open invitation for them to continue to fuck her. When our relationship ended, so did every feeling or desire I ever had for Kyle. And no meant no, whether I was his former girlfriend or not.

The thumping sound continued until Biscuit reached the first floor landing - and each thud of Kyle's head against a concrete step was like music to my ears.

BISCUIT

I would rather spend the rest of my life without ever being in another fight. The odds of that happening, however, were pretty damned slim. I'd been in more fights than any other man I'd ever met, and looking back on it, most had been instigated by someone who I perceived as being disrespectful. I could stand for a lot of things, but for a man to be disrespectful to me, one of my brothers, or a woman wasn't something I was willing to ever accept.

The world seemed to be filled with people who had very little understanding of the importance of being respectful, and although I realized it was not my *responsibility* to teach them to do so, my *ability* to convince people of my beliefs on the matter made it difficult for me not to do my best to cleanse this earth of the filth which continued to fill it. The disrespectful men on this earth seemed to swim in circles like sharks, waiting for the next weak victim to expose itself, only to be savagely devoured solely for an inability to fight back.

To think for one minute I could rid this earth of every man who resembled Kyle would be foolish on my part.

But I did my God forsaken best to make certain what little portions of this world which exposed themselves to me were free of any and all men like him.

Being raised by a father who spent all of his free time drunk and beating on my mother wasn't easy for me. When I was young, I wasn't big enough to whip him, and although I couldn't convince my mother to leave, convincing myself to do so was easy. At fifteen years old, I left and never looked back, moving damned near eight hundred miles away from my hometown.

Seventeen years later, accepting that I'd walked away from my mother - leaving her at the hands of that cruel prick - was impossible. I struggled with my decision on an almost daily basis, wondering if I should have just killed my old man and took her from the abusive hell she lived in. Wondering what my mother's life had become, and knowing men like him didn't ever change, I was forced to either accept what I had done, or live with the guilt for doing it.

The guilt suffocated me as if I were drowning, and my only way to obtain one more much needed breath was to fight my way to the surface of the water, eliminating every shark I encountered in the process.

"So I beat the brakes off this so-called Marine, tossed his ass on the couch, and bent down there and breathed into his ear. *You punk assed little bitch*, I said. And then I bit off the bottom half of his ear and spit that fucker on the floor."

I nodded my head and reached for my bottle of beer.

Axton shook his head for a moment, eventually fixing his eyes on mine, "God damn, Biscuit. Pulled a Mike fucking Tyson on his ass, huh?"

I shrugged my shoulders, still fuming from what he had done to Kat.

"Is that it? You didn't kill the fucker did you?" Axton shrugged.

"That ain't all I did, but no, I didn't kill him. I should have, but I didn't. Put the boots to him for a bit, and told him I'd have Pete butt fuck him and cut his hands off if he ever came back. Oh, and I drug his ass down the steps, three god damned flights," I chuckled as I lifted my bottle.

"By his fuckin' feet. His head bounced off each god damned step, thumpity-thumping all the way down. I think he got the point," I grinned.

"The girl alright?" Axton asked as he stood.

I pushed myself from table and took a drink of beer, "Yeah. He slapped her a few times and tried to make her suck his cock. She was pretty shook up. Too fucked up to fuck, that's for sure. I stuck around for an hour or so and just held her 'till she fell asleep. You know, the whole deal reminded me of my mother. I just wish…"

"Can't change it Biscuit. We've talked about this a million times," Axton sighed, "You did what you had to do. You did good by this girl. I'm pretty surprised you didn't kill the prick, but I'm god damned pleased you aren't in jail."

I shrugged my shoulders, not certain of what to say. Each and every time I learned of another man abusing a woman, the sensible side of my mind went somewhere else, leaving a two hundred pound fifteen year old boy to make decisions.

"She must have been worn the fuck out," Axton sighed, breaking the silence, "going to sleep at three in the afternoon."

"So did you take time to talk to her about her father's little visit?" he asked.

I shook my head and stood from my seat, "No. Kind of forgot about it at first, then when she was cryin' and fallin' asleep, didn't really want to upset her."

"You know my recommendation. Get it over with as soon as you can. That's all I've got for advice. You sure you're alright, brother?" he asked as he stood.

"I'm good. Just need to drink this beer," I grinned.

Axton nodded his head, "Well, I'm gonna get the fuck out of here, Avery's off early today and we're gonna ride out to Benton to the airport."

I raised the bottle and grinned.

Axton said as he turned toward the door, "Lock up when you leave."

"Always do, Boss," I nodded.

He stopped at the doorway and glanced over his shoulder, "Remember what I said. I don't want that fucking cop back over here looking for you any time soon."

"Gotcha," I said as I tilted my beer bottle toward him.

"And don't toss that fucking bottle in my trash," he grunted as he walked down the hallway.

After I heard him ride away, I sat in the office and thought about everything that had happened. Kat was no different than any other girl I'd ever fucked, but something about her made her more attractive to me. Unable to pinpoint exactly what it was, I wondered if her father's insistence of my leaving her was what made her more appealing.

The forbidden fruit.

After finishing my beer, I decided that wasn't the case, as I seemed to have a fondness for her long before her father showed up at the shop. After struggling with my decision for some time, eventually I decided it was in my best interest to step aside for at least a few days, and see if she made contact with me. The time away would let me make a decision without a brain manipulated by the power of pussy.

I walked into the shop, glanced down at my swollen knuckles, and tossed the empty beer bottle in the trash. As I gazed across the shop at my bike, I decided more than anything I needed to clear my mind. The only way I had found to truly rid my mind of what was bothering me was to ride, and ride hard. After pushing the bike into the parking lot and setting the alarm, I fired the engine and let it warm to operating temperature.

As I reached for the hand controls and pulled in the clutch, the iPod switched songs, shuffling randomly to the next tune it selected from my 4,000 song playlist. Strangely, The National's *I Need My Girl* blared out of the speakers and filled the parking lot with snippets of wisdom about a man in need of his girl.

For some reason, no differently than the man in the song, I felt smaller and smaller as each moment passed. After the song stopped playing, I pressed the *back* button and repeated it. Half way through it, I pulled the clutch lever, shifted into gear, and released the clutch. As the bike slowly rolled down the street, the song ended and Cypress Hill's *How I Could Just Kill a Man* began playing.

I reached for the iPod, turned the volume to maximum, and rolled back the throttle. As the bike sped through the intersection and down the street, I tilted my head back, rested my feet on the floorboards, and grinned. The random cars parked at the side of the street rushed past me like fence posts on the highway.

That's more like it.

I rounded the corner onto the highway 30 miles per hour faster than the speed limit - dragging the floorboards as I did so - sparks flying behind me until I straightened the bike up after the curve. There was no doubt the forty mile ride to Wichita would clear my mind. To me, riding my bike was like a shot of heroine to a junkie.

There was nothing in the world that could ever replace it.

Or make the itch go away. Nothing at all.

KAT

I hadn't heard from Biscuit in four days, and as much as I didn't want to let it bother me, it did. Most would probably believe all we shared was sex, and that I was a typical clingy female for feeling the way I felt, but to me although our *relationship* wasn't much more than sex, my *feelings* were based on how intrigued I was by him, my physical attraction to his handsome looks, and his ability to make me laugh on command. Lastly, I felt like when no one else ever attempted to or was able, Biscuit had saved me from the sickening piece of human garbage who continued to resurface in my life, Kyle.

Maybe to Biscuit I was nothing more than a piece of ass, and although that was what I agreed to be, my mind struggled with accepting him as no more than a cock. His love for music, lack of desire to have a television or computer, and passion for the open road made him a far more appealing man to me than almost anyone I could ever remember meeting. There was no doubt he was a tough and capable biker, he'd proven that – but there seemed to be so much more to him. He possessed a certain kindness even when we were having sex, never giving me more than I was able to handle, but making sure I got everything I needed and deserved. As demanding as he was sexually and as naturally dominant as he seemed to be, it didn't overshadow his natural kindness. The nights we sat in his living room naked, listening to music for hours after we had sex left me hoping that even if it was happening slowly, he was becoming attracted to having me in his life beyond sex.

How he held me after dragging Kyle from my home wasn't something he *had* to do. He did it because he *wanted* to. And, in the end, he didn't even try to have sex with me. He held me until I fell asleep, tucked me into my bed, and kissed me on the forehead before he left.

I wondered if he realized I knew he kissed me.

I hoped he didn't.

I suspected most people who didn't actually know me would perceive me as an immature 22 year old woman, concerned with nothing more than having a man who I could cling to, screw, and pilfer money from. Truthfully, I believed myself to be very mature, and longed for someone who was kind, funny, very masculine, simplistic in his needs, and willing as well as able to satisfy me sexually. My previous relationships, even eliminating Kyle, had been filled with sex, and excluded much reciprocating emotion. It seemed I used sex as a way to get back at my overbearing father, thinking if I fucked the men he despised; it would cause him to feel the same level of pain he imposed on me as I grew up under his oversized thumb he always pressed down upon me.

In reality, something within me directed me toward the bad boys of this earth; and a kind, calm, cute office manager with a Mercedes-Benz and an unlimited bank account wasn't attractive to me. Right or wrong, I wanted an alpha male who wasn't afraid to put me in my place when I needed it, but take care of me and cherish me along the way. I had always told myself if that person was ever to be found, I would cling to him like gum to a shoe.

In all reality, my desire was Biscuit.

But he didn't want a conventional relationship. And I gave my word

I wouldn't press the issue, and assured him I could be satisfied with a sexual relationship.

NSA.

No. Strings. Attached.

Many people did it. I had no idea how many actually *succeeded* at it, but I really didn't care. If I had to, at least for now, I'd do it unsuccessfully, hiding my true feelings until I was either able to be honest, or got disgusted with the lack of returned emotion.

I needed to step up my game. The next time I saw him, I wasn't going to let him fuck me.

I had made up my mind.

It wasn't going to happen.

I was going to turn the tables.

It was high time Kat step up to her A-game.

He wasn't going to fuck me next time; *I* was going to fuck *him*.

BISCUIT

I stood back and admired the new *Sandstone Beige* paint. The room looked significantly larger in the light beige tone than it did in the *Chelsea Red*. I turned slowly and studied all of the trim along the floor, making certain there were no spots in need of touch-up before I took the drop cloths from the floor.

Everything looked perfect.

After a satisfactory nod, I reached for the can of paint, pressed the lid onto the top, and carried everything to the garage. As I placed the can on the workbench I wondered how much I'd spent on paint over the years. It really didn't matter, a bright well-painted room was something I truly enjoyed, and if it took me three dozen attempts to get it right, I could rest easily knowing I was giving it my best effort.

As I glanced around the garage at the various half-empty cans of paint, I heard a car in the drive.

Perfect timing.

I walked to the edge of the garage, pressed the button, and opened the door. Cassie's car was parked in the front of the drive, and she was walking up the sidewalk as the door opened.

"Just come through here," I shouted.

"Oh, okay," she responded.

I hadn't seen her since the day we fucked on my back deck by the pool, but considering how long she took to prepare, and what she looked like as she stood in front of me, I wondered if I'd seen her the first time through an overly aggressive pair of beer goggles. She was far from cute, sloppily dressed, had unhealthy looking hair, and was more than likely four foot ten in height.

I glanced down. Her feet were wrapped in a pair of three inch heels. I shifted my eyes upward. The scarring on her face from what I expected was a lifetime of acne caused her to look like someone had lit her face on fire and then put it out with a fork. I shifted my eyes downward slightly.

She had no tits.

I shrugged my shoulders and reached for the door leading into the house.

"Come on in," I said as I opened the door.

"It's really cool to get to see you again," she said cheerily as she skipped toward the door.

Wish I could say the same.

"You fully understand why you're here, right?" I asked.

"Uhhm, yeah. You wanted to see me?" she shrugged.

I shook my head, allowed my mouth to curl into a shitty little smirk, and chuckled, "No. I'm going to fuck you. You came here to fuck me. That's the *only* reason you're here."

She shrugged her shoulders again and grinned, "Oh, yeah. Okay."

She obviously lost her self-esteem at the same time she lost her face cleanser. I fought the urge to tell her to leave, and decided to do the complete opposite.

I pointed toward the wide open garage door and waved my hand her direction, "Shut the door and get undressed."

She lowered her shoulder, dropped her purse, and reached for the door. As she pulled the door closed behind her, I stared blankly at her, hoping she'd change.

She didn't.

She turned around and stared, seemingly confused on what *get undressed* meant. As she stood on one side of the island, and me on the other, I continued to glare at her in a combination of disgust and regret.

"Cassie, right?" I asked.

She smiled and bobbed her head eagerly, "Yeah, you remembered."

"Get."

"Undressed," I sighed.

She glanced around the kitchen, "Here?"

"No, in the fuckin' street," I responded in a sarcastic tone.

She gazed at me with deer in the headlight eyes.

I shook my head and sighed heavily, "Yes, *here*. You'll need to do it so we can fuck. Remember? We're fuckin', it's why you're here."

"I just. I wondered if you meant *here*," she said as pointed toward the floor.

"We're currently in my kitchen. I'm going to fuck you, here in the kitchen. I really don't know why, but I like fuckin' in the kitchen. For me to fuck you, Cassie, I need your clothes in a pile on the floor. Most of them, anyway. So, take off your little shorts, those shoes, and if you think it's necessary, yank off the top. When you're done, we're gonna fuck. Understand?"

"Yes, Sir," she responded sheepishly.

Sir?

"What's with the authority?" I shrugged.

"Huh?" she said as she pulled off her shoes.

Standing a mere six feet from me, it was easy for me to be critical of everything about her which I disliked. I gazed at her as if disgusted, and to be honest, I was pretty close. After an exhausting three or four second glare, I expanded my question to hopefully allow her to comprehend my curiosity.

"I asked if you understood, and you said *yes Sir*. Why'd you say *Sir*?" I asked.

She shifted her eyes to the floor and held her gaze.

"I just read a book about a guy who was dominant and he taught a girl how to be submissive. I was just trying to please you," she sighed.

Perfect.

Another one of those.

The world needs one more confused twenty-something year old who thinks she wants to be submissive.

I tilted my head to the side and reached for my beard, "You wanna make *me* happy?"

She glanced up and nodded her head eagerly, "Uh huh."

"Get un-fuckin' dressed," I snapped.

I would have guessed, and I suspected pretty accurately so, there weren't too many men who enjoyed a rough sexual tumble with a woman much more than me. Slapping a woman's ass, pulling her hair, and fucking her as long and hard as I was able was roughly the extent of my sexual desire. The much wider offerings of the BDSM spectrum were left to the professionals and the kinksters, they weren't for me.

There was something about using the zit-faced girl with dirty hair as my willing sex toy for the next hour or so that had me feeling pretty good about my decision to ask her to come over. As she removed her shirt and tossed it on the floor, she glared at me as if confused.

"Uhhm, you're still dressed," she shrugged as she did her best to cover her non-existent tits.

I sighed and pointed to the island in front of me, "I'm well fuckin' aware…"

"Come over here and bend over," I said as I slapped my hand against the counter.

Although she seemed somewhat reluctant, she walked around the island and promptly stopped in front of me, smiled, and turned around. There was no way her short little legs were going to allow her to bend over the counter. One of the things that originally her attracted to me, and now came to mind, was her long torso. The fact she was less than five feet tall – and had a long torso – left very little to make up her bottom half.

In short, her legs were all of two feet long.

Leaning onto the countertop naked, she turned and peered over her right shoulder.

"What now?" she asked.

"Hold on a minute," I said as I raised my index finger in the air.

I walked out to the garage, grabbed a step stool, and promptly returned. After carrying it to the side of the island she was standing on, I tossed it onto the floor beside her, kicked it closer with my feet, and told her to step on top of it.

"Hop on top of that, it'll make this a little fuckin' easier," I said.

"Okay," she responded.

After a quick survey of the situation, she stepped onto the stool. Her ass was now at the proper height for me to fuck her, but I had almost no desire to do so. I leaned forward and studied her face.

Correction.

I had *no* desire.

'You gonna do whatever the fuck I tell you, you submissive little bitch?" I asked in my best imitation of what I expected to be a Dom voice.

"Yes, Sir," she responded.

"No matter what it is, you better fuckin' do it, understand?" I barked.

"Yes, Sir," she snapped.

Jesus. This is all too easy.

"You're going to fuck one of my biker buddies, understand?"

"Okay," she sighed.

I reached in my pocket, pulled out my phone, and called the only person I knew would come on a moment's notice.

Corn Dog.

BISCUIT

After a twenty minute wait for him to arrive, my boredom had peaked at an all-time high and I was ready to tell the zit-faced bartender to get her ass out of my house and go home. My promise of providing Corn Dog a piece twenty year old submissive pussy was the only thing that prevented me from doing just that. As I stood and watched her standing naked on the stool while we waited for him to arrive, I realized there was nothing even remotely attractive to me about her.

Now watching from the edge of the living room as Corn Dog tried to orchestrate the fiasco, I couldn't help but find humor in the ordeal, but felt no desire to involve myself in any way. My mind continued to fade to thoughts of Kat, wondering how she was doing after the run-in with her former boyfriend. Attempting to rid my mind of any outside influences so I would be able to enjoy the show, I turned down the music, peered through the doorway, and into the kitchen.

To satisfy my request – and more than likely his desire to have a threesome – Corn Dog arrived with an overly eager attitude and an additional female, Sloan. Sloan was Avery's best friend at one point in time, but as Avery's interest in Axton became apparent, Sloan didn't respect her or the developing relationship. Avery and Sloan lived together at the time, and Sloan's slutty attitude around Axton finally ground on Avery's last nerve. The friendship soon dissolved, leaving

Sloan alone and desiring a boyfriend who resembled Axton.

Toad, the MC's former Marine and Sergeant-at-Arms stepped in, fucked Sloan a few times, and found her to be a very willing – but extremely annoying – sexual partner. One day, after wrapping Sloan's head in Saran Wrap and fucking her until she was damned near suffocated, Toad lost interest in her, and simply dropped her off at Corn Dog's house.

Sloan, being the true slut she was, didn't seem to care who she was with, only that the person was a biker, and he was willing to fuck. Corn Dog, having just been released from prison, was more than willing to put up with Sloan's annoying personality as long she was willing to satisfy him sexually. After Toad introduced them to one another they had been inseparable.

Corn Dog stood on the stool I had provided Cassie. In front of him lying on her back, was Sloan. Her head - in an almost upside down position - dangled from the end of the countertop. As Corn Dog slowly and steadily pumped her mouth full of his schlong, saliva ran from her mouth, down to her nose, and along her forehead. Cassie stood the other end of the island with her face buried in Sloan's lap, and was at least attempting to eat Sloan out. As Corn Dog continued to pummel Sloan's throat, he craned his neck toward Cassie and sighed heavily.

"God fucking damn," Corn Dog whined as he pulled his cock free of Sloan's mouth.

"What?" Sloan responded as she wiped the slobber from her face and forehead.

He waved his hand toward Sloan and leaned to the side, "Hey. Whatever your fucking name is, *come here*."

Cassie raised her head, stood, and wiped her mouth with the back of her hand. She lowered her shoulders in apparent shame as she shuffled toward the end of the island.

"Yeah," she sighed as she sauntered toward him.

"You eat pussy about like I eat escargot. Is there a fucking problem?" he asked as she approached.

"I…I uhhm…it seems *weird*. I'll do it if you want me to, it's just…" she stammered.

He raised his hand in the air and shook his head, "Nope, you're done with the pussy licking. I can't fucking stand it. It's painful to see, and I'm about to go limp watching you do it."

He alternated glances between them and tossed his hands in the air, clearly frustrated. Sloan slid off the edge of the counter, stood beside Cassie, and waited for his instructions. After studying them both for a moment, he pointed to the counter.

"Sloan, you get up there on your back with your pussy facing me," he said as he turned to face Sloan.

Sloan climbed onto the island, rolled onto her back, and let her legs dangle off the end of the island.

He glanced at Cassie, "You ain't afraid of sucking a dick are you?"

"Uh-uh. I *like* giving head," Cassie responded.

"Show me what you got," Corn Dog snapped back as he pressed his hands against her shoulders.

She dropped to her knees and began sucking Corn Dog's dick like she owed him money, and giving him head was the pay off.

Having watched her attempt to suck my big cock in the past - and encountering a few issues with the size - made seeing her go to town on Corn Dog's average sized shaft with ease a little unnerving. It left me wishing – at least for the time being – that I had an average sized cock.

145

Sex, in itself, satisfied me. Finding a woman, however, who was able to satisfy me and make use of my *entire* cock wasn't easy. The few who were able to do so were reserved – at least in my mind – as my *go to* women.

As I stood back and shook my head at the porn-fest as it unfolded, Sloan resituated herself on the countertop, rising up and onto her elbows so she could enjoy Cassie's deep throating Corn Dog's cock. As Cassie continued to bob her head and moan, Sloan gazed her direction and grinned.

Satisfied this wasn't going to end anytime soon, I sat down on the loveseat and rested my chin against my hand. I found it oddly satisfying that although I was entertained by the show in the kitchen, I wasn't in the least bit aroused. Uncertain if it was my newfound disgust with Cassie or a combination of Cassie and Sloan – who I had *no* respect for – or the fact I perceived both women as possessing minimal amounts of pride, I relaxed into the arm of the chair as if I were sitting on the riverbank fishing.

"Alright, alright, you've got a pretty good head game," Corn Dog said as he pressed his hand against her forehead, forcing his dick to spring free from her mouth.

"Stand up," he barked.

She wiped her mouth free of saliva and stood. It appeared she was beaming with pride as she gazed up at him grinning.

"Now get up on top of her - on your hands and knees - and shove your pussy in *her* face," he said to Cassie as he motioned toward Sloan.

Cassie stepped onto the stool, struggled for a moment to climb onto the counter, and eventually straddled Sloan's face. Lying on her back, Sloan reached up, wrapped her arms around Cassie's waist, and commenced to burying her mouth between Cassie's legs. Cassie immediately arched her back and began moaning. At least it appeared Sloan was able to understand and follow directions.

Seemingly pleased, Corn Dog glanced in my direction, shrugged, and stepped onto the stool. As he stood with his rigid cock in his hand, he tilted his head to the side and grinned.

"You sure you don't want in on this, brother?" he hollered.

I grinned and shook my head.

"Not today, Dog. It's her punishment for pissing me off, she's got nothin' comin' from me," I shouted in return as I waved my hand in the air.

It sounded good in theory, but wasn't remotely close to the truth. I wanted nothing to do with Cassie, and would probably never see her again - unless Corn Dog brought her around. I imagine some men might look at me as somewhat of a hypocrite, fucking women and never allowing any kind of emotion to exist - all the while claiming I never *hurt* women - but in my mind, telling them what they *were* going to receive, and what they *were not* going to receive made all of the difference in the world. It was always their choice to become involved with me sexually, everything was explained in advance, and nothing was ever forced. As I watched them continue, it was almost as if I had an awakening of sorts. As I realized once again the live porn show wasn't arousing me in the least, my eyes became unfocused and my mind faded to questions of *why*.

What had changed within me, I wondered. Was it Cassie? Did I find her so repulsive that I couldn't watch? As I searched for answers of a question that had yet to be asked, I realized not only did Kat satisfy me, but I truly looked forward to the time we spent together. Beyond sex, we seemed to share the same love for music, hatred for authority, and desire to live a simplistic life.

Corn Dog's shouting brought me back to reality, and the charade that followed confirmed my current lack of interest in such activities.

"Your loss, brother," he shrugged as he grabbed the back of Cassie's head and forced his dick deep into her throat.

While Sloan did her best to please Cassie and stay in Corn Dog's good graces, he arched his back and groaned.

"Fuck yeah. Suck that cock, you little slut," he groaned as he glanced down at Cassie.

Sloan's face stayed buried against Cassie's mound, never letting up one bit. As Cassie bucked her hips against Sloan's face, she repeatedly bobbed her head back and forth along the shaft of Corn Dog's cock - her chin all but resting on Sloan's pussy as she did so.

"Bury your tongue in her pussy, baby. Bury it deep," he bellowed toward Sloan as he fucked Cassie's face.

Baby?

Now living a far cry from the prison he was in only a month prior, it appeared he was having the time of his life. If anyone deserved to enjoy life, it was Corn Dog. The epitome of a stand-up guy, he had done a five year bit in state prison for a crime he really didn't commit - and could have easily rolled over on - but chose not to. A man had sold him a crate of legal firearms – pistols to be exact – and Corn Dog intended to re-sell them for profit. After doing so, it was determined the pistols were stolen, and he was subsequently arrested and questioned. All he had to do was provide the man's name he had purchased them from, and he would have been set free. He refused to provide anything, and chose to spend the time in prison, and take care of the thief after he was released from prison. Most men would have crumbled at the thought of doing time for a crime they didn't commit.

But, being the hard motherfucker he was, he simply raised his chin, rolled back his shoulders, and did his time in prison. Now free and making up for lost time, he seemed to be enjoying what life outside the prison walls offered him.

He pulled his dick from Cassie's mouth and bent his knees slightly. As Cassie arched her back from the pleasure Sloan was providing her, Corn Dog pulled on Sloan's thighs, sliding her ass forward slightly. As her pussy reached the end of the island, he leaned forward and began fucking her. While Cassie continued to enjoy Sloan's tongue, she watched the Dog fuck Sloan violently, moaning in apparent ecstasy the entire time.

After a few minutes, he pulled his cock from Sloan's cock socket and grabbed Cassie's head. As she gazed at him with wide eyes, he straightened his knees and shoved his cock in her mouth.

"How's that pussy taste now?" he grunted as he smashed his hips into her face.

"Mmm," Cassie moaned.

After a few seconds of moaning and groaning on both of their parts, he pulled himself from Cassie's mouth, grinned, and shoved it between Sloan's legs.

He alternated between Cassie's mouth and Sloan's crotch, fucking each one for thirty seconds or so before switching. This very predictable and rather boring pattern continued for some time. When I was about ready to throw in the towel and go relax out at the pool, he reached for Cassie's head and held it firmly in his hands. As he spoke, he continued to fuck Sloan slowly and steadily.

"You like the taste of cum?" he growled.

"Uh huh, I do," Cassie nodded eagerly as she continued to grind her mound in Sloan's face.

"Good," he said as he began to fuck Sloan with much more force.

A few more seconds, and Corn Dog arched his back and wailed like the dog he was. Now standing on his tip-toes and attempting to catch his breath, he pulled his hips rearward and grabbed Cassie's hair in his hand.

"See that?" he grunted as he jacked his cock free of the few remaining drops of cum.

She gazed down at Sloan's cum covered snatch and nodded her head.

"Well, there you go. Make your little slut self useful and suck that cum out of Sloan's twat," he said as he pushed Cassie's face between Sloan's legs.

As Cassie began to go down on Sloan, Sloan moaned in pleasure. While I shook my head in slight disbelief, Corn Dog pulled on his jeans and walked barefoot into the living room.

"Good lookin' out on the little submissive bitch," he said as he buckled his belt.

I nodded my head.

"Can't believe you didn't join in. What'd that little whore do to piss ya off?" he asked.

"Nothin' really," I shrugged, "Just sick of her. She's yours now."

He narrowed his eyes slightly and tossed his head toward the kitchen, "Giving her to me are ya?"

I gazed past him and into the kitchen. Sloan and Cassie were on the island making out. It seemed although Cassie didn't enjoy eating another woman out, she was no stranger to kissing one on the lips.

"Yeah, but it looks like you might have a fight on your hands," I chuckled as I pointed past him and toward the women.

He glanced over his shoulder, sighed loudly, and began to shout.

"God damn it, I told you to suck the cum out of her pussy. You weren't supposed to spit it in her mouth 'till I got back in here. You need some training, don't ya?" he growled as he stomped toward the kitchen.

In my opinion, there wasn't any amount of training in the world that would fix Cassie. For whatever reason, she had become unattractive to me, rendering her useless. As Corn Dog scolded the women for proceeding without him, once again my mind shifted to thoughts of Kat.

"You guys want to hang out at the pool?" I asked as I stood.

Sloan pulled her tongue from Cassie's mouth and turned to face me.

"Can we skinny dip?" she asked excitedly.

"You can do whatever you want. I need to run somewhere for about an hour or so," I shrugged, "You alright with that, Dog?"

"Okay by me, brother, we'll be here when you get back," he responded.

Instead of walking through the kitchen and causing myself to feel more disgusted than I already felt, I opened the front door and walked down the sidewalk toward the garage. I needed to listen to some music and get a little riding time in to clear my head.

Who's kidding who?

I wanted to check on Kat.

It had nothing to do with feelings or emotion, I simply needed to check on her and make sure she was alright.

Because it was the right thing to do.

As I pulled my bike into the street, I turned up the volume. Almost immediately, Beck's *Loser* finished playing. After a half-second lull, Marvin Gaye's *Let's Get it On* began to blare throughout the neighborhood.

I grinned, twisted the throttle, and pointed the bike toward Winfield.

Let's get it On.

Hell, who am I to argue with fate?

KAT

I hadn't developed hatred toward my father, to the best of my ability to recollect, it had always existed. Recently, however, it had become more noticeable. As embarrassed as I was to admit it, I probably wasn't the only one who realized it. As much as I detested him and his way of doing things, I still attempted to be respectful toward him. As I sat on my mother's couch and he stood in front of me justifying his actions, it became increasingly difficult.

I sat and stared at the floor, not wanting to give him the satisfaction of making eye contact with me.

"I'm twenty-two years old, not thirteen," I sighed.

"All I'm trying to do is protect you," he said flatly.

I glanced up. He stood, arms crossed, wearing his protective vest over his uniform. The word POLICE in six inch high white letters made certain everyone he encountered knew who *and what* he was – as if there could ever be any confusion. Disgusted at his mere existence, I stood from the couch.

"Protect me? From what? Life?"

"Sit down, we're not done talking," he demanded as he pointed toward the couch.

I turned toward the kitchen and began walking away.

"*You're* not done talking. *I* am. And I'm done listening," I responded over my shoulder.

"You can't go from one shit bird to another, Katrina. You're going to have to learn to…"

Before he finished speaking, I turned around and interrupted him, "My life, my decision, and I'll suffer the consequences. For once, stay out of my life."

He uncrossed his arms, lowered them, and quickly crossed them in front of his chest again.

"I'll pull you out of that college so fast your head spins," he seethed.

"I swear. I got a scholarship, remember? I'm an adult. You can't pull me from anything. And you know what? You just…you make me… mad. That's what you do. You make me mad. Who digs through their twenty-two year old daughter's phone records? Who? Nobody does, that's who. Nobody but some overbearing *cop*," I fumed.

My mother's voice startled me, and provided not only a reminder that my father and I weren't alone, but confirmation I had overstepped a boundary of her's by challenging my father.

"Katrina Chadsworth!"

"Don't you start on me too," I said over my shoulder.

I heard the sound of her heels on the kitchen floor as I studied my father. Standing in front of me fuming, he seemed to be in shock, ready to shoot me, or both.

"Apologize to your father," my mother sighed.

I glanced over my shoulder.

"Seriously?" I chuckled.

"*He* needs to apologize to *me*. He's interfering with my life, going through my phone records, reading my text messages, and just being a…" I paused and turned to face him.

"A dick," I huffed, "He's being a dick."

"That's *it*," my father shouted as he thrust his hands in the air.

"Katrina!" my mother shouted.

"What are you going to do? Use your cop power to dig through my shit? You know, I bet that's against the law. I'll look into it," I said as I glanced around the room nervously.

I felt trapped. Both of them now stood in front of me, arms crossed, and glaring. As they searched for their next insult, I glanced down, grabbed my purse, and stomped toward the door.

"If you leave here…" my father began.

"Katrina…" my mother whined.

I waved my arm in her direction. She supported my father regardless of his position. Growing up, my brother had the freedom to do as he pleased, and I was constantly under surveillance. He was able to be out all hours of the night with his friends – because he was a boy. I was required to be home much earlier, and when I was out, my father often drove by or stopped in to check on me. Having an overprotective cop for a father minimized my chances at having many true friends.

I pulled the door open and turned around, "What? What are you going to threaten me with if I leave?"

"You'll disown me? Do me a favor, grant that wish. And I was serious about the text messages. I'm going to talk to an attorney," I growled as I stomped out the door.

For him to have talked to Biscuit would more than likely ruin my chances at ever having anything develop with him. I suspected it was the sole reason I hadn't heard from him in a matter of several days. As I backed my Jeep out of the driveway and onto the street, I decided if nothing else, finding out what my father did would provide me with a reason to call Biscuit and apologize. Talking to him would be nice.

Maybe I could convince him to meet me for a drink instead.

If I got a few drinks in him, I could probably convince him to fuck me. And, if we had sex, and I *really* satisfied him, maybe he'd forgive me for having a dickhead father.

Men.

Maybe they're all just pieces of shit, and it's only a matter of time until you smell it.

For some reason, I believed deep down inside Biscuit was a compassionate man. Penetrating the thick outer shell would be difficult, but I was willing to give it a try.

As I drove down the street, I began to cry. Not knowing if it was Biscuit's absence, Kyle's abusive behavior, or my father's childish antics, I pulled the Jeep to the side of the street and attempted to collect my composure.

Lately I seemed to be an emotional mess, and I needed to get my shit together. After a few minutes of sobbing for reasons unknown, I gathered my thoughts, regained my sanity, and wiped the mascara from my cheeks.

As much as I wanted to go home and call Biscuit, I needed to rest. Maybe after a good night's sleep I could call him and see what he thought about meeting for a drink. Some sleep, a three mile run, and a good breakfast should clear my mind of everything, and leave me in a good state of mind.

I pulled my Jeep back into the street and drove toward the highway. The forty minute drive to Winfield would settle my nerves and let me forget about my father being a dick.

I pushed through the controls on the back of my steering wheel, searching through the satellite channels for *something*.

As I clicked past the radio stations frantically, After kicking his shorts to the side, he glanced up and grinned. With his eyes locked on me, and my eyes glued to the eighth wonder of the world, the sound of his raspy voice confirmed this was no joke. Alt-J's *Left Hand Free* caught my attention. I pushed the *back* button until I reached the channel playing it, and listened to the entire song, a rarity for me.

Although my preference was Indie music, I preferred music that was more mellow and relaxing – music that meant something. Modern music seemed to have very little substance, and was a mixture of synthesizers, voice altering devices, and was filled with reference to money, pussy, or expensive cars.

After the song ended, Elton John's *Don't Let The Sun Go Down On Me* began to play. I glanced toward the radio, confused as to why it was playing, but pleased nonetheless. The song had always been one of my favorites. I recognized the station as one of Sirius XM's newer stations, one which alternated between a song from today and one of yesteryear.

I turned up the volume, got lost in the words, and for the next few minutes, escaped to a world where everyone was free to make their own decisions. A far cry from reality, but that's what music did for me.

It provided me an escape from reality.

BISCUIT

Riding back toward Wichita and somewhat disappointed Kat wasn't home, I twisted back the throttle and sped up to just shy of 100 miles per hour. As I sped down the two-lane highway, I realized just how *alone* I felt. My closest friends and forever riding companions - Toad, Axton, and Otis - were all tied up with Ol' Ladies. Otis wasn't technically sporting an Ol' Lady yet, but he sure wasn't far from it. Since encountering Sam in the bar that night, they had become inseparable, and if I was forced to guess, marriage wasn't too far out in the future. As I wondered if the infiltration of women was going to be the death of the Sinners or the dawn of a new generation, I gazed out at the horizon with unfocused eyes.

At the speed I was traveling, hearing the stereo was impossible, and my earbuds were at home; leaving me without music. In my head, Bob Seger's *Roll Me Away* played, one of my natural highway tunes when I was without music. As I sang the song in my head for the zillionth time, a gray Jeep shot by me in the oncoming lane at an equally high rate of speed.

I checked my rearview mirror.

The brake lights illuminated.

It seemed I was headed back to Wichita, and Kat was headed home. I slowed the bike down to a reasonable speed, pulled to the side, and turned around. Now going the same direction as the speeding Jeep, I twisted the throttle and quickly eliminated the distance between us. As I caught up to her, she slowed considerably. I pulled the bike alongside her Jeep, glanced her direction, and smiled. Still rolling along at forty miles an hour, Kat stuck her head out the window and grinned from ear to ear.

"Hey stranger," she shouted.

I nodded my head and grinned.

"Follow me?" she yelled.

I nodded once, applied the brakes lightly, and pulled in behind her. As I followed her into town, I was surprised to find my heart racing and my nerves aflutter. Convinced it was a result of lack of food, too few Red Bulls, and overexposure to live porn, I continued to follow her anxiously, literally counting the miles click away as I rode.

Although I was one of very few men who could claim I had *never* been in a relationship, I could make the statement without any hesitation. Following behind Kat, studying what little of her I could see in her side view mirror, I began to wonder what life would be like with her in it on a permanent basis. Certain I was incapable of such ridiculousness, and convinced Axton, Otis and Toad were influencing my thoughts, I backed away from the Jeep and began following at a distance too far away to see her reflection.

I pulled into the parking lot behind her Jeep. As I surveyed the lot for a place to park, I eventually pulled alongside her Jeep, turned around, and parked facing the rear of her vehicle. As I stepped off the left side of the bike, she opened the door and smiled.

Regardless of our agreement regarding the elimination of emotion, and even as I reminded myself she was nothing more than a piece of ass to me, I couldn't deny her beauty.

She sat in the Jeep with the door open and gazed my direction, her blonde hair hanging loosely alongside her face. I don't really know that I had ever seen a woman more beautiful than she was at that moment, at least not in person. Kat was unique in many respects, her gorgeous appearance being only one of them. As I stared at her blankly, she eventually questioned my sanity.

"What? What's wrong?" she asked as she stepped out of the Jeep.

I shook my head, "Nothin'."

"Is there something wrong? My makeup's a mess, I know that," she sighed as she shut the door.

"You look good, that's all," I shrugged as I locked the bike, "You busy?"

She turned around and shook her head, "Not at all. I just got back from my parent's house. And if you've got time, I'd like to talk."

"Sure. What's up?" I asked as I turned toward her.

With her book bag over one shoulder and her purse over the other, she tossed her head toward the apartment building, "Let's get out of this heat. Come on."

I followed her up the stairs and into the house. After grabbing two beers out of the fridge, and plugging her iPod into the stereo, she walked into the small living room and sat beside me on the couch. My mind immediately went to thoughts of Kyle and the day I beat his ass on the couch. I glanced to each side of where I was sitting, surprised there were no bloodstains on the fabric.

"So, what's goin' on?" I asked.

She glanced in my direction, held the gaze for a moment, and eventually took a long drink from her beer. As I considered that maybe

I forgot to ask the question, or that she didn't hear me, she responded.

"I'm sorry about my father," she sighed.

I shrugged my shoulders, "No big deal."

"It is a big deal," she said, "He's a dick."

I chuckled, took a drink of my beer, and nodded my head, "He's a cop."

"Cop. Dick. What's the difference?" she shrugged.

"Sounds like somethin' I'd say," I said as I tilted my bottle toward her.

She reached toward my bottle with hers and clanked them together.

A blues tune with strong guitar played on the stereo. For the life of me I couldn't make the artist. I hated to ask, but eventually the curiosity got to me.

"Who's this?" I asked as I tilted my head rearward.

"Big Sugar," she grinned, "Oh crap. It's uhhm, *Goodbye Train.* They're Canadian."

"Canadian? They sure don't sound it," I shrugged.

As the music continued, I nodded my head, "Good shit."

"I like it," she grinned.

As I relaxed, I realized I was under no pressure to do *anything.* If I didn't bring up sex, Kat would probably be satisfied with simply spending time together. A nice departure from the norm, I sipped my bottle of beer and listened to the music as it played, becoming more and more relaxed as the time passed. We sat silently, drinking our beers and enjoying the music, I admired Kat's beautiful face and blemish free complexion.

"You ever have zits," I asked.

"Not really," she responded, "You?"

I nodded my head, "Yeah as a kid."

"So, why don't you do relationships? I'm not complaining, but just out of curiosity, why not?" she asked.

Shocked that she had the courage to ask, but glad she did so, I sighed and relaxed into the back of the couch. After a long minute, I inhaled a shallow breath, held it for a few seconds, and exhaled.

"I'm gonna to tell you the truth," I began.

"That's nice to know," she responded in a sarcastic tone.

I stared down at the floor and cleared my throat, "I think, or I thought, or whatever. Anyway, I always said God put me on this earth for one reason and one reason only."

She turned and glanced over her right shoulder, "Which is?"

"Fuckin' women," I responded.

Her eyes widened and she coughed a laugh, "You're serious?"

"Uh huh. One, I'm hung like a horse. Two, I've got a tongue like a giraffe. And three, I can recover from sex in about ten or fifteen minutes and go again. So why else would he give me all of those sexual gifts if he didn't want me fuckin' women?" I shrugged.

She finished her beer and stood. As she walked to the kitchen, I waited for her response. With her head stuck in the fridge and me regretting having spoken my mind, she responded.

"I don't know. Maybe to make one woman *really* happy," she said, "Ever consider that?"

I stood and finished my beer. She had a valid point, and as stupid as it seemed to admit it, I had never really considered what she said as being God's intention with me.

Growing up in Alabama, dropping out of school at fourteen and leaving home at fifteen left me feeling as if I wasn't a very smart boy. Over time, I believed I had developed into a man who could be perceived as smart, but I always felt I lacked true intelligence. As a boy, I was required to go to church, and as a man, although my belief in God persisted, my participation in Church services stopped.

I always felt if I stepped a foot into one, I'd burst into flames.

"No, never did," I shrugged as I tossed the empty beer bottle into the trash.

"Ever been in love?" she asked as she handed me a beer.

"Nope," I responded, "You?"

"Hard saying," she responded, "Maybe. Maybe not. Truthfully, I doubt I know what love is."

"Ever been close?" she asked.

I shook my head, "Never even had a girlfriend."

She narrowed her eyes and wrinkled her nose slightly, "Seriously?"

I nodded my head. Admitting it seemed strange, and I waited for her to begin to chastise me for never having committed to a woman. Although she never began to scold me or complain, she glared at me for a long minute before continuing.

"If the right woman came along, do you think you'll ever settle down?" she asked.

I gazed across the floor toward a decorative wooden box. It was filled with various throws and small pillows. After staring blankly at it for some time, I shifted my eyes around the room, making note of all items which reminded me of a woman. Although the apartment was small, there were several flower arrangements which I hadn't noticed in the past that stood out as being rather attractive and well put together.

"Did you make those or buy them?" I asked as I tilted my head toward the two vases on the end table on the opposite side of the room.

She glanced toward the flowers and grinned, "Made them, why?"

"They're nice," I responded.

"So, did you not want to answer the other question?"

I shifted my eyes toward her, and after a moment, my head followed. Now facing her, I pressed the beer bottle between my legs, exhaled, and responded.

I intertwined my fingers, extended my arm and cracked my knuckles, "Right woman? I'd always said there was no such thing. For some reason, starting oh I don't know, say two hours ago, I began to wonder. If a woman came along that sparked my interest, I may give it a try. Hell, everyone else is."

"Because everyone else is?" she chuckled, "Who's everyone else?"

"The fellas I run with, Otis, Axton, and Toad. Pretty much they're all hooked up with Ol' Ladies," I sighed.

She turned, placed her beer bottle on the end table, and turned my direction. Standing in front of me in cut-off sweat shorts, a Southwestern College tee shirt, and Converse sneakers, she looked adorable. As I studied her and attempted to guess her height, she tugged at the bottom of her tee shirt and twisted her hips slightly.

"So, has anyone sparked your interest lately?" she asked.

It bothered me having her stand over me and talk. One of the few things that irritated me - and something I couldn't stand for more than a few seconds. I pulled the beer from between my legs, glanced to my right, and realized there was nowhere to place the bottle. Without responding, I stood, stepped past her, and leaned toward the end table sitting beside her.

I placed the bottle beside hers, straightened my posture, and inhaled a shallow breath. The smell of her perfume filled my nostrils and caused me to smile.

Couture La La.

I closed my eyes for a split second and inhaled through my nose lightly, and it was then that I remembered. It was the girl from the grocery store who eventually moved to Ohio. The only woman I spoke to regularly without ever trying to fuck. She wore the same scent, and I had asked her once what it was. Couture and a warm smile each time I went through the checkout line were her two signatures.

"Only you," I responded as I opened my eyes.

She stood a mere two feet away from me fighting the urge to smile. "Good. I feel the same way. You know, I don't buy into the entire love at first sight shit. Boy meets girl, and they say *I knew the moment I met him...*"

"I'm an acquired taste," I chuckled, "Nobody is going to meet me and say they love me. How'd we jump to love, anyway?"

She shifted her eyes to the floor and held her gaze for a moment.

"I was just saying. But if you say I sparked your interest, and I say you sparked mine, why don't we see if we can make something work between us?" she asked as she shifted her eyes from the floor.

I studied her for a moment. Her eyes were brown with little flecks in them. Her hair appeared to be a little more blonde than I remembered it being. Her skin was the golden brown color most women strive to achieve through the course of the summer. In summary, she was nothing short of beautiful. As I studied her for some type of imperfection, the response came to me.

I crossed my arms in front of my chest and sighed heavily, "You know, I spent fifteen years bein' exposed to a man and a woman in a relationship that just didn't work. She hated him, but was afraid to leave, and he hated everyone and settled for taking out his hatred on her. Hell, he couldn't remember her birthday and vice versa. They didn't really know one thing about each other. Not a fuckin' one. But they stayed together because of me."

"Your parents?" she asked.

I nodded my head, "Yep."

"Do me a favor?" she asked.

I shrugged my shoulders, "Huh?"

She widened her eyes slightly, "Will you do me a favor?"

"Suppose so," I responded.

"Turn around," she sighed.

I cocked one eyebrow and reached for my beard, "Excuse me?"

"Humor me. Turn around," she said as she pointed toward the floor and turned her index finger in a circle.

I turned around and shoved my hands into the pockets of my jeans.

"Over your left eye there's a scar. It's small, but it separates your left eyebrow in to two almost identical halves. Your nose has a mole on it on the, oh shit, hold on. Left, it's on the left side. It's small too, about the size of a piece of sand. You've got a scar on your upper cheek that goes down and disappears into your beard. It looks like one that wasn't professionally taken care of, because there aren't any scars from the holes beside it where it would have been stitched," as she hesitated I heard her inhale a shallow breath.

Amazed, I started to turn around.

"No, stay right there," she demanded, "I'm not done."

"Your tooth in the front, the incisor or whatever they call it, it's got a line down the center. It looks like it was broken or fractured. And the knuckles on your right hand are so covered with scars that it's hard to

167

tell where they start and stop, but I think it's weird that your left hand really doesn't have any. Let me see, oh, and your tag on your bike is a personalized one, it says RFOF," she paused, inhaled a shallow breath and exhaled, "I guess that's it, you can turn around now."

I turned around slowly and removed my hands from my pockets. I was truly impressed with not only her attention to detail, but the fact she had made a mental note of all of the things she recited about me. As I studied her in disbelief, a strange feeling of comfort washed over me. After a short minute of uncomfortable silence, I crossed my arms and sighed. .

She was grinning from ear to ear.

"There's only three types of people I let get close enough to me to touch me," I said flatly.

"Huh?" she shrugged.

"My license plate. RFOF. Ride Fuck Or Fight. The fellas I ride with, whoever I'm fuckin', or the person who I'm beatin' the shit out of. Those are the three who get close enough to me to touch me," I explained.

She pressed her hands to her hips, "Well, I don't ride."

I grinned and shook my head.

"Wanna fight?" she asked as she raised her clenched fists.

I shook my head, "Sorry, don't fight women."

"Well, that only leaves one thing," she sighed as she lowered her hands.

"Damn the luck," I responded as I uncrossed my arms.

"Yeah," she breathed as she lowered her chin slightly.

Her hair fell into her face. As she gazed down at the floor in obvious thought, I reached for the strands that dangled from the sides of her head.

"About that question earlier," I said as I brushed her hair behind her ear.

She glanced up and blinked her eyes, "Yeah?"

"Let's give that a try. Let's get to know each other a little better and see what happens," I said, "That's about all I can promise."

"Enough for me," she shrugged.

As much as I hated to admit it, it was all I could offer her.

But for me, it was a huge step.

And more than likely, all I would be able to handle.

At least for a while.

KAT

In the two weeks following our discussion about attempting to make something work between us, we had seen each other every day. Although we didn't have sex on every single day, we came close. I found it rather reassuring that I no longer felt a need to have sex, only a desire. My problem seemed to be the same as Biscuit's. My desire was overwhelming, leaving our sexual downtime as the only opportunity to truly get to know one another.

"I think it's funny you never asked what my name is."

The low rumble of his voice prevented me from falling asleep totally. I was probably a few seconds away from it, floating in the almost dream-like state that always seemed to precede my passing out. I blinked my eyes, confused on where I was and what was going on. The warm sun against my skin and the sight of him beside me reminded me of where we were and what was happening.

I opened my eyes and began to fumble along the side of the lounge for my sunglasses. He rolled to his side and laid his head flat against the cushions of the chair. After finding my glasses and shading my tired eyes, I responded.

"I uhhm. I never really…I don't know. It's not that it didn't matter, but it didn't matter. I figured when you were ready to tell me you would. I guess I didn't want to pry. I know from talking to Avery that you're a private bunch of men, I was just being respectful, I guess," I said.

"Dalton," he said as he turned his head toward the sun.

I nodded my head and grinned, "I like it."

"Ain't got a middle name. They never gave me one. Last name's Biskette. It's where Biscuit came from, but that ain't too difficult to figure out," he said as he sat up in the chair.

He wiped the sweat from his brow as he stood, "I'm gonna hop in. It's hotter'n grits on a motherfuckin' griddle out here."

His speech patterns, funny sayings, and the slang he used led me to believe he grew up elsewhere. Not wanting to insult him, but curious about his upbringing, I stood from my lounge and tossed my glasses against the towel beside my chair.

"Where did you grow up again?" I asked as I followed him across the concrete deck.

"Alabama," he said as he dove into the pool.

He was an extremely graceful man in many respects. To watch him walk was nothing short of entertaining. There was a certain gate to his walk, not what most called swagger, but a small pattern. It was almost as if he had a bad hip or knee, but I knew he didn't. With each step of his right foot, his right hip would dip forward. Not only did it make his walk interesting, but there was a certain grace to his walk, almost like watching a ballerina. Seeing him dive into the pool made me believe he had at least taken diving lessons at one point in time. His body entered the water in a manner that produced virtually no splash, and made me quite envious.

As I dove into the pool, I wondered what my splash looked like.

"Have you taken swimming lessons? And diving lessons?" I asked as I cleared the surface of the water.

He wiped the water from his beard as he nodded his head, "At the Y. Figured when I bought the house I'd need to know how to swim and stuff, so I took lessons for a few years. You'll find out I don't do anything I can't do properly. Ain't nothin' worse than someone tryin' to do something and lookin' like a fuckin' idiot doin' it."

"Do I look like an idiot when I dive in?" I asked.

"No," he chuckled.

"You lying?"

"Maybe a little," he said as he swung his hand over the top of the water's surface, splashing it into my face.

"You fucker," I howled as I attempted to do the same.

Now in a heated splashing fight, we both swung our arms violently, splashing and screaming like children.

Being with Biscuit was so much different than being with Kyle. With Kyle, I was always on edge and wondering what his next complaint was going to be, and how he was going to treat me as a result of it. The tension between Kyle and I was thick, and I remained nervous throughout the entire relationship. At the time, I was convinced it was simply part of being with a man and the differences between men and women.

Actually being accepted by a man and not having to worry about being criticized for every mistake I made was a pleasant change, and certainly something I would have to get used to. I found myself waiting for the axe to fall with Biscuit, and it never did. Oftentimes I would do or say something I fully realized Kyle would explode about, and wait for Biscuit to do the same.

But the anger never came.

Truly grateful to have met him and pleased at our ability to be ourselves in each other's presence, I swung my arms like a flailing fool. Eventually we both stopped. Declaring a winner would have been impossible; he had better precision, but I possessed more determination.

"Now I'm exhausted," I sighed, "I'm glad it's Saturday."

"What's that got to do with anything?" he asked as he tossed his hair out of his eyes.

"Well, not everyone works on their own schedule. I've got the day off and no school, so I'm pretty happy. I get to relax," I said as I waded across the pool away from him.

"Relax?" he said as he splashed water my direction.

I turned to face him as I pulled myself from the pool. As he gazed up at me, I pulled my bikini top down as if to resituate it. Intentionally, I pulled it a little too far, but acted surprised as my boobs popped free of the material.

"Yep," I said as I glanced down at my breasts.

"Shit, they popped out, didn't they," I chuckled, "It's tough to keep these big fuckers in here."

"You tease," he said as he splashed water at me.

"Tease?" I laughed as I pulled my top out and over my boobs, "I don't think so."

He nodded his head and stuck out his tongue.

"That's teasing," I sighed.

"Not if I'm willin' to use it," he responded.

I glanced around the deck. The entire pool area was protected from the neighbor's view by a very tall privacy fence in every direction. I reached back, untied my top, and pulled my top over my head. As I reached for my bottom, he waded toward the side of the pool. While he was pulling himself from the pool, I relaxed onto the soft cushions of the lounge.

I sighed heavily as he walked my direction.

"I hate tan lines," I said as I reached for my glasses.

"Damn shame," he said, "I'm gonna lick that little pussy till you got a tan line of my head on your inner thighs."

"Promises, promises," I sighed as I put on my sunglasses.

As I felt his wet beard between my legs, I inhaled a deep breath and held it. Although I knew what was next, there was never anything I could do to prepare myself for it. No one could. The equivalent of riding a rollercoaster, jumping off a cliff, and witnessing a miracle all at the same time, having him lick my pussy was an entirely different kind of pleasure.

As his tongue slowly penetrated me, I exhaled and reached for his head. I lightly gripped it in my hands as he raised his chin and smiled.

"Fuck yeah, grab my head, Kat. Grab it and fuck my tongue," he said through his teeth.

Being caught off guard by his unexpected request, I stared down at him through my sunglasses without responding.

I held his head loosely in my hands as he lowered his chin and began to lick me softly. As his tongue began to press against my lips, I felt myself open up like a flower, inviting him into my warm, wet folds.

I closed my eyes and sighed. Somewhat lost in the feeling of his tongue, the warm sun, and my developing love for his being, his consistent moaning reminded me of his request.

You better fuck his face, Kat. You don't want to make him mad.

I gripped his head in my hands lightly and slowly raised my hips.

He pressed his tongue deeper, held it, and curled the tip into my g-spot.

I lowered my hips slightly.

175

His pulled his tongue from inside of me and flicked the tip against my clit.

Holy hell. I could get used to this.

I raised my hips again.

He presses his tongue deep inside of me and curled the tip into my g-spot. I held my hips against his face. The g-spot licking continued until I was dizzy and lightheaded.

I lowered my hips.

He licked my clit.

Well, he did say fuck my tongue, didn't he?

As Bill Wither's *Use Me* began to play over the stereo, I grasped his head in my hands firmly and began grinding my hips to the sound of the music. After a few seconds, I was grinding my hips against his face like it was my last chance. Completely separated from all that surrounded me, I continued until I had an orgasm in his mouth.

I pulled his head rearward and inhaled sharply.

"You okay?' I breathed.

He raised his hand and wiped his beard, "Be a lot better if you'd fuck my face for a while. I don't do this 'cause I think you like it. I do it 'cause I love it."

"Now fuck my tongue," he demanded as he lowered his face into my lap.

And who was I to argue with a demand like that?

I pressed my hands into the edges of the lounge and raised my ass from the surface of the chair. I held myself in position and released the edge of the chair. Using every muscle in my stomach, I ground my crotch into his face as I pulled against the back of his head with both hands.

His tongue deep inside of me, I had no intention of allowing him to catch a breath until I was done. Right now, this was about me, and I was going to take advantage of the situation fully. As I held his face against my swollen mound, he continued to curl his tongue against my g-spot. The tingling deep within me began and I held my eyes closed until I reached a heightened state of sexual sensation unlike anything I had ever experienced.

My breathing became choppy as I reached climax. I released the tension in my stomach and slowly collapsed into the chair, still holding his head tight against my pussy. As he worked his tongue in and out of me with great precision, I sighed, relaxed every muscle in my body, and released his head.

A tingling sensation between my ass, crotch, and nipples began. I felt pressure building inside of me. I opened my eyes and gazed into the sky, uncertain of what was happening. As his tongue pressed deeper and flicked against my g-spot one last time, I reached for his head and held it in place. I had no idea what was happening, but I knew I didn't want it to end.

As I reached the peak of climax, I felt as if something inside of me had burst. The feeling continued for what seemed like forever, but couldn't have been any longer than a second. I released his head, flopped my and to the side, and heaved a sigh from the depths of my soul.

"What happened?" I asked blankly as I felt him release his weight from the chair.

"Fuck yes!" he growled as he stood.

I blinked my eyes and stared.

"What?" I shrugged as I attempted to sit up slightly.

"You came in my mouth. Like a ton. You squirted," he grinned,

"That was fuckin' hot."

"I what?" I gasped.

"You squirted. You came in my mouth like a faucet," he said as he wiped his hand along his beard.

"Seriously?" I shrugged.

He released his beard and reached for his shorts, "Fuck yeah. We're gonna have to practice that."

"That was awesome by the way, I'm exhausted," I sighed as he untied the drawstring in his shorts.

"What are you doing?"

He shrugged his shoulders and widened his eyes, "Well, I can't fuck you with them on, now can I?"

I felt like I was still having an orgasm. My mind confused, and my body hypersensitive to everything, I sat and stared. The thought of sex wasn't currently on the forefront of my desires. As he began to stroke his cock, my thoughts on the matter began to change. After a few seconds of watching him stroke his hand along the swollen shaft, I rolled onto my stomach, stuck my ass high in the air, and sighed.

"Come and get it, *Dalton*," I breathed.

I felt the chair twist as he climbed onto it. With his chest pressed against my back and his thighs grazing against my ass as he situated himself on the flimsy chair, he moved his mouth to my ear.

With his lips pressed lightly against my ear, he inhaled a deep breath, sending chills down my spine. As I tilted my head his direction, attempting to force his mouth away, he bit my earlobe and growled into my ear once again.

"Come and get it? No, Kat. I'm gonna *take* it," he whispered.

"Oh God," I sighed.

"You know why?" he breathed into my ear.

"Because it's yours?" I squeaked.

He released my earlobe from between his teeth. "That's right. *My* pussy," he whispered.

Hearing him say it made me a melt. As I felt the tip of his cock pressing against my still throbbing pussy, I inhaled sharply, exhaled as he penetrated me, and bit my lower lip in anticipation of what was sure to come.

Slowly and steadily, he began to fuck me. With each stroke I was one step closer to collapsing in a pile on the lounge chair. Still recovering from the squirting, and feeling rather exhausted, I was providing very little to the sexual act with the exception of a wet willing hole.

I moaned as his pace and depth slowly increased. When he reached a point that he was stroking me with every inch of his cock, he dug his fingernails into my shoulders and forced me to arch my back.

"That'll hit that spot," he growled into my ear.

And he was right.

The tip of his ever so lovely cock was grinding against my g-spot with each stroke. No differently than someone shoving their fingers into my armpit and tickling me, his stiff cock was positioned perfectly and tickling me sexually.

He released my shoulder, and reached for my breasts. As he squeezed them in his hands, he continued to pull me rearward, forcing his swollen tip into my tingling g-spot.

Although I had no real way of knowing if all women shared my sexual chemistry, my boobs were connected by a direct sensual string to my pussy, and I enjoyed it immensely. As he squeezed them in his hands firmly and continued to fuck me, my body, mind, and spirit began to reach a heightened state of being.

"My tits," he said as he squeezed them firmly in his hands.

"Yours," I sighed.

"My fucking ass," he said as he released my right boob and slapped his hand against my ass.

"Oh God yes. *Yours*," I said through my teeth.

He slapped his hand against my ass again harshly, and then again. The force of his swats were a huge turn on, but took my breath completely from my lungs. As I attempted to catch my breath and focus on his cock, his hand gripped my neck.

As he squeezed my neck in his hand and turned my head to the side, I peered upward. His mouth opened slightly and he encompassed my lower lip in between his upper and lower lip, biting it slightly.

As he bit down with slightly more force, I groaned in pleasure. Certainly not for everyone, but a far cry from abusive, this was exactly what I desired in a sexual relationship - rough forceful sex at the hand of a bad boy who was, above all things, a good man.

As he released my lip and began biting along my shoulder he continued to squeeze my neck in his hand. With his left hand steadily squeezing my boob and pinching my nipple, he maintained a direct connection to my throbbing g-spot.

I was close. It was almost time. Reaching a point of sensory overload, my eyes began to open and close rapidly. His cock continued to pound against my g-spot with each stroke, bringing me one step closer to climax.

After dragging his teeth along my shoulder and up my neck, he breathed into my ear.

"Ready?"

"Uhhm," I stammered.

He released my neck, pressed his hand against the back of my head, and forced my face deep into the bottom cushion of the lounge. Startled, I naturally tried to resist. As I arched my back against his hand, he pushed harder, pressing my face firmly into the bottom of the chair. Now incapable of speaking and barely able to moan, my muffled groans melted into the fabric before they escaped onto the deck of the pool as nothing more than silence.

My helpless state left me feeling sexually owned. Not abused. Not taken advantage of, and certainly not anything but the sexual property of Dalton Biskette. I had become Dalton's, wholly and completely and he knew it. As he pulled against my hip with his free hand, I groaned into the chair and raised my ass high into the air.

I whimpered into the chair as he pounded himself into me harder and deeper than he ever had. Although I couldn't see him, I suspected he was standing on the balls of his feet, forcing himself into me as deep as his cock, my pussy, and the laws of physics would allow. As his hips pounded against the cheeks of my ass, my swollen muff throbbed like a beating heart.

As I felt myself reaching climax, I screamed into the chair, his hand still pressing against the back of my head. For the sake of reassuring myself I was owned by the right man, I attempted to raise myself from the chair. A growl in return and a firm hand on my head reminded me I'd chosen the only one to properly tame me.

"Hold still, little girl, we're almost done." He growl as he continued to punish me with his throbbing shaft.

I cried out into the chair as I reached climax, sorry the entire neighborhood wasn't able to hear my screams of pleasure.

I wanted the world to know I was satisfied.

For now, I'd settle for Dalton knowing.

As I felt his cock swell inside of me, I knew he was close to climax. As I bellowed my tune of ecstasy into the cushion, I felt his cock slowly pull from my dripping pussy. He moved his hand from the back of my head, causing my shoulders to naturally lift slightly.

"Turn around, I want you to see this," he said under his breath.

With my boobs still resting on the chair and my ass still high in the air, I craned my aching neck to look behind me. As my gaze met his throbbing cock, I watched him stroke it twice before it exploded between my ass cheeks.

He stroked it a few more times, spurting warm cum onto my ass and pussy with each stroke. Some girls may have been repulsed. Some might have felt belittled or less of a woman as a result.

I felt blessed.

Because for that moment - as the cum ran along my ass and dripped onto the lounge - not only was I truly his, but he was mine.

And in *my* mind at least, there was no denying it.

KAT

Perfection. My life had become the definition of perfect. I prayed it would never change, tried to live with nothing more than a little hope - and cast any and all expectations to the wind. I would have never thought Dalton and I would have become so close, but I was sure glad we had.

As we sat across from each other in P.F. Chang's eating, I couldn't help but wish the night would simply last forever.

He spooned more of the chicken and rice mixture into a leaf of lettuce and rolled it tightly. As he lifted it toward his mouth, he gazed past it and fixed his eyes on me.

"You suppose those fuckers in China or whatever actually eat this shit, or is it all a bunch of Americanized stuff?" he asked.

"Americanized. I don't know. Yeah, I'd say Americanized," I shrugged.

He took a bite of the lettuce wrap, swallowed it, and grinned as he pointed the remaining portion of the wrap toward me, "Well, either way, I fuckin' like it."

"I do too," I said as I grabbed a wonton with my chopsticks.

"Ain't figured out how to drive those damned things yet. You're gonna have to teach me," he said as he finished the last bite of his lettuce wrap.

"Okay," it's easy, "Lay one across your finger like this…"

I placed the middle of the stick in my web of my hand and rested the end of it on my middle finger. Carefully, I placed the other stick beside it and pinched it between my thumb and forefinger.

"And the other like that," I said, "Now, you just click the ends together."

"We'll have to get us some of 'em and practice. I ain't lookin' to be somebody's fool up in here," he said as he glanced around the restaurant.

"How are you two doing?" the waitress asked as she approached the table, "Does everything taste good?"

Dalton nodded his head as he wagged his index finger in the air, "Tastes damn good. Can you bring us another plate of the lettuce wraps? While she was eating those little dumplin's I ate all the lettuce wraps. And bring me another glass of water if you don't mind."

"I'll get that right out," she said, "Anything else?"

"Not yet, but keep checkin' back, we'll come up with somethin', I'm sure of it," he responded.

He leaned forward, rested his elbows on the table, and ran his fingers along the edges of his beard, "You know, I ain't even gonna try and bullshit you one bit. Kat, I like you. I like you a lot. I'm thinkin' this deal we got between us is one of them every single fucker on this earth wants, but can't get. Guys will hop from girl to girl lookin' for the one. They never find her, so they keep lookin'. Well, I'm gonna announce it right now. I'm fucking done."

"Done what?" I asked, not sure of what point he had made.

"Lookin'. I'm done lookin'. Found what I was lookin' for. You make me happier'n fuck. Hell, six months ago I'd a never guessed I'd be sittin' in some Chinese joint eatin' shit wrapped up in a piece of lettuce and lovin' it, but I am. You're good for me," he said as he continued to gaze at me admiringly.

"Thank you. You make me happier'n fuck too," I giggled.

He released his beard and leaned away from the table as he nodded his head. After a few seconds he leaned forward and grinned.

"When you get outta college, we should shack up and see how things go," he said.

Tickled pink by the mere mention of it, I nodded my head repeatedly, "We should. I think I'd like it."

"I know *I'd* like it," he said with a nod.

His eyes were hazel, and the specific mix of color I'd always wondered if anyone truly had. After seeing his, I decided everyone else's eyes were just stupid. As I attempted to stare into them and figure out what made them so different, he tilted his head to the side.

"That was quick," he said as the waitress placed the plate on the table.

"And there's a water," she said as she slid a fresh glass of water beside his empty one.

"Anything else?" she asked.

He shook his head.

"Can I say something?" the waitress asked.

"Say whatever you want," Dalton shrugged as he shifted his eyes to meet mine.

I nodded my head in agreement.

"You two are like the cutest couple in the world. I mean, I don't know. It's just that you're like so happy together and it shows. I just wanted to tell you that," she said with a grin.

My mouth shot into a smile so quickly it hurt.

"Oh, thank you," I said as I covered my mouth with my hand.

"She's beautiful, huh?" Dalton asked as he tilted his head toward me.

"She is," the waitress agreed.

"You ought to see inside of her. She's twice that pretty on the inside, and that's a damned fact," he said.

Officially falling in love.

I moved my hand away from my mouth and mouthed the words. "Thank you."

As the waitress walked away Dalton reached into the glass container in the center of the table and removed a pair of chopsticks. After placing them just as I'd shown him into the web of his hand, he reached for the mixture, picked up a piece of chicken, and poked it into his mouth.

"Impressed," I said as I clapped my hands together lightly.

"Good teacher," he responded.

After a few more bites with his chopsticks, he rolled another wrap and held it in his hand.

"We get done here, you think you can just stay at my place tonight?" he asked.

"I nodded my head, "Sure. No school tomorrow, so I don't see why not, why?"

"Well," he said as he took a bite of the wrap, "After all the fuckin' and swimmin' we did earlier, I'm wore out. Thought maybe we could eat, ride to my place, and just lay around in bed naked, you know with our bare skin just touchin' each other. Maybe fall asleep like that. It'd be nice."

And, no differently than Dalton had said earlier, I was done.

The search was over.

I had fallen face first and landed in a puddle of love.

BISCUIT

There wasn't too much I enjoyed other than riding, fucking, and fighting. Well, until now. As I attempted to lay still and breathe easily, Kat's leg was draped over my thigh and her bare chest was pressed against mine. After fifteen minutes or so of me being as motionless as I had ever been, she began to stir.

As she began to moan, she rolled to the side. Lying flat on her back with her head pointed up at the ceiling, she opened her eyes. Upon realizing where she was, she immediately rolled right back on top of me.

"Mornin'," I breathed.

"Morning," she said.

After a quick kiss, she ran to the bathroom. A few minutes later she walked into the room, still naked and as beautiful as ever.

"What day is it?" she asked.

I gazed at her for a long minute before responding. Her body, hair, skin...everything - was perfect. She was truly a god send. After I cleared my mind of what a fortunate man I was to have her in my life, I responded.

"Monday," I responded.

"And the time?" she asked.

I glanced at my watch.

"Almost six," I responded.

"Shit. I've got to go. I need to get home, take a shower, and go to damned school," she said as she started picking up her things.

"I feel like crap," she said as she pulled on her shorts.

"Probably wore smooth out," I said as I rolled off the bed.

"No, I feel sick," she responded.

I shrugged my shoulders, "Probably the Mexican food from last night, or hell maybe the Chinese from Saturday?"

She pulled on her top and grabbed her purse.

"Maybe. I'm sorry, but I've got to get," she sighed, "Time?"

I glanced at my watch, "Six straight up."

"Shit. Okay," she said as she leaned toward me.

After she kissed me on the lips she stood back, stared for a minute, and kissed me again.

"Miss you already," she said as she turned toward the door.

If you had any idea.

"Miss you," I sighed.

As I watched her Jeep back out of the drive, I realized lying in bed naked with her was my new favorite thing in the world. I had no intention of telling the fellas, or Kat for that matter, but I damned sure couldn't wait until she came back and we could do it again.

She was a true one and only.

And she was mine.

KAT

Standing in my bathroom shaking, I stared down at the test I had taken an hour prior, still in absolute shock. The last thing a twenty-two year old girl who has an extremely independent bad boy biker for an *almost* boyfriend wants to see is a positive pregnancy test – especially nine months prior to her completion of college. I sighed and set the test on the side of the vanity and opened the second test, one capable of telling me the amount of weeks I was pregnant.

I squatted, peed on the indicator, and waited.

After a long stressful period of hoping the first test was inaccurate, I opened my eyes and looked down.

Please…

The indicator said "3+". From my interpretation of the instructions, it meant just what I was afraid of – the baby was older than 5 weeks old.

Fuck.

My body's reaction to the birth control I used wasn't typical nor were my periods. Some months I had one, some months I didn't, and yet other month's I had a miniscule period which included light spotting. My most recent period was eight weeks back, and I had dismissed my missed period as nothing more than another month of my not-so-typical periods.

I had only known Dalton for approximately four weeks, and if the test was accurate, it could only mean one thing.

The baby would be Kyle's.

And it was conceived almost immediately before he went to jail, and after he beat the woman half to death.

He had come to my home in a drunken stupor, and demanded sex. After refusing him, he slapped me, choked, me, and held me down until I was exhausted. As I cried and whimpered, hoping for him to stop, he had sex with me and promptly left.

It was the last time we had sex, and I was afraid it was the day the child I carried inside of me was conceived.

I felt sick.

I stood, leaned over the vanity, and vomited.

After a long period of crying, and a longer period of denial, I walked to the living room and called my doctor.

And afternoon cancellation allowed me to make an appointment forty-five minutes from now, almost the exact amount of time it would take me to drive there.

I grabbed my purse, tossed my phone inside, and wiped the tears from my cheeks as I stepped out onto the landing.

There's no sense in torturing yourself over this until you're certain, Kat.

I walked to my Jeep in a daze, trying to figure out what my life was going to become if the child was truly Kyle's. In my opinion, raising a fatherless child wasn't an option, nor was abortion. Spending my life with Kyle, however, wasn't something I could even begin to imagine.

But if the child was truly his, I felt it was my only option.

I leaned against the Jeep, pressing my hand against the hot metal as I attempted to prevent myself from collapsing onto the asphalt parking lot. As I stood and waited for my head to clear, my stomach convulsed once again.

And I vomited between my feet.

The thought of Kyle made me ill.

I wanted a life with Dalton, but I seriously doubted the child was his. A life with him which included raising a child wasn't something I could see happening in the near future.

As I reached for the door handle, I began to cry again. I closed my eyes, tilted my head toward the sky, and prayed.

I don't know what's best, and you do. All I ask of you is this:

Do whatever you can to make sure I raise this child safely and to the best of my ability.

That's all I ask of you.

You take care of me, and I'll take care of the baby.

I opened my eyes and opened the door, knowing I had done all that I was able. The rest was up to God.

And the father.

BISCUIT

I had wondered for a large portion of my adult life if anything would ever happen to improve my way of living, thinking, or being. I eventually dismissed the thoughts, convinced the manner I lived my life was as good as I was personally able, therefore life was as good as it would ever become.

I stood in the living room gazing blankly into the bedroom. My choice of colors for the room never seemed to last more than six weeks at best, but something about the beige appealed to me. It looked calm, peaceful, and bright – without being over the top.

I nodded my head, grinned, and turned toward the kitchen. Satisfied my room was just as I wanted it, and my life wasn't far behind, I walked to the fridge and opened it. An entire shelf of Red Bull's looked back at me. I reached in, grabbed a yogurt and a Red Bull, and closed the door.

As I scooped the yogurt from the container and sipped the Red Bull, I closed my eyes and said a quick prayer to the man in charge.

You and I know I paint that room because it's the only thing in my life I feel I have control over. If I can look at it and be satisfied, it must mean I'm satisfied with my life. I just want to let you know I appreciate you having Kat and I run into each other.

I ain't always been...

Damn it, I mean 'I've not'. That's what I meant to say. 'I've not' always been the best man I could be, but I'm gonna give it an honest shake this time. I like this girl, and while I'm eatin' my yogurt here, I just need one thing, Boss.

Help me keep from doin' dumb shit.

That's all I need.

Amen.

I finished the yogurt, drank the remaining red Bull, and grabbed one for the road. I stumbled out to the garage, hopped on my bike, and opened the can. As I sat silently on the bike, I slowly sipped the beverage, thinking of how Kat allowed me to feel like it was okay to just be me. Grateful for her being in my life, I began to wish she wasn't in college, but with me, able to enjoy my life with me on a daily basis. Eight more months and I wouldn't have to worry about her being in college.

Anxious to see what the future for us held, I finished the drink, tossed the can in the trash, and started the bike. As the engine warmed up, the exhaust echoed throughout the neighborhood. After a few moments of chuckling to myself about what my neighbors must think of me, I pulled in the clutch and shifted the bike into gear.

I inched forward, pressed the remote clipped to my fairing, and watched in the rearview mirror as the door slowly closed. After turning up the music to a dull roar, I slowly rolled into the street and stopped.

Hell, I ain't done a burn out in longer than I can remember.

I pulled in the clutch, revved the engine until the rev limiter stopped me, and released the clutch. As the bike's rear tire began to smoke, the bike inched forward slowly. As the rear tire continued to screech and spin wildly, I realized as soon as it got a little traction I would lurch forward like I'd been shot out of a rocket.

Within a few seconds, the neighbor across the street stepped onto the porch, pressed his hands to his hips, and shook his head.

I released the controls with my left hand, waved, and continued to twist the throttle back.

Smoke bellowed from the rear fender.

I twisted the throttle a little further.

And, as the neighbor watched in disgust, I grinned. Working the throttle back and forth, I screeched the tire in a smoky burnout, bellowing smoke from the fender, and leaving a black mark stretching along the street the width of my neighbor's yard.

As I continued to grin and twist the throttle, my rear tire exploded into a thousand pieces. Rubber flew from the rear of the bike down the block behind me about a hundred feet. Almost instantly the bike fell six inches to the street and the wheel began to screech on the asphalt.

I released the throttle and shook my head, knowing not only that I'd ruined the tire, but that I'd possibly damaged my wheel beyond repair.

I glanced at the neighbor as I shut off the bike. His hands were now on his knees, and he was laughing uncontrollably.

I might have known what I wanted out of life, but for me to think for one minute that I was anything more than a great big kid would have been an absolute lie. As the neighbor finally caught his breath and stood up straight, I stepped off the bike and attempted to push it back into the garage.

Pushing the nine hundred pound bike alone on the steel wheel without a tire was almost impossible.

Within a few seconds of my huffing, puffing, and shoving, the bike began to float easily along the pavement. I glanced over my shoulder. The neighbor was bent over, his hands against my saddlebags, pushing for all he was worth. Within a few minutes, the bike was parked safely in my garage.

"Appreciate it. I'm Dalton Biskette," I said as I extended my right hand.

He chuckled as he reached for my hand, "Quite a show. I'm Randy Devlon. Hell, you've lived here for ten years and we've never met."

He had an average build, roughly six feet tall, with salt and pepper hair that seemed to be out of place for what I would guess to be a man in his latter thirties. Dressed in designer jeans and an untucked dress shirt with loafers, he looked like a desk jockey. .

"Ain't never been much on mingling with people I don't know. Appreciate your help, though, I really do," I said as I released his hand and gazed down at my bike.

"I understand. You know, you'll never know anyone if you don't mingle. I guess that's another way to look at it," he shrugged.

"Well, stop by sometime, we can have a beer," I said as I glanced in his direction.

"I'll do that," he nodded, "Nice meeting you."

"Likewise," I grinned.

As he turned and walked away, I realized I had lived across the street from him for the ten year period he'd indicated without meeting him. Feeling almost guilty, I turned toward the house and walked into the kitchen. I grabbed a Red Bull from the fridge, opened it, and stared down at the can.

I was in a half-assed relationship with a woman, for once in my life had no desire to be with another, and had actually met one of my neighbors.

What the fuck was my life becoming?

I turned toward the door leading into the garage and opened it. My bike sat on the rear wheel, which was clearly ruined. I tipped the can up and drank half of it. I gazed at the bike. I drank the remainder.

I tilted my head back and stared up at the ceiling of the garage.

You've got a sense of humor, don't you?

I tossed the can in the trash can beside the door, stepped into the garage and gazed out toward the street. Pieces of tire littered the block for a hundred feet in front of my house.

If anyone was going to keep me from doing dumb shit, it wasn't going to be God, it was going to be me.

Well, this new way of living is going to take some getting used, to, that's for sure.

KAT

Having a friend you truly trust and can count on regardless of what type of situation your life presents is invaluable. Jennifer was that type of friend for me. We didn't always agree with each other, but I always knew she would be truthful with me about her opinions when so many others might not. As we sat at the coffee shop on College Road and waited for our drinks, she began to look nervous.

"So what's the deal, Kat? Why are we meeting *here*?" she said as she looked around at the various hipsters drinking their mocha-choka-lattes.

"I don't know," I shrugged.

"Kat!" the barista hollered.

"I'll be right back," I said as I stood from my overstuffed chair.

I walked to the bar, picked up our two smoothies, and walked back to where we were seated. After handing Jennifer her drink, I sat down and stared at my cup. It resembled a milkshake. I sucked on the straw until some of the frozen beverage escaped into my mouth.

Holy shit, this is good.

I nodded my head and raised my cup, "Holy shit, this is good."

"So…" she said as she studied her cup of frozen beverage.

Talking to Jennifer about it would be easier than talking to Biscuit or my parents. I figured if nothing else, discussing it with her would provide me with a little experience. Beginning the conversation, however, is always the hardest part.

"I'm pregnant," I sighed.

"Excuse me? I thought you said you were pregnant," she responded.

I nodded my head, "I am."

She leaned forward in her seat - almost off the front edge. She lowered her hands between her knees as her eyes widened drastically.

"Holy shit, what are you going to do?" she asked, "What's Biscuit or whatever his name is going to say?"

"Well, that's what I wanted to talk to you about. And before you go ballistic, let me finish," I said.

"Okay," she sighed.

"It's Kyle's. From when he came over and all but raped me that night after he got arrested. Remember me telling you about that?" I asked.

"Oh my God," she gasped as she covered her mouth.

"What are you going to do?" she whispered.

I gazed down at the floor and began to explain my intentions. "I've already told Kyle. I'm going to do the only thing I can do. We're getting back together. I'm not going to raise this baby in a fatherless home. I can't do that to him or her. We'll just have to work out our differences."

"It'll never work Kat. I hate to say it, but you and I both know it won't work. He's mean, abusive, and violent. He's a douchebag, I'm sorry. He needs help, and it's not help you can provide," she paused and sat up in her chair.

I raised my hand and held it between us, "Please. Don't say that. I've decided it's what's right. And, no matter how difficult it is, I'm going to do it. For the baby. Maybe he'll change once the baby is born."

"Maybe," she shrugged, "But I doubt it. I'm sorry, but I hate him. You're better than that. And what about your parents? Told them yet?"

I shifted my gaze from her toward the floor. As my eyes went unfocused, I began to speak, "Well, that's an entirely different issue. My father will be pissed. Truthfully, he'll probably be glad it's Kyle's and not Biscuit's. He doesn't know how violent Kyle was, by the way."

"And Biscuit?" she asked.

"Dalton. His name is Dalton," I said as I shifted my eyes to meet hers, "Here's what sucks. I love him, Jen. I really do. I know it's going to seem weird to you, but I love Dalton, and I'm going to be with Kyle, and I can't...I can't..."

And that was it. The pain in my heart was unbelievable.

I began to blubber, crying uncontrollably. The thought of Dalton not being in my life was one I didn't want to think of, but it was all I could think about. Being with Kyle was going to be torturous at best, but it was what had to happen, like it or not, for the baby.

"Kat, it'll all be fine. It will," Jen said as she placed her hand on my knee.

I continued to cry, alternating my eyes from the floor to Jen, "I'll never...I'll never be able..."

"I won't be able to...see him...and it's going...it's going to hurt," I blubbered.

I was a lot of things, but one thing I wasn't was a cheater. If I was going to be with Kyle, there was no way I could ever see Dalton again – or talk to him. It wouldn't be fair to Kyle, me, the relationship, or the baby. I was going to have to cut ties to him in any and all respects. Realizing it caused me pain that was over and above any pain Kyle ever caused me.

Because my heart belonged to Dalton.

BISCUIT

It's never too late to change. I'd heard people say that phrase, from time to time, for my entire life. I'd heard it so many times I had actually begun to believe it. Like almost everything clsc do-gooders say, it was false. Luxuries most men and women of this earth are afforded don't apply to me. The rules don't apply to me.

Because I am a Sinner.

Sinner Forever, Forever a Sinner.

She glanced down at her feet, crying. I didn't know whether to hug her, tell her to kick rocks, or stare up at the sky and scream. I felt like life was a great big lie. For the first time in my life I cared for a woman - actually liked her - yet keeping her was out of my control.

What upset me more than anything was my knowing the child was going to be brought up in an environment no different than the one I grew up in. A life exposed to violence between his or her parent's would do to the child what was done to me. Nothing good would come of an upbringing in such an environment. In fact, it would cause permanent damage to the child, and its ability to discern right from wrong – regarding violence – when it was an adult.

"So that's it? The decision's made?" I asked as I kicked my boot against the grass, digging a small hole with my foot as I did so.

She nodded her head and wiped the tears from her eyes, "I'm sorry.

I can't…"

She turned away.

"And we're not going to talk to each other?" I shrugged as I shifted my eyes upward.

She turned to face me and wiped the tears from her face, "I'm sorry…"

I'd never been in love, and I knew nothing about it. I couldn't say whether what I felt for Kat was love or something else, but I knew the pain I felt from thinking about never seeing her or talking to her again was greater than any pain I had ever felt in my life – and I had my fair share of pain in my days.

"Alright. I'll respect that. Kat," I paused not quite knowing what to say, especially if it was going to be my last words with her.

"Yeah," she said.

Her voice was dry and full of emotion.

I raised my hand to my beard and caressed it in my hand, "What we had was real. I want you to know that."

"I love you, Dalton," she said.

And she turned and walked away.

BISCUIT

In the week following Kat's departure, my life had gone into a whirlwind of activities, none of which were good. I'd spent all seven days drunk, depressed, and in pain. The club found out a fully patched member was an undercover ATF agent, and it was all I could do not to kill him. In the end, we decided to make a deal with him, giving him a chance to live – as long as he didn't testify against us.

My knee jerk reaction upon learning we had been infiltrated by the ATF was to kill the agent. After learning he had a wife, kids, and a desire to right what we believed was wrong, I didn't go soft, but I considered things I never would have thought I'd consider in the past. Still uncertain if our decision was in the club's best interest, I spent my days wallowing in the pain of living life without the woman I desperately wanted to share my days with.

"You need to sober the fuck up, Brother," Axton said.

"Ain't drunk now," I shrugged.

"It's eight o'clock in the morning, I'd sure as fuck hope not," he responded.

"I can't convince myself that killin' Gunner wasn't the right choice. Lettin' that fucker walk was wrong. He was gonna have us all doin' time in club fed if he had any say," I said as I stood.

Axton crossed his arms and flexed his biceps as he narrowed his eyes slightly.

"We've been over this every day for a god damned week," he growled, "I don't like it, but it was our *only* choice. Killing him would have had the ATF in here in a matter of fucking minutes. As soon as he didn't report in, they'd have come looking for him. Talking about it makes me think of it, and I'm done with both. How about *don't fucking bring it up again?*"

I cleared my throat and shook my head as I shifted my eyes to the door, "It's eatin' on me, Boss."

"I've got some news for you. What's eating on you is the girl, not Gunner," Axton sighed.

I glanced toward Axton, somewhat surprised with his statement. Slightly embarrassed, but fully understanding Axton wouldn't embarrass me further or poke fun at me like the other fellas might, I responded honestly.

"Bein' honest, it's a little of both," I shrugged.

"Well, from what you told me, there's no changing it. She's going to try and make things work with that kid. You need to respect that," he said as he uncrossed his arms and turned his palms upward.

I fixed my eyes on his for a long minute and eventually shifted them toward the tips of my boots. As I studied my scuffed up boots, I responded the best I felt I was able.

"You know, when my iPod fucks up, or when my air ride fucks up, most times I can smack the fuck out of it and fix it. Just hit it real hard one time, and whatever's fucked up fixes itself. I wish I could smack this deal and fix it, Boss," I said under my breath.

"Everything happens for a reason, Brother. Can't say I know what the reason is behind this one, but there is one. It'll make you stronger or it'll kill you," he said as he approached me.

He wrapped his right arm around my back and pulled me in for a bro hug. As he slapped his hand against my back, he continued.

"It just depends on whether you choose to accept it, or let it eat you up. Let's lock this fucker up and go for a ride. We can go see if Jack and Toad are done cutting the grass. If they're done, maybe we'll all go for a ride out to Benton and have a little late breakfast, how's that?" he asked.

"Sounds good," I responded.

"Hell, maybe you'll meet someone out there," he said over his shoulder as he walked toward the door.

The thought of any woman in my life other than Kat was unthinkable. Not only was I in pain from not having her in my life, I felt terrible for all of the women I had wasted my time with, wondering if I wasn't busy with them if it would have been possible to meet Kat sooner, before she got pregnant, changing the outcome of my life, her life, and the life of the child.

"Don't wanna meet someone. Don't care to ever meet another woman as long as I live, Boss," I seethed.

"We'll see how long that feeling lasts," he chuckled.

I followed him through the door and into the shop without speaking. There was no need for me to respond. Hell, if I did, he wouldn't believe me.

I was done.

I needed to change the plate on the back of my bike to ROF.

Ride or Fight.

Those were the only two options left.

And I was ready to do both.

KAT

Trying to accept Kyle as my partner in life wasn't something that was easy to do. To agree to have him as my husband or even significant other was almost impossible for me. Although in the last week we had taken the time to discuss marriage, the thought of it was repulsive to me and it would be nothing more than a shotgun marriage and I knew it.

On a nightly basis I prayed for the ability to forgive him for his past actions, and accept him as not only the father of our child, but my lover. As much as I wanted everything to work between us, I had accepted that I would be living my life feeling alone and in love with someone I would more than likely never see again. So far, I had not made love to him, and spent my time thinking of Dalton, and making excuses for not being able to make love to Kyle. My heart belonged to Dalton.

And it hurt.

Realizing I was doing this not for myself, but for my child, allowed me to understand the bond a mother has with her child, even if unborn. Some of the decisions I'd seen young mother's make in the past - wondering all the while why they made them - began to make perfect sense.

We sacrifice ourselves for the sake of our children.

And my sacrifice was huge.

Gazing out into the living room as Kyle drank a beer I proceeded with cooking our dinner. Staying at Kyle's house made me feel uneasy and exposed. I had always felt more comfortable in my home when we were together - primarily because I always believed I could kick him out if need be. Living in his place left me feeling vulnerable and full of fear.

As I poured the noodles into the colander I wondered just how long the uncomfortable feelings would last. As with anything, I decided, in enough time I would probably forget his past behavior as long as what he expressed in the future exhibited growth and change.

After draining the noodles, I placed them in the pot on the stove, turned down the heat, and added the vegetable and meat mixture I had sautéed. Almost more than I feared Kyle and his potential for violent behavior, I feared getting fat throughout my pregnancy. Unlike some women who were able to eat as they pleased and remain thin, I was different. I had to constantly exercise, eat healthy foods, and count my daily caloric intake to remain in the physical condition I was in.

The whole wheat pasta, chicken, and fresh vegetables sautéed in olive oil would be a healthy dinner for us both, but satisfying nonetheless. After stirring the pasta, I opened the oven and removed the bread I had prepared.

A whole wheat loaf drizzled with olive oil, basil, and garlic.

As I placed the bread on the counter, I turned toward the living room and sighed.

"Dinner's ready," I shouted.

"Be there in a minute," he responded, "We're about to make a touchdown."

There was no doubt Monday nights were going to be one of my least favorite nights of the week. Kyle spent the majority of the time glued to the television watching football and shouting if the game didn't go the way he wanted it to. As his choices for football teams could easily be compared to his choices in life, rarely did his team of choice win.

Some women may simply accept the life of having a man in front of the television, and take him his food on a platter. I'm not that woman, nor would I ever become her. Kyle and I would learn to eat dinner as a couple; regardless of what was going on in our home, a thirty minute break from it to come together as a family wasn't too much to ask of anyone. As I carefully placed the pasta on the plates, he began to scream and cuss at the television.

"Call it both ways, ref. Motherfucking offsides!" he bellowed.

"God fucking damn. Cocksuckers went offsides and sacked the fucking quarterback," he screamed.

"Son-of-a-bitch ref doesn't call it both ways," he grunted as he kicked the end table, knocking his can of beer onto the floor.

"Fuckers," he sighed as he walked toward the kitchen.

I did my best to act interested by shaking my head.

"We're getting our asses kicked, I'm just going to take mine in there and watch this," he said as he reached for his plate.

"Let's sit down and eat. It's not even half time, it'll just take a few minutes," I responded as I sat down on the stool.

"I'm eating mine in there," he said as he gazed down and studied the plate.

I glanced upward and fixed my eyes on the top of his head.

"Sit down," I said through my teeth.

He tilted his head back, met my gaze, and wrinkled his nose, "What the fuck is this shit?"

"Dinner," I responded as I dropped my fork onto my plate, "It's what I fixed for dinner. It's pasta."

213

"Where's the fucking meat?" he asked as he stirred his finger through the pasta.

"There's chicken in it, sit down please," I sighed as I reached for my fork.

"Ain't eating it. Looks like shit," he said as he turned toward the refrigerator.

Seriously? You insensitive prick.

I glanced over my shoulder as he pulled another can of beer from the refrigerator. After opening it and taking a drink, he began to walk the length of the kitchen and toward the living room.

"Sit down," I demanded as I turned in his direction.

He reached up with his free hand as he passed me, and slapped me on the top of the head, "You eat it. I'm watching the game."

Don't you dare touch me.

As I ran my hand over my head to smooth my hair, he walked to the couch and sat down.

I took a bite of my pasta, chewed it, and dropped my fork onto the plate. Only a week into our new relationship and he was already being a dick. I really had no idea why I'd expect him to be otherwise, but accepting it wasn't something I was willing to do. I was going to make this work regardless of his willingness to participate. I stood from my stool, walked to the couch, and crossed my arms in front of my chest.

I sighed heavily. He turned to face me. I lifted my elbows and allowed them to drop onto my stomach heavily, sighing again as they did so. As he glanced in my direction, I opened my mouth and spoke my mind.

"Get in there, sit down, and eat. It's time for dinner," I said flatly.

He gazed my direction, shook his head, and laughed. As he turned toward the television, I continued.

"I'm serious," I huffed.

"Fuck off. I'm watching this," he said as he waved his hand my direction.

"Is this how it's going to be?" I asked, "After our baby is born? Are you just going to tell me to fuck off when I want something?"

"Depends on what you want," he shrugged.

"You're a selfish prick," I said as I turned away.

"What did you say?" he growled.

"You heard me, you selfish prick," I responded over my shoulder.

I heard him get off the couch and begin following me into the kitchen. To think I would have to beg him to take time out for dinner was unnerving. As I sat down on the stool, I noticed he wasn't walking toward his stool, he was walking toward me.

And he was beet red.

"Don't ever talk me like that again, you mouthy bitch," he bellowed.

The blur of his hand caused me to lean back in the stool, but I didn't lean far enough. As his hand impacted my jaw, everything went black. I realized as I tried to stand that he hit me so hard he had knocked me off the stool. Before I had a chance to shed a tear, and long before I was able to stand, he leaned over me.

For an instant, I thought he was going to help me up.

I was sadly mistaken.

The sound of his fists hitting my face was sickening. I raised my arms to try and block his hands from hitting me, but it did little good. Within a few seconds my arms were at my sides and his hands were pounding against my head.

I attempted to stand and the force of his fist against my shoulder knocked me flat onto the floor. My eyes already swollen so severely that I was almost blind, I attempted to gaze around the room and find a way to get away from him. I hoped the few second lull in the beating meant that he was done.

As I pressed my hands into the floor and tried to stand, something hit my head.

And everything went dark.

BISCUIT

Looking back on my life, I couldn't say I had ever lived a day that I was depressed. Somehow or another, whatever life tossed my way seemed to roll off of me like water from a duck's back. Never one to dwell on the bad, I always considered myself fortunate in that I was able to accept life as being nothing more than the system which haphazardly supported my existence.

Living in a carefree manner allowed me to accept *life* as being no more than my continued existence on this earth. The clock proceeded to tick regardless of the state of mind I was in, so why not live every day wearing a smile? Incapable of changing my surroundings, and only able to slightly modify what was at my fingertips, I realized early in life I was in charge of my own fate.

If I exposed myself to very few outsiders, and lived a life of solitude, life was as easy as breathing.

My exposure to Kat, as much as I regretted nothing I had done, caused me to realize letting people into my life was a risk. With each and every one, I exposed myself to potential harm, pain, and feelings I wasn't necessarily eager to accept as necessary.

Surrounded by my brothers, I had always felt safe from harm. We supported each other wholeheartedly, and offered a hand of assistance and a shoulder to lean on whenever it was necessary. If the world were filled only with my brothers and people like them, it would truly be a better place to live.

"Not a one? You telling me you don't have a single solitary story to tell?" Toad asked as he leaned back in his chair.

I glanced at Jack, shifted my eyes toward Axton, and shrugged, "Nope."

"You need to see a doctor. Something's wrong, Brother," he sighed as he leaned forward.

I glanced at my untouched bottle of beer, "ATF deal has me all shook up."

"I'm telling you, that guy isn't going to say shit. We've got devices in his kid's backpacks, in their laptops, on his cars, shit…" he paused and took a drink from his bottle of beer.

"He isn't going to go anywhere or do anything to risk harming his wife and kids. I'm thinking he regrets ever taking that fucking job. What are your thoughts, Slice," Toad asked as he tilted his bottle toward Axton.

"Agreed," Axton nodded.

Toad tilted his head toward Jack. Jack nodded his head.

"I'll agree," Jack said.

"See?" Toad sighed, "Nothing to worry about."

"Don't mean I got a story to tell. I'll be fine in a couple days," I said as I reached for my beer.

The bottle felt warm in my hand. I glanced around the table, realized everyone was almost done with their beers, and that I hadn't so much as took a sip.

"You want this?" I asked as I slid my bottle toward Toad.

"Fuck I'll drink it," Jack said.

"Drink it," Toad said as he slid the beer toward Jack.

"My gut hurts," I said as I pushed myself away from the table.

We had ridden to Stearman Airfield in Benton, Kansas. An old airfield originally designed to support the few Stearman bi-wing airplanes that collectors in the immediate area had, it increased in size over the years, and added a very nice bar alongside the runway. With large glass garage doors lining the entire wall, patrons could sit and watch the airfield regardless of the weather. Today was warm, sunny, and had very little wind, so the doors were open, and the planes were flying touch-and-go's roughly every five minutes. The bar was also one of what had become fewer and fewer places that were biker friendly, always welcoming bikers in the establishment.

As I sat and stared out onto the runway, a bi-wing plane came rolled toward the fueling station. With my mind fading off into somewhere else, a buzzing in my pocket reminded me I was losing grip with reality.

I leaned rearward in the chair, knowing the only person not in the group was Otis.

"Any of you fellas heard from the big O?" I asked as I reached into my pocket.

"Out fucking Sam is all I know. It's all he does anymore," Toad shrugged.

"Ain't that the truth?" I blurted as I pulled the phone from my pocket.

I found the similarities between us almost laughable.

As I stared down at my phone, I realized it wasn't ringing, but that I'd received a text message. After unlocking my phone and opening the text screen, a message from Kat was highlighted. Nervous, excited, and full of wonder, I pressed the message with my thumb.

Can I call? I need to talk.

Without thinking, I pressed my thumb onto the keypad and typed my response.

Yes.

I pressed send.

"Otis?" Toad asked.

I glanced at him and shook my head, "Nope. Someone wanting to know if they can call."

Almost immediately, the phone rang. I stood from my seat and began pacing along the length of the garage door as she spoke, anxious to see what she needed to talk about. Her request when we last spoke was clear.

No contact whatsoever.

"Can you talk?" she asked.

"Sure, what's going on?" I asked.

She started crying uncontrollably. After roughly fifteen seconds of worry, she regained her composure and cleared her throat.

"I'm sorry. Uhhm. Can you come get me? Maybe let me stay with you for a few days or something? I don't know what else to do," she stammered.

Not necessarily wanting to open myself up to even more pain, but feeling I needed to do what I could to provide her whatever it was she needed, I pressed her for a little more information.

"I thought we weren't going to have any contact, out of respect to you and your relationship?" I asked.

After I spoke, I felt like maybe I should have just kept my big mouth shut and said yes. The phone went silent for several seconds, but it seemed like an eternity.

"He beat me. Bad," she said.

My eyes widened and I held the phone at arm's length and gazed at it for a long minute.

"Excuse me?" I said as I raised the phone to my ear.

"He beat me, Dalton. He beat me bad, I'm in pretty bad shape," she cried.

"Where are you? I'm on the bike, can you ride?" I asked, trying to remain calm.

I felt my body temperature increase twenty degrees. As the warmth of my anger washed over my face, I regretted not killing that prick when I had a chance.

"I'm home. He's at his place. I'm done Dalton. I promise, I'm done with him. Yeah, I can ride. I look like hell, but I can ride," she responded.

I bit my bottom lip so hard as she spoke it should have burst.

"Be there in twenty," I said as I released my lip.

"Kat?" I asked.

"Yeah?" she responded.

"You have a gun?" I asked.

"No. Just a knife," she said through the obvious tears.

"I might bring one of the fellas, just in case. Kat, everything'll be fine, I'll be there in twenty."

"Okay, Dalton. I'll be here. I love you."

"See ya in a few."

I pressed the *end* button and stared at the phone for a few seconds. After inhaling a deep breath and attempting to clear my mind, I turned to face the fellas.

"Fellas," I sighed.

"We got a situation," I said as I reached for my wallet.

I tossed a fifty dollar bill on the table and pushed my wallet into my rear pocket.

"That kid beat Kat. The Marine I beat the shit out of a few weeks back. Sounds like she's busted up pretty good. I need to go get her, and I don't know when he's gonna be back. Who's rollin' with me?" I asked.

"Where's he stay," Big Jack asked, "I'll take care of him, you go get the girl."

I shook my head.

"Just want some back up, who's in?" I asked.

"Following you," Toad said as he stepped over the short fence that separated the restaurant from the runway.

"Lead the way," Big Jack said as he hurdled the fence.

Axton simply gazed my direction and winked, "Everything happens for a reason, Brother. Lead the way."

And lead the way I did.

KAT

Kyle had beaten me the night before. Whether I had a concussion, was knocked unconscious, or he had merely beaten me into a state of mental incompetence, I didn't wake up until the next morning.

When I woke up he was asleep. While I gathered my things and attempted to get cleaned up, he got up and apologized - blaming his drunkenness for the beating. When I explained I was leaving, he laughed - saying I was sure to return. The look on his face as I walked out the door was one of worry and possibly shame. As I drove from his house in the country to my apartment in Winfield, I decided I never wanted to see him again no matter what the circumstances.

Having lived in Winfield for just shy of four years, I had seen the Sinners on many occasions. More frequently, I had *heard* them. Living almost a mile from their clubhouse, I could still hear them when large groups rode in and out of their parking lot. Several times over the years, when I was eating pizza or having a beer at the little bar by the college, the hair on the back of my neck would raise as the sound of them riding by would fill the air. Hearing them several seconds before they appeared did very little to prepare me for the sound of their passing by, nothing on this earth sounds like a dozen Harley-Davidson's with loud pipes.

Nothing short of a tornado.

Or maybe the rapture.

As the windows of my house began to shake, the sound of the motorcycles in the parking lot became more and more prominent. The unmistakable rumble of them circling the lot and coming to my building provided me with a feeling of relief I had waited almost twelve hours to feel.

The pounding on the door startled me.

I peeked through the peephole. Daltons beard filled the viewport.

I dropped the knife on the floor and opened the door.

As the door opened, he gasped. He tried to mask it, hide it, and act like he wasn't startled by my looks, but I noticed. The look on his face did little to disguise how he truly felt. His eyes conveyed love while his face was unmistakably washed with anger.

"Bad huh?" I asked.

"Not bad at all," he lied.

"You look great, Kat. He ain't here is he?" he asked as he peered over my shoulder and inhaled a deep breath.

I shook my head.

"You're a shitty liar, I look like ass. And the asshole is probably at home. He took the day off work. I think he's afraid you're coming," I said.

"Where's he stay?" he asked through his teeth as he studied my face.

"Halfway between here and Wichita. Maybe ten minutes away, I don't know. Up by Udall," I shrugged.

He held my chin in his hand. As he lifted his hand slightly and tilted my head back, he fixed his eyes on mine, "Where *specifically* does he stay, Kat? I need to know."

"First house south of Udall on the east side of the street. It's back away from the road by the river. His name's on the box, Kyle Coffman,"

I responded.

After a moment, he inhaled a deep breath and glanced upward. As he shifted his eyes downward, he reached out, exhaled, and wrapped his arms around me. While he held me in his arms I felt his body shaking.

"This'll never happen again," he sighed into my ear.

"Grab anything you think you'll need," he said as he released me.

I lifted my shoulder and patted my purse with my hand, "This is it."

"Need me to carry you?" he asked as he looked down the length of the landing nervously.

"I'm a big girl, I'll be fine. Hell, he didn't break my legs - or my pride for that matter," I said as I stepped in front of him and locked the door.

We walked down the stairs side by side, with his arm over my shoulder. Even so, I felt slightly nervous and slightly apprehensive.

As I stepped off the bottom landing and into the parking lot, I gasped at what I saw. Three men, all tattooed, massive, wearing cuts and covered with muscles, stood beside their motorcycles with their arms crossed in front of their chests.

My protectors.

Seeing them caused my heart to begin to pound in my chest so hard I felt it in my throat.

"Don't wanna take her to my house just yet, Boss. I'm gonna need to see if she can stay in the shop for a bit. I gotta go take care of this," Dalton said as we stepped past the men and toward his bike.

Although I attempted not to face the men for no other reason than embarrassment, the one with a few days growth of beard and one hell of an expressed attitude reached out and held my shoulder. He was a massive man with huge arms, a wide chest, and shorter brown hair that was slightly curly.

"Turn around for me, Kat," he said.

His voice sounded like what I would expect a bear to sound like - if a bear could speak. I stopped and reluctantly turned to face him.

His cut had a patch on it that said *President*. Knowing what I knew about Avery, I realized this was her boyfriend, Axton – who went by the club name *Slice*. From what she had shared with me, he was not a man anyone should ever fuck with. As I stood staring down at the parking lot, embarrassed to look up, he lowered his head and gazed up at my face. After a very audible sigh he released my shoulder.

"Bylaws say she can stay there *without* your approval if you've got your name marked on the board with an "X", and you don't. Other than that, she can only stay *with* your approval if she's your Ol' Lady. Didn't write them, brother, but I've got to enforce them," Axton responded.

"She's my Ol' Lady, mark it on the board if you got to, I don't give a fuck," Dalton growled.

My heart immediately swelled to ten times its size. I swallowed heavily and turned toward Axton. He uncrossed his arms and turned toward the remaining two men. As he exchanged glances with them it was almost as if they were speaking without speaking. The message was clear. Axton had business to take care of and the other two men were agreeing.

"Fellas," Axton sighed.

"You heard the man," The dark skinned one with jet black hair and a buzz-cut said as he turned toward his bike and nodded his head.

"Biscuit, you trust me?" the muscular tattooed man asked as he stepped over the seat of his bike.

He was covered in muscles, tattoos, and looked like he just got out of prison. The patch on his cut said *Big Jack*. His hair was blonde and cut short, but not as short as the one with black hair.

"You're a fuckin' Sinner, ain't ya," Dalton said over his shoulder as he climbed onto his seat.

"Let *me* take her to the shop. You fellas go take care of business," Big Jack said.

Dalton glanced at me. I shrugged my shoulders.

"I got to do this, Kat," Dalton sighed.

To my rear, it sounded like Axton was growling. The dark skinned man was mumbling audibly. Although I couldn't make out everything he said I heard portions. It was apparent he was so angry with what Kyle had done to me he was mumbling his intentions under his breath.

"You're going to cut off his hands?" I asked Dalton sheepishly, remembering what he had said to Kyle the day he slapped me.

He shook his head and gazed down at the parking lot.

As he glanced upward and met my gaze, he responded, "Afraid it ain't gonna be that simple."

I don't even want to know.

I nodded my head, "I'll ride with him. You're going to come back for me, right?"

"You've got my word," he said under his breath.

I pursed my lips, did my best not to start crying, and nodded my head.

Dalton raised his hand in the air and spun it in a circle, "Let's roll!"

As the three of them sped out of the lot, I was scared, relieved, and a little curious.

Whatever Kyle received in punishment wouldn't be enough.

"He'll be back, don't worry. I'm Big Jack," the man on the motorcycle said as he stepped off and extended his hand.

"Kat," I said as I shook his hand.

"Nothing'll happen to you from here on out, least not on my watch," he said in a low rumble.

"Thank you," I sighed.

"Ready?" he asked.

I nodded my head, "Yep."

As I got on the bike he tilted his head to the side, "Got a first-aid kit in the shop. While we're waiting on the fellas, I'll get you doctored up and looking like new."

"Miracle worker?" I asked.

"According to some," he chuckled.

Angels in Selected Sinners cuts is more like it.

He released the clutch and slowly started to pull out of the lot. As I reached around his mid-section and pressed my shaking hands against his stomach, I began to believe all of the Selected Sinners were just that.

Protective angels.

BISCUIT

Maintaining a clear state of mind during stressful times had always been one of my strengths. Similar to an experienced combat veteran, stepping into a dangerous situation, confrontation, or walking right into the middle of a fight never bothered me. I realized I wasn't invincible, but I knew I was pretty god damned close. As we rode in Tater's truck along the back side of the river I wasn't nervous - and I damned sure wasn't scared - but a clear state of mind wasn't something I possessed.

Toad immediately went into full U.S. Marine mode and directed our approach to the house as if it were a military operation. We followed a line of trees along the south side of the home, as the south side had only one small window – more than likely a bathroom – and was the least probable to be occupied. The three of us were armed with handguns, and Tater remained with the truck along the river. After agreeing we wouldn't break the doors down unless we had to, Toad low-crawled toward the back door as Axton and I remained crouched along the south side of the house.

After reaching for the door handle and attempting to open it, he gazed in our direction and shook his head.

Fuck.

Half way back to where we were positioned on the south side of the house, Toad stopped, tilted his head to the side, and raised clenched fist.

As he appeared to be listening to something, Axton and I exchanged awkward glances. As Toad rose into a low crouch I turned to face Axton.

"What the fuck is he doing?" I whispered.

Axton shrugged his shoulders.

And Toad disappeared toward the front of the house.

"Fuck," Axton sighed.

"What do we do?" I asked.

"Hold tight," Axton whispered.

"Fuck that," I responded.

Axton narrowed his gaze and clenched his jaw muscles, "He told us to hold tight. Hold tight. He's got about ten years of experience doing this shit on a daily basis, we'll follow his lead."

Axton no more than finished speaking, and the sound of Toad whistling came from the front of the house.

Axton stood. Somewhat reluctantly, I stood.

"All clear," Axton said as he began to walk around the rear of the home.

I wrinkled my nose slightly and tilted my head his direction, "You two do this shit all the fuckin' time?"

Axton grinned his shitty little grin.

As we came around the front of the house I immediately noticed the garage door was open. It was closed when we had driven past the home the first time. Although Toad wasn't immediately visible, as we stepped into the garage, he was.

He had Kyle in a Marine choke hold, and was grinning from ear to ear.

"Fucker was trying to get in his truck and get out of here," Toad grunted.

"You motherfucker, I'm going to kill you," I seethed, "Can he hear me?"

"He can hear you just fine. Can't respond though," he said.

"Let him go," I growled as I stepped toward the driveway and started to peel off my ridiculous rubber gloves Toad had made us wear.

"We already talked about this, and leave those god damned gloves on," Axton snapped back as he turned to face me.

We had discussed all of the possibilities Toad could come up with for capturing Kyle, and lightly covered what we intended to do with him after we caught him. Although I agreed at the time not to beat Kyle – primarily to shut Axton up – honoring the agreement wasn't easy.

"I took a Beretta nine from him when I grabbed him. Think he knew we were coming," Toad said over Kyle's shoulder as he tilted his head toward the front of the truck.

"Devil looks after his own, it'll save us from searching for one," Axton said as he walked toward Toad.

"Biscuit, shut the garage door," Axton said flatly.

"Toad, drag his ass in the house. Take him to his bedroom," Axton said as he bent over to pick up the pistol.

Toad walked backward toward the door that led into the house. Still fuming with anger about what Kyle did to Kat, I followed close behind, and shut the garage door with the wall mounted button as I stepped into the threshold of the door. .

A quick search of the house by Axton revealed two bedrooms, one with a bed and one full of weight lifting equipment. Toad drug Kyle into the room with a bed while I followed. As Toad rolled onto the bed with Kyle in his arms, Axton bent over and grabbed a pillow.

"We're going to need to fire two rounds…"Axton began.

"Nope, just tell me when you're ready," Toad grunted.

Axton narrowed his eyes and glared at Toad, "He's got to have residue on his hands."

Toad nodded his head, "He will. Just tell me when you're ready."

"Got anything you want to say to him?" Axton asked as he turned to face me, handing me the pillow.

Faking a suicide wasn't near as satisfying to me as beating Kyle to death with my bare hands. For me to beat him and *not* beat him to death would have probably been impossible. According to Toad and Axton, beating him would have left my DNA all over his body, and eventually I would have been caught. Even in my state of mind, what they said made perfect sense. So far, as we were all wearing rubber gloves and stocking caps, leaving our DNA at the scene wasn't impossible, but it was far from probable.

Kyle's eyes were wide and bulging as Toad continued to squeeze him in the chokehold. I stared at him blankly as his face contorted with each movement on Toad's part. As much as I felt I needed to say *something*, I didn't want to give Kyle any satisfaction knowing how I felt, nor did I want to allow him to understand he played a part in causing me to feel the grief that filled me as a result of what he had done to Kat.

I clenched my jaw and alternated glances between Axton and Toad, "Nope. How's this work?"

"I'm going to knock him unconscious. It'll last about ten or fifteen seconds. You cover his face with a pillow, wrap his hand around the weapon, and use *his* finger to pull the trigger. Your gloves aren't torn are they?" he asked.

I glanced down at my hands and inspected my gloves. I shifted my eyes toward Toad and shook my head. Axton slid the slide on the pistol rearward slightly, checked the breech for a round, nodded his head, and handed it to me.

"It's ready," he said.

Toad positioned himself on the side of the bed, holding Kyle in front of him with his legs dangling over the edge of the bed. In this position, it would appear to any investigator that Kyle regretted what he had done, sat in the edge of his bed, covered his face with a pillow, and shot himself.

His fingerprints would be on the weapon, the weapon was his personal Beretta, and his hand would be covered in the residue from firing the gun.

A simple suicide.

I glanced toward Toad, gripped the pistol in my hand, and nodded my head once.

In a blur of a movement, Toad released Kyle from the chokehold and immediately struck him sharply in the neck with the back of his palm. Kyle collapsed onto the bed. Quickly, Toad shifted onto his back and held Kyle upright by his lower back as he lay behind him.

"Hurry the fuck up," Toad howled.

As I pressed the pillow into Kyle's face Axton reached around me and held it in place. I grabbed Kyle's limp arm and attempting to position his finger through the trigger guard of the pistol. After a few seconds of awkward fumbling, I held his hand in mine. I twisted his arm into place, pressing the pistol into the pillow and against his face.

While trying to make sense of it all in my head, Kyle began to regain consciousness. Nervously, I clenched his hand in mine, pressed against his finger, and waited.

The sound of the pistol firing was almost deafening. As much as I had fired guns at various objects and in multiple situations, I had never fired one in the confines of a bedroom. As my ears rang and the taste of cordite filled the air, Toad rolled to the side and Kyle slumped onto the bed.

"Don't touch anything. Leave him lay there as natural as possible," Toad said as he jumped from the bed.

Toad began to brush the imperfections from the comforter with a decorative pillow.

I gazed at him slightly confused and a little uneasy about everything. Beating the life out of Kyle seemed a natural choice to me, and shooting him - now that it was over with - seemed instantaneous, permanent, and almost criminal.

I would have never guessed a feeling other than satisfaction would have filled me, but I was wrong. Although I wasn't remorseful about what we had done, it was apparent part of me regretted the manner we chose to do it.

After smoothing the comforter free of all of the wrinkles except the ones Kyle's limp body created, Toad clutched the decorative pillow in his arms - leaving the one with the bullet hole on the bed - and turned toward the door.

"You alright, Brother?" Axton asked as he patted me on the shoulder.

I nodded my head.

With each step we took toward the river, I became more at peace with shooting Kyle. Although ridding this earth of Kyle wasn't necessarily my responsibility - or anyone's for that matter - doing so prevented him from repeating what he had done to Kat with anyone else. It also eliminated the possibility of him raising a child in the same atmosphere I was raised in. As we approached the truck, I wondered what my life would have been like if my father would have been absent throughout my childhood.

The thought of growing up without my father in my life satisfied me completely, further convincing me what happened to Kyle was ultimately what needed to happen exactly when it needed to happen. As I gazed down at the riverbank, Axton gripped my shoulder.

"You getting in?" he asked.

I nodded my head toward the river and sighed.

"We're telling her he wasn't home, right?" I asked over my shoulder as I slid into the front seat of the truck.

"We came here and he wasn't home. What happened today stays here, with us. And this is the last we'll discuss it," Axton responded.

I sat quietly and gazed through the windshield as Tater drove along the edge of the river and toward the county road. As I considered exactly what we had done, I realized completely it wasn't Axton's or Toad's first effort. The precautionary steps that were taken, the pillow, lack of DNA and fingerprints – even the smoothing of the bed with the pillow...

I glanced over my shoulder.

The pillow Toad had used was positioned between them in the rear seat.

I shifted my eyes to the windshield and gazed with unfocused eyes as the trees lining the edge of the river passed us, wondering just how many people the Selected Sinners had eliminated from the bowels of society.

And what a fractionally better place the world was as a result.

KAT

My time in the shop with Jack passed quickly, and was very entertaining and informative. We discussed his time in prison, being released recently, and his accepting the ATF agent who arrested him as *only doing his job*. He also confided in me that he and his sister, Toad's fiancée, had grown up in and out of orphanages, and eventually landed at a foster home, living with an overbearing preacher for several years.

His insight into the difficulties of a child growing up in a broken home – and without parents – caused me to wonder just what the future might hold for my baby. Ultimately, regardless of the environment the child was reared in, growing up without Kyle in his or her life would be much better than growing up in *any* environment with him.

After Jack did what he could to clean me up and make a repair to a cut high on my left cheek, I reapplied my makeup. I now resembled the girls in school I made fun of – the one's with too much makeup – but at least I did not look like I had been beaten.

As we sat and talked in what he described as Axton's office, the sound of approaching angels filled the air.

"Sounds like they're back," he said as he stood.

"Thank you, for everything," I sighed as I stood from my seat.

"Anything for the Ol' Lady of a brother," he nodded.

Hearing him describe me as Dalton's Ol' Lady seemed odd. In no

237

more than a few days my life had again changed, sending me in another direction altogether. I was certain the change was for the better, but accepting it as reality wasn't first nature for me by any stretch of the imagination.

As we walked into the hallway, the rumbling sound of the motorcycle's exhaust stopped. I gazed out of the hallway and into the garage. Toad, Axton and Dalton stood beside their bikes talking.

"Did you hit him once for me?" I chuckled as I walked toward Dalton.

"Motherfucker wasn't home," he shrugged, "Hell, we looked all over the fuckin' country for the prick. Finally gave up and came back. Cocksucker's gonna get it when we finally find him."

"A-fucking-men to that," Toad said as he pounded his hand into his fist.

"Probably a good thing he wasn't there," Axton growled as he turned my direction.

"You're looking much better. Did Jack clean you up?" Axton asked.

"He did," I said as I turned toward Jack and grinned.

Axton nodded his head toward Jack. I glanced toward Jack. Jack nodded his head in return. As Dalton wrapped his arm around my shoulder, he leaned over and studied my face. After a few seconds, he nodded his head once and grinned.

He shrugged his shoulders and glanced toward Jack, "Hell, I can't even tell."

"Damned sure wasn't the first time I had to doctor somebody up. Damned sure won't be the last," Jack responded.

I realized although at that particular moment I felt safe, and free of Kyle's abusive tendencies, I couldn't keep away from him forever.

Sooner or later, as he always seemed to, he would find me. When he did, there was little remaining doubt that he would be civil and kind. Dalton held me against his shoulder as I stood listening to the men talk, wondering all the while what Kyle's next visit might bring. I glanced around the group, silently hoping they would find Kyle before he found me – and that whatever their punishment consisted of would be sufficient in convincing him to leave me alone forever.

I didn't know for certain what the laws were regarding visitation of a child, but I suspected Kyle would have certain rights regardless of what my concerns were. Even the thought of him coming into contact with my baby sickened me to no end. As I stood at Dalton's side not paying so much as an ounce of attention to what they were talking about, I turned my head toward Dalton and waited for him to finish speaking.

"I bet he retires from fightin' long before anyone beats him," Dalton said as he waved his hand toward Axton.

"What's on your mind, Kat?" he asked as he shifted his eyes to meet mine.

I grinned and shrugged my shoulders, "Nothing really."

"Probably worn the fuck out, aren't ya?" he asked.

I nodded my head.

"Well, let's get my truck and come back to your place and get your stuff. You alright staying with me?" he asked.

Oh hell yes.

"I'd like that," I responded.

"Well, fellas, as much as I'd like to stay and mingle, I better get this poor girl home," he said.

"If you need *anything*," Axton said.

I melted into Dalton's shoulder, feeling more secure than I had previously.

"I'm talking to you. You sure you don't have a concussion?" Axton asked.

"I'm sorry. Were you talking to me?" I asked.

"I said *if you need anything*...I just want to let you know, whatever it is you need, you just let Biscuit know. We'll get it handled for you," Axton said.

"I'm sorry. I didn't realize you were talking to me," I responded.

He narrowed his eyes slightly and crossed his arms. "Well, I was. Don't forget what I said, either."

"I won't. Thank you," I responded.

"If you need any help with that makeup, have Biscuit give me a holler," Jack chuckled.

"I'll do it," I responded.

Toad leaned over to hug Dalton, and I stepped aside. As he pulled away he slapped Dalton on the back and grinned.

"If that fucker shows up, give me a call. I want first jab at him," Toad said.

"You can have him when I'm done," Dalton grunted.

"Maybe you could hold him while I kick him in his nuts," I said.

"Oh shit," Axton chuckled, "We got us a little fighter."

"You can count on it," Toad responded with a nod.

"We're headin' out before it gets too late. If he shows up, I'll get at ya," Dalton said as he opened his saddlebag.

"Throw your purse in here," he said as he extended his hand.

He placed my purse in the saddlebag and latched it. After he got on the bike, I got on the back and relaxed into the seat. Being on the bike with him I felt safe – almost incapable of being harmed. I wanted to retain the feeling forever, but realized nothing in this world is forever. As he pulled out of the garage and into the street, I wondered just how long he'd have me stay with him.

When we were at the apartment he did claim I was his Ol' Lady.

I wonder just what that means, anyway?

As we pulled away from the stop sign and along the street leading to the highway, I squeezed him lightly in my arms. When we got to his house I'd text Avery and have her explain biker protocol to me.

Hopefully being his Ol' Lady meant he was going to keep Kyle away from me for a long, long time.

But nothing lasts forever.

KAT

Four days had passed since anyone had heard from Kyle, and even his boss contacted me regarding his whereabouts. Dalton had driven to his house twice trying to find him, but each time Kyle was gone. I began to feel more comfortable about his being away, and hoped he had simply decided to leave the area for fear of what may happen to him if he didn't. I chose not to press the issue with Dalton regarding my staying at his house, and decided just to enjoy it as long as it lasted.

I would have never guessed that anything could have increased my sexual desire, but being pregnant acted as some type of an accelerant to my already overly active sexual cravings. We had spent every spare moment either fucking, recovering from fucking, or seeking nourishment so we could fuck again. Jokingly, Dalton had shared with me the previous night that he was afraid he'd met his sexual match.

If there was an upside, I guess it would be that I didn't have to worry about getting pregnant.

With his weight against my back and his mouth pressed against my ear, he inhaled a deep breath and exhaled into the side of my face. As his beard tickled the skin on my neck, I raised my shoulder for any relief I might be able to receive. He pressed with a little more force, moving my head and shoulder apart even further.

"Don't fight me, Kat," he breathed into my ear.

"I'm not. I'm just…"

"Just what? Done?" he asked.

His warm breath against my ear sent chills down my spine. I blinked my eyes a few times, focused on the headboard, and shook my head.

I was thirsty, worn completely out, and my pussy felt as if it were on fire. We'd been fucking on and off for almost two hours, and my arms were not only bound together at my wrists, but secured to the headboard of the bed. On my belly with my ass in the air and my tits pressed into the comforter, I truly wondered if I could outlast him.

For him to get me to give in, he'd have to fuck me to death.

"No. I'm not giving up," I growled as I arched my back against him.

"Fuck it. Have it your way," he said as he shifted his weight to the side.

I peered over my shoulder and watched him as he walked to the dresser and removed a small plastic bag. After removing what looked like a tube of toothpaste, he turned toward the bed.

"Turn around before I slap that ass again," he said as he climbed onto the end of the bed.

Resting partially on my forearms and partially on my elbows, I turned toward the bed and sighed.

Oh fuck he's not going to…

I felt the lubricant between my ass cheeks. As I began to speak, he pressed one hand against the center of my back lightly and attempted to comfort me.

"Shhh," he whispered.

I felt his finger along the crack of my ass, gliding back and forth lightly through the lubricant. As the tip of his finger slid across my anus each time, my sphincter would tighten and my entire spine would tingle.

As much as I wanted to hate what he was doing, I began to enjoy it immensely.

After a few more strokes of his finger, I felt light pressure against my anus. Within a split-second, his finger was in my ass.

And I loved it.

In and out his finger slid, causing me to moan in pleasure with each stroke. I buried my face into the comforter, not necessarily wanting him to understand how much I was enjoying what he was doing.

I pulled against the restraints. Acting as if he was doing everything against my will provided me with even more satisfaction. As I yanked against the binding which held my hands to the headboard, I arched my back and mentally begged for him to never stop.

I wondered if I was supposed to enjoy it, and felt almost guilty for doing so. After a few seconds, I felt more lubricant on my ass, and sighed into to the comforter relieved and excited he intended on continuing. His finger repeatedly slid in and out of my ass slowly. My pussy, which I was certain fifteen minutes earlier was done for the night, began to tingle. Whatever he was doing was working.

I wanted more cock.

I lifted my head from the comforter, craned my neck rearward, and growled.

"Fuck me."

"Believe me," he said as he continued to fuck my ass with his finger, "I intend to."

I felt his hand slide up the center of my back and grip my hair. As he pulled my hair taught, I arched my back in response.

"That's right. Arch that back good, Kat. I want to get that spot. You know the one," he breathed.

Do I ever...

"Do it," I growled, "Do it..."

After a second of slight pressure against my pussy, it opened up like a spring tulip, allowing his length to easily slide inside. As he slowly began to fuck my pussy with his massive cock, his finger continued to fuck my ass. The sensation of both holes being filled at once was embarrassingly sensual. I bit my bottom lip, hoping the sensation would last forever, but knowing I was a matter of minutes from collapse.

He pulled against my hair sharply. As I arched my back further, the tip of his cock pressed against my g-spot. A tingling sensation throughout my lady bits reminded me once again of Dalton's sexual strength.

He knew how to fuck me right.

And he had the equipment to do it.

"You like that little finger of mine in your ass, Kat?" he asked through his teeth.

I lifted my head from the bed, "Yes. Yes I do."

His cock slid back and forth, sending a sensation throughout my lower body with each *in* stroke. His speed increased and within a few seconds he was pounding himself into me with tremendous speed, his hips pounding against my ass and his tight scrotum slapping against my clit with each stroke. His finger continued to fuck my ass, causing a tingling that seemed to connect my ass to my pussy. My mind had gone into sexual sensory overload. It was almost as if my brain was incapable of realizing all of the feelings my body was experiencing in *real time*.

My body began to tense into one solid contracted muscle.

This was going to be it.

I was going to die.

I clenched my eyes closed and focused.

And he stopped.

He slowly pulled his cock from my sopping wet pussy, and his finger from my perfectly satisfied virgin ass. I opened my eyes, turned my head to the side, and pulled against the restraints.

"No, don't stop. I was…" I begged.

I realized I was out of breath and attempted to take another gulp of air and speak my mind.

While my mind worked to catch up with my body and my tongue sought a little guidance to form the words I desperately needed to say, I felt pressure once again against my ass.

Thank God.

I sighed and pushed my face into the comforter.

But it wasn't his finger this time.

A light vibration and a little more girth caused me to open my mouth and widen my eyes. I had no idea what he'd snuck out of the dresser and onto the bed, but whatever it was…

I loved.

With my mouth agape and my mind reeling to accept a totally new feeling of sensual and sensual bliss, I willingly allowed him to explore my ass with his buzzing butt toy.

In and out of my ass he slid the joyous delight. I bit my lower lip, knowing I was enjoying the experience far more than I should. I had no idea if this was punishment, an effort on his part to get me to scream *uncle*, or if he intended for it to be pleasurable, but I was loving every minute of it, and every stroke of my little buzzing friend. I pulled against the restraints, released my lip, and began to breathe heavily.

I desperately needed to rub my clit and cast myself off into space.

"You like it when I fuck that tight little ass, Kat?" he said through his teeth.

I opened my mouth and craned my neck slightly. The words came a few seconds later, cast from my lungs in a bust of warm breath.

"Love it," I heaved.

"I'm going to fuck it good for you, Kat. I'm going to make you give up. I'm going to win," he breathed.

I lowered my head to the comforter and pressed my face flat against the fabric.

"Do it…" I grunted.

I wanted it all. Every girlfriend who'd ever spoken to me about anal told me it was dirty, nasty, and painful. I had no idea who was fucking them in the ass, but obviously it wasn't Dalton. As he continued to work his magic in and out of my ass, I felt guilty, dirty, nasty, and absolutely satisfied.

A few more strokes with my newfound buzzing friend, and he pulled it from inside of me. With my ass still tingling, and my mind begging for more, I grunted the word no into the surface of the bed. I needed to gain the strength to raise my head and protest, I wanted more.

Anal sex was my new escape, and I needed to become lost in it.

Face down and ass up as they say, I attempted to gain the strength to beg for more. Try as I might, I could not. I was completely exhausted and pretty damned close to extremely satisfied.

He pulled against my hair with his hand, causing me to raise my head and arch my back. He pulled steadily, and with more force. As he pulled, I arched my back ever further, knowing regardless of my desire to win this ridiculous competition; I was going to have to throw in the proverbial towel. As I no more than opened my mouth, I felt pressure against my anus again.

"Breathe, Kat. You need to breathe," he whispered.

He was right. I was going to pass out if I didn't watch myself. I was a mental mess.

As I tried to decide whether to thank God or scream for him to stop, I felt the unmistakable girth of his cock slowly penetrate my anus and begin to slide into my ass. My mind said no, but my ass was saying yes. Within a few seconds, my ass won the argument, and my mind eventually agreed.

And my mind drifted off into heaven.

"You got something to say, Kat?" he growled as he pulled steadily on my hair.

I shook my head.

"Not a fucking word?" his laugh was almost sinister.

I bit my lower lip and shook my head once more.

"You like that big fat cock in your tight little ass?" he asked as his hand came down against my right butt cheek.

Oh fuck yes. Slap it.

"Fuck...yes," I blurted as he continued to slowly fuck my ass.

The sensation was indescribable. Whether it was a combination of previous feelings – or his cock in my ass alone was causing it – I didn't care. All I knew was that it felt so far beyond amazing.

His hand slapped my ass again, sending a stinging feeling along my thigh. I pressed my face into the comforter and breathed against the material, feeling my breath surround my face each time I exhaled. After another obvious squirt of lubricant, he maintained his perfect rhythm of slowly fucking my ass deeply, carefully, and perfectly.

And then his free hand found my clit.

It was too much. I would have stopped him if I could, but with my hands tied, I wasn't able to do anything but writhe against him on the surface of the bed.

"Dalton…" I begged.

"Shhhh, not a word," he whispered.

I lowered my head and bit into the fabric. As I clenched it in my teeth, he carefully fucked my tight ass and flicked his finger against my swollen nub. My nipples began to ache. I released the comforter from my teeth and howled out into the room.

As he slowly and steadily fucked my ass while fingering my clit, I felt as if my body burst into pieces and was thrust out into the room - pieces of me traveled in each and every possible direction. I felt like a human firework, exploding into thousands of small fragments and being cast out into the sky for all to enjoy.

As my screaming echoed throughout the room, he carefully pulled his cock from my ass. Within a few seconds I heard him groan and I felt his warm cum against my back, and along the crack of my ass.

I collapsed into the comforter.

This time, I was truly done. To continue would kill me.

His chest pressed against my back lightly and his beard tickled my cheek.

"Truce?" he breathed into my ear.

I tilted my head to the side.

"No winner, no loser?" I whispered.

"Yep. Two winners. Deal?" he asked under his breath.

"Deal," I responded.

I realized as he reached to untie me that not only was Dalton different than anyone I would probably ever meet, but that he was caring, kind, and always considerate of me. His huge heart was disguised by a beard, tattoos, gauges in his ears, and an outer bad-boy shell as tough as diamonds.

And I wouldn't have it any other way.

KAT

I could recall when I was young and my grandmother died from breast cancer. The feeling deep in the pit of my stomach when my parents told me she passed away wasn't anything I could compare to another feeling. The pain was deep, dull, and lasted for what seemed to be a lifetime. Since her death, I had never felt anything comparable, but I had not had to deal with death again either.

When I was a little older, my brother won the bull riding competition at the state level. The bull they selected for him was a tough one, feared by most men, and known for breaking bones, maiming riders, and just being downright mean. Upon learning which bull he was to ride that night, we all felt as if he could certainly die trying to ride it for the eight second requirement.

His ride was nothing short of perfect, he scored an 88, and he won the competition. The feeling I felt for him, the level of joy, and the depth of my pride was the polar opposite of what I felt when my grandmother died.

That level of joy, at least for me, had yet to be matched.

Until now.

"So, you ready to talk?" Dalton asked.

I took a bite of my eggs, and as I chewed them, glanced in his direction, "Sure."

"Alright then," he said as he placed his fork on the plate.

"I want this baby to be *mine*. I wanna adopt it or whatever I have to so you and I can raise it like a family. And, I guess it goes without sayin' that I want you to stick around here forever," he said flatly.

I dropped my fork onto the plate. Although I meant to place it there, my mind disagreed. It fell the twelve inches from my hand to the plate with a loud *clank*.

"You don't have to do that," I responded.

As the words escaped my mouth, I felt like a fool. I was elated, overjoyed, and beyond grateful.

"I don't have to do anything. I realize that, Kat. I *want* to. Been thinkin' about it for some time now. No matter what becomes of Kyle, I want that baby to be mine. Well, you know, ours. I want that. What do ya think?" he asked.

He was so calm. So matter-of-fact. It was difficult for me not to jump up, bounce across the table, and hug him.

"I think that would be nice. I like the thought of it," I responded.

I was going to start crying. There was no two ways about it. It was coming, and I could tell.

"Axton's Ol' Lady, Avery, works for an attorney. I'll see what we have to do to get something done, but I just want you to know, I want to raise that baby like it's my own. I want you to know that, Kat. No need in havin' that kid grow up like I did, none at all," he said as he reached for his fork.

"None at all," I agreed as I shook my head.

I covered my hand with my mouth and coughed.

"Bathroom," I said as I tossed my head to the rear and stood.

He nodded his head.

As I turned away, I began to softly cry. On my way to the bathroom, tears of joy ran down my cheeks and onto the floor. Once in the bathroom, I turned on the exhaust fan and the faucet to mask the noise.

And I cried tears of happiness while thinking about having a child and living with the man I truly loved.

All at the same time.

When the tears finally stopped, I wiped my face, grateful it was early in the morning and I hadn't done my makeup yet.

I glanced in the mirror and grinned.

I walked into the kitchen and sat down. After studying my plate for a moment, I glanced in Dalton's direction. He had bitten a hole in the center of his piece of toast and held it in front of his right eye, peering through it as if he were looking through a knot hole in a fence.

"You know," he said, "Lookin' through this piece of toast like this is the shits. You can only see what's right in front of ya. And when I move it to the side…"

He moved the toast beside his face and let it dangle from his fingers.

"Well, then you can see it *all*," he grinned as he surveyed the entire kitchen.

I nodded my head and eventually began to laugh.

"I'm thinkin' I had *toast eye* for my entire damned life and meetin' you was like chuckin' the fucker to the side," he said as he tossed the toast toward the sink.

I glanced toward the sink. The toast landed perfectly in the center. I turned to face him, still giggling at the analogy he'd created.

"Toast eye?" I chuckled.

"Not anymore," he said.

Dalton wasn't a difficult man by any means.

But he was complex. Complex in a very simple way.

And as simple as that, Dalton had made me comfortable that not only did he want to raise another man's child as his own, but that he attributed the broader field of vision in his recent life to having me as a lover.

Well, that and knocking the toast away from his eye.

KAT

Regardless of the resentment I felt toward my father, he was still my father. As much as I wanted to go against his each and every wish, from time to time his desires and mine were either similar or exactly the same. It was infrequent that he agreed with me, but when he did it allowed me to understand he had the ability to be human.

"I don't know. We were together three years," I sighed, "To try and count them now would be impossible."

"Educated guess?" my father shrugged.

I gazed beyond him and toward the people seated at the far side of the coffee shop, "Fifteen or maybe twenty."

"Actual beatings? Where he *hit* you?" he asked, trying to keep his rage from showing.

I bit my lower lip and nodded my head slightly.

"Not like *this* time, but yeah. You know, slapped me. Pushed me against the wall and slapped me. Sometimes he drug me around the house by my hair. I don't know what you want to call it all, but I call it bullshit. I mean looking at it all now, I call bullshit. At the time I was just, I don't know. I think I told myself it was part of it. You know part of what it was like to be in an adult relationship. Fuck, I don't know," I sighed.

"Watch your mouth, Katrina," he said through his teeth.

"Seriously? Watch my mouth? Okay," I huffed as I glanced down toward my shoes.

"Listen," he said as he reached for my shoulder.

I shifted my eyes upward and met his gaze. His face portrayed his true feelings for once. He was sorry.

"Why didn't you ask me for help? Why didn't you tell me what was going on?" he asked softly.

I shrugged my shoulders, "Because you didn't raise a pussy. You're a cop, and don't get mad, but you're a dick cop. You raised me like I was another son. My best friend growing up was my bull riding brother. I'm not soft, and I don't complain. It's over, and I lived through it. I'm a stronger person now. You know, what doesn't kill you makes you stronger, right?"

"A dick cop?" he half chuckled and half cried.

Without responding, I widened my eyes slightly and tilted my head to the side in affirmation as I turned my palms upward.

He reached up and wiped his finger along the bottom of his eye as he turned his head to the side slightly. After a long sigh, he faced me again.

"So, you're staying with Biskette now?" he asked as our eyes met.

"His name is *Dalton*. He's not a suspect in a crime, so don't call him Biskette, please," I sighed, "And yes."

"And you say he came to your house and *saved* you? He drug Kyle outside and kicked the shit out of him?" he asked.

"Sure did," I nodded as I reached for my vanilla bean smoothie.

"What threats did he make afterward? Upon Kyle's departure he had to tell him something. What did he say?" he asked.

I was beginning to feel like I was under investigation. My father, try as he might, was always a cop first, and a human being later. Seeing no value in telling him the complete truth, I shrugged my shoulders and told my version of the story.

"He, he Kyle, not he Dalton. He was forcing me to suck his dick. He had me…"

"Stop," he interrupted as he raised his hand in the air, "No need for the graphic details."

"So you want me to sugar coat it for you? Lie to you?" I asked as I placed the cup on the table beside me.

He glanced around the coffee shop and eventually fixed his eyes on mine, "I wish you hadn't picked this place to meet. I wish you'd have met me at our house."

I widened my eyes as my mouth curled into a slight smirk, "When we're at your house you have the upper hand. At least here we're closer to even."

He shook his head and leaned to the side and turned to face me, positioning himself much closer to me.

"Continue," he whispered.

"So he had his little dick in one hand and my hair in the other. He tried to force me to suck his dick. When I refused, he slapped me. I don't know, it seems like I stood up and told him to leave. Then he slapped the absolute fuck out of me and knocked me down. He picked me up by the hair and was trying to shove his ratty little dick in my mouth again, and Dalton burst into the room," I paused and took a shallow breath.

"He broke into your apartment? Knocked the door down?" he asked.

"No, god damn it. The door was open, Kyle left it open. Dalton's not some thug, Dad," I sighed.

"So anyway, Dalton grabbed him, beat the shit out of him, and drug him downstairs and made him leave. He told Kyle if he ever came back, he'd give it to him again," I shrugged my shoulders and reached for my drink as I waited for his response.

He widened his eyes slightly, "And that was it?"

"Maybe you should have been there. It was enough. Dalton beat the absolute shit out of him," I responded.

"And then what?" he asked.

I shrugged my shoulders as I slid my lips over the end of the straw. After sucking half of the remaining vanilla lusciousness from the cup I lowered it to my side and responded.

"He carried me to my room, held me in his arms, and I fell asleep. When I woke up the next morning, he was gone," I responded.

"And after that time? What about the most recent time? What did Dalton do?" he asked.

"Jesus, dad. He came to get me, they fixed up my face with some butterfly stitches, cleaned me up, and they went looking for him. It's been five days and so far, nothing," I said as I reached for my drink.

"When was the last time they went looking, do you know?" he asked.

Back under investigation.

I swear.

"Yesterday, I think," I shrugged.

"Still trying to find him, huh?" he asked as he relaxed into his seat.

"Uh huh," I nodded.

"Katrina, I've got some news. I don't know how you're going to take it, but I need to tell you. I don't want you to hear it from anyone else but me. I want to be the one who's here for you through this," he said.

Oh my god. Mom's got cancer, doesn't she?

I bit my lower lip and nodded my head, not wanting to hear whatever he had to say, but knowing whatever it was needed to be heard.

"They found Kyle, this morning. An apparent suicide. It appears he's been dead for five days," he paused and inhaled a shallow breath.

I sighed heavily and the words escaped my mouth as I exhaled.

"Thank god," I heaved.

His eyes narrowed and he looked confused.

"He's dead, Katrina," he said as he shook his head.

I nodded my head. I had no idea how I should have felt, but I was nothing short of relieved. Whatever feelings I had for Kyle in the past, regardless of what they were, vanished the day he beat me the way he did the last time. Now, there was nothing left. Nothing at all. With Kyle gone, I could truly begin a new life with Dalton without worry or fear of him returning someday.

"I got that. And I'm happy," I said as I raised my cup.

He gazed at me with a look of clear confusion.

"Dalton said he wanted to adopt the baby. We found out he couldn't without Kyle's consent. This just makes everything easier. Dad, he was an animal. A fucking beast. He probably realized exactly what he did, regretted it, and killed himself in a drunken stupor," I said.

"Alcohol played a part. The county investigated it, but I've seen the report. His toxicity was…"

I raised my hand in the air to stop him from speaking, "La la la la I don't care."

He shook his head and grinned, "You really don't care, do you?"

"Nope. I want to celebrate," I said as I stood from my chair.

"Lunch, my treat?" he asked.

"Depends," I said as I reached for my purse.

I shifted my eyes upward as I stood. He gazed back with wide eyes, waiting for me to continue. I stared at him for a moment and sighed lightly. He looked happier than I had seen him in some time, and I had no idea what about our mid-morning coffee would have pleased him so much.

"On?' he eventually asked.

"You going to leave Dalton alone? Let us be?" I asked.

"Are you truly happy?" he asked.

I nodded my head, "Never been happier."

"Is there any fear that one day he'll harm you?" he asked.

I shook my head, "The complete opposite. He's sweet, Dad. He really is. Not only will he never hurt me, he'll make damned sure no one else does, either."

He nodded his head and opened his arms, "All I want is for my little girl to be happy."

"She is," I said as I hugged him.

As he held me in his arms, I sighed. And, although my father didn't raise a pussy, a tear escaped my eye and ran down my cheek.

It was the first time in my life I could remember my father holding me in his arms that I didn't want him to let me go.

I love you, Dad.

BISCUIT

There's two things that will make a 1%er's asshole pucker for sure. One is an unscheduled visit from the police, and the other is a former girlfriend showing up at his door with a baby in her belly. I'd never had a girlfriend show up pregnant, and until now, I'd never had a cop show up at my house.

"I've got a gun on the bench beside me, and if you come in my god damned garage I'll drop you where you stand, Cop. Your threat didn't settle well with me," I said as I turned his direction and reached for my pistol.

"Katrina tells me you're not a violent man, Dalton. I'm beginning to wonder," he said as he continued to walk up my driveway.

"I'm not," I said as I placed my hand against the grip of the pistol, "But you threatened to kill me. Kind of made matters personal when you did that."

"I'm not here as a police officer. I'm here as Katrina's father," he said as he stopped at the edge of the garage door.

I released the grip of the pistol, wiped my hands on a rag, and turned to face him. As I crossed my arms in front of my chest and did my best to swell to twice my size, I studied his six foot six frame. Whipping him in a fist fight would be an all day job for sure.

"Sure look like a cop to me," I shrugged.

"I just got off duty. Got a minute to talk?" he asked.

I shook my head, "Don't let cops in my house, sorry. Garage is part of my house. There's nothing in here for ya. None of your god damned business what I got or what I'm doing."

He shook his head and began to laugh, "Typical biker."

I inhaled, flexed my biceps, and pushed my chest forward, "Typical fuckin' cop, tryin' to make his way into a biker's house so he can fuck with him."

"Well, now that we've got that out of the way, do you care to talk about your relationship with my daughter?" he asked.

Relationship?

He seemed calm, accepting of what he was saying, and his hand didn't hover over his pistol.

"I'll listen to ya. But it won't be in my house," I lowered my arms and glanced around the garage, "And it won't be in here, either. Hold on a minute, I guess you can sit beside the pool and talk. I'll let you in the side gate."

I turned toward the door, pressed the button to the garage door, and watched his body disappear as the door went down. After the door was fully closed, I stepped into the kitchen, grabbed two Red Bulls, and walked out the back door. As I opened the gate, he stood a few feet behind it, grinning from ear to ear.

"Somethin' funny happen while I was away?" I asked as I studied him.

"Just find your protective nature humorous, I suppose," he shrugged.

"Downright comedic, huh?" I chuckled as I turned away.

I pointed toward the table and chairs situated on the deck surrounding the pool, "We can sit here."

I pulled the cans of Red Bull out of my pockets and slid one across the table. As I pulled my chair from the table and sat down, I opened the can and drank half of it in one swig. He studied the can, opened it, and raised it to his lips. Almost immediately his face contorted and he held the can at arm's length.

"That tastes like shit. You like this stuff?" he asked.

"Best shit ever," I nodded, "So if sharin' a Red Bull with a biker wasn't your reason for comin', what brings you to this part of town, Cop?"

He shook his head and grinned, "Dave. My name is Dave."

I raised my can and grinned, "What brings you to this part of town, Dave the cop?"

He shook his head.

"Sorry, sometimes I just can't help myself," I chuckled.

"My daughter tells me you kicked the everloving shit out of that scumbag who slapped her around in her apartment?" he said.

I stood from my seat, pointed toward the gate, and sighed, "Investigation's over, Cop. I'll lock the gate behind you."

He stood and shook his head as he laughed a shallow laugh.

"I'm here to thank you. And to tell you I appreciate you coming to my daughter's aid. She said your friends helped her out and doctored her up afterward. I want to express my gratitude for their assistance in the matter. She also told me you and the gentlemen you ride with have been looking for the scumbag on a daily basis. I appreciate that as well," he said.

I relaxed, pulled out my chair, and sat down.

"Have a seat," I sighed as I pointed toward his chair.

He sat, leaned over the table, and raised the can of Red Bull. After

265

reading the label, he took another drink and shook his head.

I leaned forward, rested my forearms on the table and sighed. I shifted my gaze toward his face and held it. As he realized my focus was on him, he locked eyes with me and lowered his chin.

I widened my eyes and sighed lightly. "I don't ride with *gentlemen*. They're my brothers. We have a brotherhood and a bond someone like you will never understand. Each and every one of those fellas would and will do whatever they must to protect her - because they're my brothers."

"I know a little about that. When I call for backup, I put my life in the hands of *my* brothers. Each and every one of them would and will do whatever they must to protect me, and to protect *you*, Dalton, from harm," he paused and took a sip from the can of Red Bull.

I shook my head, "It's not the same."

He nodded his head, "You'd be surprised."

I sighed heavily and shook my head. "Change the subject."

He leaned back in his chair, inhaled a deep breath, and exhaled heavily.

"So, she tells me you'd like to adopt the baby?" he asked.

I nodded my head. Talking to him about it seemed much different than talking to Kat. Somewhat uncomfortable, and not necessarily wanting to get into an argument with him about *anything*, I decided to minimize my speaking and keep things simple.

"That's right," I responded.

"Do you love her?' he asked.

I leaned back in the chair and stared beyond him with unfocused eyes. Love was something I wasn't even sure existed. I'd never been in love, and I had my doubts, other than Kat, if anyone had truly ever loved me, short of the love my brothers in the club had for me. After a long minute of thinking, I focused my eyes on him and began to explain my thoughts.

"Don't know that I even know what love is for sure. A feelin', I suppose. Not knowin', it's hard to say. I can tell ya this for sure. When your daughter's with me, I feel like my life is kinda perfect for the first time. When she's gone, like when she went back to Kyle, life ain't much worth livin'. Never felt that way about anything before. You know, she came back, and everything that was broke immediately was fixed. I ain't gonna shit ya, *Dave*. I've been with my share of women, and I ain't never had one make me feel like Kat. So, maybe it's love. But whatever it is, I'd like to make a commitment to her, and I suppose to you," I paused and took a drink.

I lowered the can and leaned forward, "I want that baby to see me as it's father, and know nothing different. We can raise that kid up never knowing any different. Kid deserves that."

He shifted his eyes from the can in front of him toward me and nodded his head.

"What is it you do for a living?" he asked.

"Off the record?" I asked.

He nodded his head.

"Murder for hire," I said flatly.

He nodded his head again, "Comedian?"

"According to some," I grinned.

I shook my head and leaned forward, resting my arms on the edge of the table.

"I build high performance Harley motors. Between you and me, I make a hundred grand a year. House is paid for, bike too. I claim about forty to help on taxes, it's an all cash business. I do pretty well. Save most of it," I said.

He studied the can for a moment and eventually shifted his eyes to meet mine.

"They found that kid. Kyle. Found him this morning," he said as he stood.

"Got him in custody?" I asked as I stood from my seat.

He shook his head, "Suicide. Been dead four or five days."

"Damned shame," I said flatly.

He gazed down at his feet and continued.

"Sure is. You know, the county investigated it. Ruled it a clear case of suicide. Kid used his personal pistol, shot himself in the face. He used a pillow for some reason, I personally found that strange, but anyway," he paused as he shook his head slightly.

"You know another thing I found strange?" he asked.

I shook my head and shrugged, "No idea."

"I've known that kid for three years. He was left handed. The residue from the weapon discharging was on his right hand, and the pistol was still in his right hand. So I thought, *why would this kid use his right hand to kill himself - if he was a natural leftie?*" he asked.

I shrugged my shoulders.

"I didn't bother telling the officer in charge what I knew. I just couldn't see any sense in it. God has his way of weeding out the bad on this earth, you know. Sometimes it's at the hand of a cop," he paused and locked eyes with me.

"And sometimes it's not," he sighed.

"Investigation's over?" I asked.

He nodded his head, "Closed case."

"And you're alright with Kat and me? Me adopting the baby?" I asked.

"I've accepted it. She says you're good for her. She loves you, you need to know that, Dalton," he responded.

I tilted my head toward the back door.

"Come in for a bit, Dave?" I asked.

He glanced toward the door, turned to face me, and smiled.

"I'd love to," he responded.

"Follow me," I said as I turned toward the door, "We need to have us a little talk."

As I walked toward the door I realized he and I were similar in at least a few respects. No differently than he had a preconceived notion about me being a dirty biker, I had the same about him being a chicken-shit cop. In the end, all he was trying to do was the same thing I had tried to do.

Keep Kat from being harmed.

Together, if we could see eye to eye, there was no doubt in my mind that Kat could live a life not only safe from harm, but as a very, very happy woman.

And I'd be a very happy man.

BISCUIT

After painting our bedroom *Fair Fieldstone Taupe*, I painted the spare bedroom a combination of light blue and pink. Two opposing walls were pink, and the opposite two walls were light blue. For now, the color combination satisfied me, and would be satisfactory regardless of the sex of the baby.

I stood in the doorway, admired the new colors, and studied the trim for imperfections. As always, I found nothing that needed touched up. My anal retentive nature prevented me from walking away from a job that wasn't perfect.

I sighed, inhaled the odor of the drying paint, and looked into the living room at the boxes of new furniture I'd purchased - a crib, changing table, and dresser, all in need of assembly. I glanced at my watch. It would take some hard work, but having it assembled and in place by the time Kat got back from shopping should be doable. A quick shower on my part afterward, and we should make Cash's patch in party without any problems.

It was nice to see Kat and Avery becoming close friends. Sydney was attached to Avery's hip, so there was no doubt they'd all become close. There wasn't much better women on this earth than those two, and as tough as Avery was, I wasn't so sure Sydney wasn't a little tougher. Making it out of her childhood with the peaceful, upbeat, and always eager attitude was a feat in itself, and left me impressed with who she was and what she stood for.

Having a little of her rub off on Kat would suit me just fine.

I closed the door to the bedroom and allowed the room to vent out into the yard through the open windows. After cleaning up the paint supplies, I knelt down on the floor and began to assemble the furniture.

Three and a half hours later, I cleaned up the mess, carried the furniture into the room, and moved it into place. I glanced around the room at the changes. A year prior, if someone would have brought up a baby being in my life, I would have laughed until I pissed myself. Now, looking around the room at the furniture and bright colors, I was excited, eager, and more than willing for the change.

The reward, at least in my mind, was my knowing there wasn't another man on this earth who was going to be as devoted to raising the child properly as me. A man has one chance to do what's right in his being a father, and there's no room for mistakes. As inexperienced as I was at being a father, I had years of exposure and a complete understanding of what *not* to do.

I'm sure a man accepting another man's child or children as his own is a far more difficult task than accepting his own children. In my current state of being, I was incapable of producing children, and as far as I was concerned, the baby wasn't another man's child.

The child was mine.

I had come to accept that what I shared with Kat could be nothing short of love, and if she and I loved one another - and I wasn't able to produce children - God had done what he felt was necessary.

His provision of a child wasn't something I perceived as being a mistake, burden, or complication.

To me, it was nothing short of what it truly was.

An opportunity to right a lifetime of wrongs.

A gift.

And a blessing.

As I heard Kat's jeep rolling into the drive, I glanced around the room, making sure all of the evidence was cleaned up. I wanted the room to be a surprise, and I hoped to show it to her in a few days.

As she rushed into the house and dropped her bags, she wrinkled her nose and stared.

"Smells like paint," she hissed.

"Painted the room one last time," I responded.

"Last time?" she chuckled.

"I'm thinkin' so," I grinned as I walked into the kitchen.

"Look," she said as she reached into one of the bags.

Dangling from the end of her fingers was a Harley-Davidson shirt. White, orange, and black, it was suitable for a boy or a girl.

I grinned and nodded my head, "It's cute."

"Cute? Seems funny hearing you say that," she responded.

"I've got bags of stuff," she said as she pointed to the bags sitting on the floor.

I was time for both of us to get ready for the patch in party, but I couldn't resist. After a good solid thirty minutes of going through each and every item one by one, we decided to shower together to save time, water, and satisfy our sexual needs.

"Better hurry the hell up and decide, it's going to be six thirty before you know it," I said as I glanced in the room.

"Do I look fat?" she asked as she twisted her hips in front of the mirror.

She looked beautiful. Her hair flipped around in a circle behind her as she twisted back and forth. Although she really hadn't begun to indicate she was pregnant from her appearance regarding weight or size, something about her had changed. She had a certain glow about her that was unmistakable and incapable of accurate description. It had to be seen to be believed.

Whatever it was worked well for her, and reassured me that not only was I fortunate, but I was with the most beautiful woman in the world.

"Tough for you to look fat, you're skinny," I shrugged.

"These jeans look good?" she asked as she turned her ass toward the mirror and gazed over her shoulder.

"Better'n any I've ever seen," I responded.

"Any?" she asked.

"Any," I responded.

"Ready?" she asked as she reached for her purse.

"Suppose so," I sighed.

"So what exactly is this again?" she asked.

"Patch in party. A kid's been prospecting for a year, and finally paid his dues. Tonight we eat, drink, and raise hell. It's a party for him to celebrate his becoming a fully patched member of the club," I said as we walked toward the garage.

"Sam, Avery, and Sydney said they're going too, so it'll be fun for me," she grinned.

"Better get that hair tied up, or you'll be spendin' the night untanglin' it," I chuckled as we stepped into the garage.

"I think I'll just let it blow," she said with a nod.

"You sure?" I asked.

She nodded her head and grinned, "I like it that way. I don't know, it's hard to explain. But it just kind of makes me feel free. Like a bird or something, I just can't really explain it, but I love how it makes me feel."

She turned to face me and shrugged her shoulders. I leaned forward and kissed her, something I was still getting used to, but enjoyed more than almost anything.

"No need for explanation," I said as our lips parted.

I knew exactly what she meant.

KAT

I had always looked up to Avery. She was a year older than me in school, and one of the best volleyball players I had ever seen. Not admiring her for what she'd done for the team and what she'd done with her career would be difficult. It seemed she was as fierce as a legal assistant as she was on the volleyball court. Having her act now as my equal seemed strange, but I welcomed it; accepting the fact my life was slowly changing. As we stood in a circle talking, I turned almost giddy in excitement thinking about my future with the three women as my lifelong friends.

"You can't tell anyone, not yet. Dalton hasn't told everyone, and I don't know when he will. I think maybe Axton knows, but that's it," I glanced over my shoulder as I finished speaking, seeing where Dalton was.

He stood with Otis, Axton, and a few others in a circle talking. As always, it seemed he was telling a story, and the others were listening to him.

"Okay what is it?" Sam asked.

She was as beautiful of a woman as I had ever seen. I gazed at her hoping when I was her age I could be half as beautiful as her. Her hair was long and blonde, and her body was phenomenal. I gazed down at her Chuck's, and quickly noticed Sydney and Avery wore the same shoe. Aggravated I'd chosen to wear boots, I shifted my eyes to meet Sam's and smiled.

"I'm pregnant," I whispered.

"Oh dear God," Sam gasped, "That's so exciting."

Avery already knew, but I acted like she didn't. Sydney stood back, grinned, and raised her finger to her lips. As she did, Avery turned toward her, placed her hands on her hips, and inhaled a deep breath. Sydney stood with her finger pressed to her lips and began to giggle.

"You little bitch," Avery blurted, "You little fucking bitch. You aren't, are you?" Avery seethed.

Sydney nodded her head as she lowered her hand, "Shhh. We haven't told anyone. I mean no one. Not even his parents. We want to make sure everything goes good. I mean it, you can't tell a soul."

Sam turned toward Sydney and started to softly cry. As she wiped her eyes, Sydney opened her arms and sighed.

"What is it, Sam?" Sydney said.

Sam shook her head, "I'm just happy for you two. It's just…I don't know. Otis and I split up over my wanting kids when we were twenty-one years old. I don't want them anymore, I'll settle for him. It's just…when two people can have it to share, and they both want it…it's special."

I nodded my head, "We're both really happy."

"Cambio wants twins. He's freaking crazy," Sydney chuckled.

"Twins," I coughed, "Oh my God. That would be insane."

Sydney nodded her head, "I know. But he wants two at the same time so bad it's like an obsession."

I shook my head, "I think I'd die."

"You fucking hooker, I can't believe you didn't tell me," Avery fumed.

Sydney shrugged as she twisted her mouth to the side. The thought of one of the other girls having a baby at roughly the same time as me was very exciting to me. As I stood and considered how much life was going to change, I was truly grateful it wasn't going to change for me and me alone. Having Sydney go through the changes with me was something I welcomed with open arms.

As we all stood and talked about men, kids, and life in general, the sound of Axton's voice over the stereo reminded me this party wasn't for us, but for someone else.

"So, without further ado, we'll get back to it. Todd Parker, known by the club as Cash, has fulfilled his requirement of prospecting for twelve months. All patched in Selected Sinners in favor of his advancement into the club and acceptance as a fully patched member respond in the form of *aye*," Axton said.

"Aye," everyone wearing a Sinners cut screamed.

Axton nodded his head and waved at the crowd.

"Requires a one hundred percent vote to be a Sinner, any opposed respond in the form of nay," he said into the microphone.

I glanced out into the crowd at the one they called Cash. He was hugging his wife and preparing to walk toward Axton.

"Well, it appears…" Axton started to say

"Nay!" someone shouted from the crowd.

"Oh dear God," Sam gasped.

"What?" Avery asked.

"Otis. He's opposed. Oh dear God," Sam shrieked.

"Do I have one opposed?" Axton shouted.

Otis nodded his head and waved at Axton.

I shifted my eyes toward Cash. He released his wife and began to run toward Otis.

"Yes you do. My vote is *nay*," Otis screamed.

Within five seconds, and as Sam began to walk toward Otis, Cash got in front of Otis and started screaming. Otis swung one punch and knocked him flat on his back. Dalton, Axton, and Toad walked toward them both and helped Cash up to his feet.

Axton walked Cash into the house.

"Holy shit. Guess he didn't make it," Avery said, "Axton didn't like him anyway."

"But he did his part or whatever, right?" I asked.

"Not that easy," Avery said as she shook her head, "It takes a one hundred percent vote. Otis must have had a reason for not wanting him in the club. This is a tight knit bunch of guys, you'll learn that. And to call them brothers wouldn't even come close to describe the bond."

I nodded my head, "I see."

Cash's wife began screaming out the back door of the house toward Otis. Almost immediately, Otis, Dalton, Toad, and Axton ran into the house. Sydney turned toward me and shrugged her shoulders.

"Haven't you ever had a friend that one day you decided wasn't such a good friend?" Avery asked.

I nodded my head, "Yeah."

"Well, imagine if you were stuck with your friends forever because you made some silly pact or blood oath. That's what these guys do when they accept someone. They're in for life. So, they've got to be careful about who they choose. You're Biscuit's Ol' Lady, his brothers are your brothers. Be proud that your brothers are the best of the best," she said.

"I nodded my head and grinned, "I will be. I mean I am."

Avery nodded her head and grinned as she turned toward the house.

Dalton walked out the door, turned, and began walking our direction. His head hung low, as if he was upset about something.

"We're gonna need to get out of here. Cops will be here pretty quick. Cash offed himself," he said.

"Huh?" I said, confused at the phrase he'd said.

He shook his head, "He killed himself, Kat. Right in the kitchen in front of his wife."

"Oh my God," I gasped.

He shook his head.

"Cambio?" Sydney screeched.

"Everyone's fine. They're covering up the body and talkin' to his wife - it ain't nothin' you wanna see," Dalton explained as he reached for Sydney's shoulder and hugged her.

"I'm sorry," I sighed.

Dalton shook his head, "Far as I'm concerned, just proves he was too weak for the club. Good call on Otis' part."

I thought about the suicide, and what someone must be feeling to commit the act. Kyle's suicide was no doubt a result of his guilt and grief for what he'd done. Cash's was probably because he felt incompetent, or worthless. Maybe, the more I thought about it, Kyle felt worthless as well.

As he should have.

I stared down at the ground, closed my eyes, and said a small prayer.

Bless them anyway, Lord.

They were your children.

KAT

I sat nervously in the courtroom, waiting for the judge to enter. Dalton sat beside the court appointed attorney in the front of the courtroom, looking rather dapper in the clothes I had bought for him. Although he refused to wear slacks, he allowed me to buy him a pair of new jeans, a button-down shirt, and a pair of black boots. With is freshly waxed beard, slightly trimmed hair, and perfectly waxed eyebrows, he looked fabulous.

"All rise," the bailiff howled.

We all stood as the judge walked into the room. I had asked Dalton to tell the club about his court date, but he refused. I felt having Avery with me would ease my mind, but he insisted that she not know of the hearing either. As I stood on shaking legs, the judge reached his seat and sat down.

"You may be seated," the judge said.

I sat down and pressed my palms onto my shaking knees. After looking on the internet at the severity of the charges, I learned Dalton could very well spend five years in prison for beating the men he beat in jail. Hopefully the judge would see that he wasn't a troublemaker, and although he'd been arrested several times, he'd never been tried and convicted of a felony or a violent crime.

"Will the defendant please rise," the judge said.

I stared at Dalton as he stood, wondering what the procedure would be. I suspected no differently than on television, people would give their testimony, Dalton would give his, and the jury or the judge would decide the case. Maybe after hearing what everyone had to say, I would feel better about the entire situation.

I gazed blankly across the courtroom with unfocused eyes. The thought of losing Dalton was something I chose to deny as even being a possibility. Raising our baby without him would be extremely difficult, and thinking about it made me cry. Even after Dalton gave me keys to the house, instructions on operating the pool equipment, and the combination to the safe, I refused to accept his incarceration as being even a slight probability.

A hand lightly touched my shoulder, startling me. I turned to my right and glanced upward.

Dad?

"It's getting ready to start," I whispered.

He raised his index finger to his lips and whispered his response, "It's getting ready to *end*. It'll be over before you know it."

Huh?

I wrinkled my nose, shrugged my shoulders, and stared. He grinned. I slid to my left and patted the wooden bench beside me. He shook his head lightly, winked, and mouthed the words *I love you* as he reached for the door beside him.

Before I could respond, he opened the door, slipped into the hall, and walked away.

That was weird.

I turned toward the courtroom and blinked my eyes a few times as I tried to focus on the judge's statement.

"…therefore, considering the electronic files were damaged while in evidence, rendering them useless and leaving the court without video, we would be required to rely solely on the testimony of the plaintiff's to prosecute this case. As fate would have it, both plaintiffs have no recollection of the events on the day in question," the judge paused and peered over the top of his glasses.

After a moment, he reached up, removed his glasses, and studied Dalton.

"Considering your plea of innocence has been maintained, Mr. Biskette, it saddens me greatly to announce the county has no ability to prosecute this case. In the matter of Sedgwick County versus Biskette, the case has been dropped by the county due to lack of evidence," he hesitated, pounded his gavel onto the wooden block and shook his head.

"Mr. Biskette, you are free to go," he sighed.

Oh my God.

I clapped my hands silently and stood. Dalton turned around and winked. I gazed at him for a moment, turned toward the door my father had walked through, and stared.

With my gaze frozen on the door, I mouthed the words.

I love you, too.

KAT

I couldn't believe the time had come for us to find out the sex of our baby. As I scrambled to get my hair finished, Dalton stood in the doorway with his hands on his hips. He seemed excited, but by no means as excited as I was. I couldn't seem to contain myself. Finally, I shook my head from side to side, let my hair fall slightly into my face, and settled for the loose ponytail I was wearing.

"I'm almost ready," I said as I ducked under his arm, ran past him, and into the bedroom.

The room looked great in the new colors, but I had my doubts how long they'd last. The baby's room was better than great, and I was so in love with it I brought my mother and father both over to see it. Seeing my father get along with Dalton, considering he was a cop and Dalton was an outlaw seemed almost too good to be true.

They sure seemed to get along well, and my father laughed at his stories and jokes as he told them. Dalton never said one cross word about my father since the day he said my father stopped by to visit him. It was almost as if they'd somehow made peace with each other on that day.

I pulled my shoes onto my feet and cocked my head slightly to the side.

"Is the bike running?" I asked.

He rubbed his beard in the palm of his hand his hand as he nodded his head, "Yep."

"Sorry," I sighed.

"Ready," I shouted as I sprung to my feet.

"Grab your purse," he said as he motioned toward my purse.

I grabbed my purse, followed him through the garage, and stopped in the driveway. As I checked my ponytail, I glanced down at the back of his bike. Rumbling through the exhaust and shaking, the back fender shook from side to side.

I glanced at the back of it with unfocused eyes, repositioned my purse, and started to get on.

Something in my head registered a few seconds late.

His plate was different.

I stepped back, studied the license plate, and narrowed my eyes as I stared at it.

"Your plate doesn't say RFOF anymore," I said as I stared down at it.

He climbed off the bike, turned to face me, and crossed his arms, "Nope."

I read the letters out loud, "W.Y. M. M."

"What's it mean now?" I shrugged.

"Figure it out. Been on there for about three weeks waitin' for ya to see it," he huffed.

I stared down at the tag.

While. You. Might ...

Wont. You.

What. You're.

I shook my head and stared. Shit like that had always bothered me.

I hated not being able to figure out license plates. I gazed at it with unfocused eyes and thought.

W.Y.M.M.

Will. You Marry.

Holy shit, no way. He's not that…

I glanced up at him. Standing with his arms crossed and his mouth covered with a full on smirk, he studied me. I gazed down at the letters, not certain of their order.

W.Y.M.M.

"Will you marry me?" I whispered as I studied the plate.

I glanced upward after I spoke. I had said it louder than I intended to, and was slightly embarrassed. As the words escaped my lips, my heart raced.

I wondered if I guessed right.

"As a matter of fact I will," he said as he reached into his jeans pocket.

"Been carryin' this fucker for three weeks, since right after I asked your father if it was okay. Had to spend my bond money on somethin' when they gave it back, figured this was as good as anything. Katrina Chadsworth…" he paused as he knelt down in front of me on one knee.

You asked my father?

"Will you marry me?" he asked.

I raised my hand to my mouth and nodded my head as the tears rolled down my cheeks. He reached out, held my left hand in his, and slipped the ring onto my finger.

"Not as pretty as you, but damn close," he said.

I glanced down at the ring, still in shock over what had happened. After a few minutes of absorbing the beauty of the ring, I shifted my eyes to meet Dalton's and gazed at him in a semiconscious state.

"I love you, Kat," he said as he kissed me on the lips.

"I love…I love…you," I blubbered as our lips parted.

He glanced at his watch. His eyes widened and left hand immediately shot into the air. As he extended his index finger, he twirled it in a circle.

"Saddle up," he shouted into the air, "Let's roll."

I laughed into my clenched hand as I climbed onto the bike.

Life with Dalton Biskette was a lot of things.

Wild.

Crazy.

Fun.

Adventurous.

Full of love.

But there was one thing it wasn't.

Predictable.